JUSTICE BURNING

OTHER TITLES BY SCOTT PRATT

JUSTICE BURNING

SCOTT PRATT

THOMAS & MERCER

Text copyright © 2017 by Arthur Scott Pratt
All rights reserved.

Published by Thomas & Mercer, Seattle

www.apub.com

Amazon, the Amazon logo, and Thomas & Mercer are trademarks of Amazon.com, Inc., or its affiliates.

ISBN-13: 9781542045605
ISBN-10: 1542045606

Cover design by Cyanotype Book Architects

Printed in the United States of America

This book, along with every book I've written and every book I'll write, is dedicated to my darling Kristy, to her unconquerable spirit and to her inspirational courage. I loved her before I was born, and I'll love her after I'm long gone.

Life's filled with trauma. You don't need to go to war to find it; it's going to find you.

—*Sebastian Junger*

PROLOGUE

A cold breeze was blowing as I walked down the dark sidewalk toward the bar. I was wearing a dark-brown jacket with a black wool sweater beneath it, a black stocking cap, black jeans, black running shoes, and black socks. My hands were covered by a pair of black cold-weather running gloves. A Beretta pistol was shoved into my pants, secured by my belt, at the small of my back. I slipped into a creek bed and moved up close to the gravel parking lot outside the bar. To my surprise, there were only two vehicles in the lot. One was a brown Chevrolet that had been parked by the door earlier in the day. I assumed it belonged to the owner, a man named Sammy Raft. The other was Donnie Frazier's girlfriend's pickup truck.

I considered my options. I could wait out there in the cold until they came out, which might not be until closing. The door said closing time was 2:00 a.m. on Fridays. That was six hours away. Or I could walk into the bar and improvise. It took me about five seconds to decide.

"Fuck it," I said out loud and headed toward the door. When I walked in, Sammy was standing behind the bar, polishing a glass. I knew what he looked like because I'd ordered a cheeseburger from him earlier in the day while checking the place out. The bar smelled of stale beer, cigarette smoke, and hamburger grease. Donnie Frazier and Tommy Beane were in a booth against the wall to my right. A Merle

Haggard song called "Momma Tried" was blaring on the jukebox. I sat down at the first bar stool, and Sammy walked over.

"A little slow for a Friday, isn't it?" I said.

He shot a glance toward the booth behind me. "It's them two. They done run everybody off. Want the place to themselves. Probably be best for you if you don't stay long."

"I'll take a Budweiser, longneck," I said. "Appreciate the heads-up."

Sammy turned and reached into a cooler. He popped the cap off the bottle and set it on the counter.

I didn't touch it. Instead, I leaned toward him as though I wanted to draw him into a conspiracy. "Can I ask you a personal question? I know it might seem a little strange, but is your mother still alive?"

Sammy looked to be around sixty, pudgy and balding, with bright-blue eyes. He gazed at me curiously. "She passed about ten years ago. The cancer took her."

"I'm sorry to hear that. Were you close? Did you love her?"

"My momma? Are you asking me if I loved my momma?"

"I'm sorry," I said. "You'll understand in a minute."

"I loved her to death. She was the finest woman I ever met, even better than my wife, Linda, and that's saying a lot. Now tell me why you want to know if I loved my momma."

"Because I loved mine, too, and those two insects in that booth over there raped her."

I saw Sammy swallow slowly. His blue eyes locked on to mine, searching for an answer to a question he was afraid to ask. Finally, he asked the question. "Are you planning to do something about it?"

"I am."

"Here? Now?"

"Afraid so. You know those boys well?"

"Well enough to know I don't much care what happens to them, but I don't see myself sitting back while you kill two men in my place of business."

I'd told him they'd raped her, but the two men in the booth had killed my mother. I'd done a lot of planning, taken some serious risks, and had driven a long way to get revenge. The man standing in front of me had done nothing to me, but I wasn't going to let him stop me from doing what I'd come there to do. If I had to kill him, too, I was prepared to do so and chalk it up to unavoidable collateral damage.

"I'm not asking you to sit back. I'm asking you to take a little trip to the bathroom," I said. "There'll be some noise. Wait until the noise dies down, and then come back and call the police, but take your time about it. Tell them you went into the bathroom and heard shooting start. You were afraid to come out. When you finally came out, they were dead."

"Why would they rape your momma?" he said.

"It's a long story, something you don't need to hear. Those boys are going to die in the next couple of minutes. You can either go into the bathroom or you can die with them."

"Why should I believe you?"

"You don't have to believe me, but fate has put you and me and them in this bar together at this moment, and something is about to happen."

"What if I pull this sawed-off shotgun out from under the bar and blow your head off with it?"

"You better be quick," I said.

He stared at me again for a long minute. His expression changed to one of resignation, and I watched him make his decision. He began slowly walking around the bar. He walked behind me, past Frazier and Deane, to the end of the bar, turned left, and disappeared behind a black door that said **Restrooms**.

By this time, Merle Haggard's song was done playing, and Johnny Cash was singing "Folsom Prison Blues." I got up off the bar stool, took a deep breath, and was surprised I wasn't more nervous. I pulled the Beretta and hid it behind my back. I flipped the safety off and walked up to the booth. Beane was to my left with a cigarette hanging from his lips. He looked just like the photo I'd been given: Elvis Presley hair and sideburns, dark eyes, thick neck. Frazier had a dark-blond ponytail and greenish-blue eyes. Both of them had tattoos on their necks and on their hands. Their arms were covered with shirtsleeves, but I was sure they were also covered in prison tats.

I looked them over for a couple of seconds before Frazier said, "What the fuck you lookin' at, boy?"

Without saying a word, I put three rounds into Beane's chest. The noise inside the small bar was deafening. Beane melted into the booth, blood already oozing from his shirt. Frazier froze and looked up at me, his eyes wild with fear. I didn't feel a bit of sympathy for him or for the man I'd just shot three times. My heart rate was steady. My hands weren't shaking. More than anything else, and for the first time in a long time, I felt in control.

"My name is Darren Street," I said to Frazier. "Ring a bell?"

I pointed the Beretta at his forehead as his eyebrows raised and an "Oh shit" look came over his face. "This is from my mother."

Those were the last words Donnie Frazier heard. I pulled the trigger, and a hole opened up between his eyes. I shot him seven more times and then put four more rounds into Beane to make sure he was dead. The Beretta locked open on the slide, indicating the gun was empty. I stuck the pistol in my waist and walked out the door. I walked quickly to my car but didn't run. I got in, fired up the Monte Carlo, and headed out of town toward Tennessee, the same way I'd come in.

An hour and a half later, I pulled into a mostly deserted rest stop off the interstate, near Charleston, West Virginia. I walked into the restroom, took a look in the mirror, and realized I had small dots of blood spatter on my gloves, glasses, and forehead. I was sure it was on my jacket and fake beard, too, but it wasn't noticeable. I found myself reluctant to wash it off.

Having Frazier's and Beane's blood all over me gave me a visceral feeling of power. It felt like war paint, and I wanted to wear it for all the world to see.

PART I

CHAPTER 1

Six weeks earlier

My name is Darren Street, and as I settled into the seat the doctor had pointed out, I felt a sense of dread come over me. I suddenly wanted to get up and run out the door, like a child who is afraid of being given a shot. The doctor hadn't done anything to frighten me, at least not intentionally. In fact, she'd been quite pleasant.

Laura Benton was a board-certified psychiatrist who ran a boutique practice from her home in the posh Bluegrass neighborhood in Knoxville, Tennessee. She charged $200 an hour, cash only, and was supposedly quite good at what she did. The appointment had been arranged through my girlfriend, Grace Alexander. Grace knew Dr. Benton because both of them volunteered at the Second Harvest Food Bank. I'd been falsely convicted of a murder and imprisoned for two years—one year in a federal maximum security penitentiary—and I'd had some problems adjusting to being free. So Grace had thought some psychiatric assistance might be in order. I wasn't thrilled about it, but I knew I was struggling. Grace had offered to pay for the first session, so I'd finally given in and agreed to go.

Dr. Benton appeared to be around forty, a few years older than I was. She wasn't an ugly woman by any means, but she wasn't particularly attractive, either. She had brown hair and eyes and a studious, prudish look about her. Her sky-blue blouse was buttoned to her throat, and her loose-fitting black skirt fell below her knees. Her calves were pale and without definition.

We were in an airy, open room with a high ceiling, plenty of windows that looked out over the manicured lawn outside, and several pieces of overstuffed furniture. She settled into her seat across from me with a yellow lined notepad in her right hand and a pen in her left.

"You're a southpaw," I said, just to break the proverbial ice.

"Beg your pardon?"

"Wrong-hander. Lefty."

"Are you nervous, Darren?" she said.

"Sorry. Yeah, I guess I'm a little nervous."

"Why do you think you're nervous?"

"Because you're a stranger and you're going to ask me questions about things I probably don't want to talk about."

"I'm here to help you. Do you believe that?"

"I suppose I do," I said.

"Good, then how about we start by you telling me what you believe is your most serious difficulty right now. Grace has told me quite a bit about you, so I feel as though I know you pretty well, but I'd like to hear what you think might be bothering you."

"I can't sleep," I said.

"Do you mean you can't go to sleep, or you wake up easily?"

"Both. I can't go to sleep because I don't really want to go to sleep. I don't want to go to sleep because I know what will be waiting for me over there. When I manage to get to sleep, what I dreaded is always there, and I wake up quickly."

"So you have nightmares."

"Constantly."

"And these nightmares, do they seem real, or are they dreamlike?"

"They seem real. It's like all my senses are intact. I can see and hear and smell and feel the things that are happening."

"What kinds of things do you dream about?"

"I dream about being chased by the police. I dream about being beaten by prison guards. I dream about being handcuffed and shackled on a bus for months at a time. I dream about being strip-searched. I dream about being stabbed."

"So all those things happened to you when you were in prison?"

I nodded. "I wasn't chased by the police. They just walked into a restaurant and arrested me and then helped frame me for a murder I didn't commit. But all the other things happened to me."

"And I understand you're a lawyer, correct?"

"Yes. Criminal defense. It's all I've ever wanted to do."

"So you continue to visit jails and go to courtrooms and do all the various things associated with practicing criminal defense law. You see men and women in restraints every day, deal with police officers and prosecutors and judges, and you deal with guards at the jails you visit."

"I do."

"Do you fight a lot of battles for your clients?"

"Every day. That's pretty much all a criminal defense lawyer does. We fight and argue and scrap, trying to make sure the government plays by its own rules."

"Those things probably aren't good for you, Darren."

"They're all part of it. I have to make a living. I did four years in college, three more years in law school, and then another seven building my practice before everything came crashing down on me. I went to prison for two years, was finally exonerated, and fought to get my license back. I've been going hard for a year now and am starting to reap some benefits, at least financially, from my efforts. I can't just walk away."

"Would you rather die?" she said.

"Come again? I don't think I understand."

"If you keep going the way you are, if you keep exposing yourself to these stressors, these triggers, it will eventually cause you some serious health issues. It's already affecting you mentally and emotionally, and to be honest, you're in a dangerous area mentally."

She wasn't telling me anything I didn't already know. The anxiety I felt all the time, the grinding of my teeth, the violent dreams, and the occasional thought of taking my own life in order to be free of the terrifying nightmares were all things I knew were dangerous.

"I know I'm in a dangerous area mentally," I said. "That's why I'm here."

"You could be in danger of losing all faith in the principles that have guided you to this point in your life. Do you know what a nihilist is, Darren?"

Did she think I'd become a nihilist? I didn't. I still had my mother, my son, and Grace. I loved them and felt close to them. I needed them. Nihilists didn't need anyone. They didn't care about anyone or anything.

"If I'm not mistaken, a nihilist is someone who thinks life has no real meaning."

"Exactly."

"I'm not a nihilist. I have feelings. I have people I love. I look forward to the future."

"But you could be heading down that road if you continue to expose yourself to these stressors and triggers on a daily basis. Because what you're describing to me is classic Post Traumatic Stress Disorder, and PTSD, left untreated, can lead to even more serious difficulties."

"Is that even a real thing?" I said. "I mean, I've heard of PTSD, but I've always thought it was just sort of a cop-out for people who have been through something traumatic and wanted to wallow in it."

"You tell me if it's real," she said. "You're the one who can't sleep. Does the lack of sleep cause you to be lethargic during the day? Do you have trouble concentrating? Have you developed a fatalistic attitude toward life in general? Do you have violent thoughts?"

I didn't want to answer, because the answers to all the questions would be affirmative. "It isn't that bad. I just need some more time. Time heals all, right?"

"You need to stay away from the triggers, at least for a couple of years. Can you go back to school, find another way to make a living?"

"I don't want to find another way to make a living." I felt a sudden surge of anger, and my voice rose involuntarily. "I'm not a quitter. I'm not going to just give up my law practice because you say I have PTSD."

"I've upset you," she said. "I apologize."

"Apology accepted." I stood and started walking toward the door.

"You're leaving? We still have a lot of time."

"I'll show myself out." I dropped the two hundred on a table by the door. "Have a nice day."

CHAPTER 2

As I looked out over the football field four days after my visit to the doctor, I felt a sense of peace and satisfaction I hadn't felt in a long time. I knew it was only temporary, but it was nice just the same. It was Tuesday night, late October, and it was mop-up time in the Boys & Girls Club city football championship game. The team I was helping coach, a group of fifth- and sixth-grade children from one of the poorest neighborhoods in the city, was on the verge of winning.

Bob Ridge, a high school and college buddy of mine and a long-time Knoxville cop who played four years of football at the University of Tennessee, was the head coach. I coached the linebackers and called all the defensive signals during the games. Bob had been coaching kids who attended Stratton Elementary for seven years. He'd won two city championships during those seven years and was about to win his third. He'd asked me to help not long after I was released from prison, saying he thought it would be good for me, and he was right. This was my second year coaching, and it was one of the most pleasurable things in my life. I still couldn't sleep, but at least there weren't any prosecutors or judges that I was arguing with, and no clients that were lying to me and stiffing me out of my fees. And I genuinely cared about the kids. Winning and losing didn't matter that much to me, but I cared about how they were doing at home, how they were doing in school, how they got along with each other. I thought about Dr. Benton and her suggestion that I was becoming a nihilist. Nihilists didn't care about groups of youngsters. Nihilists didn't volunteer their time to help needy kids.

The group of kids we coached were diverse in terms of skin color. We had fifteen black boys, fourteen white boys, and five Mexican boys. The one thing they all had in common was poverty. I'd learned that poverty didn't discriminate. It was equally cruel to all who were held in its viselike grip. About 80 percent of the kids we coached came from broken homes. Many of them lived with grandparents or aunts and uncles or foster parents. Several were being raised by single mothers, some that worked multiple jobs, and some that were substance abusers and lived off government assistance.

Many of their fathers were in jail or prison, and many who weren't locked up were abusive. We would see bruising occasionally around the eyes or mouth and ask what had happened. Inevitably, the boy would say he ran into a door or fell down some steps. One boy, whose name was Chuckie Stone, was thrown off his front porch by his father. When he landed, his femur snapped. Chuckie's brother, who was also on our team, witnessed the incident and told Bob and me about it. It was a difficult dilemma for us, because the father actually had a job and provided for the family. If we'd had him arrested, he would have gone to jail, and the family would have been devastated. So we—the entire coaching staff—decided to pay Daddy a visit. There were eight of us, led by Bob Ridge, who was a six-foot-seven-inch, 280-pound wall of muscle. We went to Chuckie's home and invited his father outside. When he came out, we informed him that if we ever caught wind that he had so much as cursed at either of the boys again, we would come back and break both of his legs and both of his arms. He wet his pants right there in front of us, the coward, and threatened to call the police. Bob pulled his badge out of his pocket and said, "I *am* the police, motherfucker."

Some of the boys went to bed hungry at night, but Bob and I and the rest of the coaches did everything we could to make sure that they were all fed after practice every day during the football season. Feeding thirty-four hungry boys five days a week was expensive. We'd become creative about it—we held fund-raisers and solicited donations from local businesses and restaurants and food banks. Somehow, we managed to pull it off, but like I said, it was only during the football season, which ran for three months. The other nine months of the year, the boys were pretty much on their own. Bob and I talked about them often. What frustrated Bob more than anything was that he couldn't help much beyond the football field, and that the kids moved on through so quickly. They would be on the team for two years if they stuck it out the entire time, and after that, he might never hear from them again.

As the clock wound down, a sixth-grade boy named Julius Antone walked up to me and spread his arms. I wrapped my arms around him and picked him up off the ground. Julius was the team's middle linebacker, a smart, tough, incredible kid.

"Congratulations, Julius," I said. "You're my man."

I set him back down, and he stood there, grinning from ear to ear.

"Thank you, Coach," he said. "You've taught me a lot."

"You've taught me more," I said.

I knew Julius didn't have a phone—only a couple of the kids on our team did—so I said, "I'll come around and see you at Christmas. How's that sound?" I knew where he lived. I knew where all the kids lived, because I'd hauled them all home at one time or another. Julius lived in a small house in an old government housing project with his mother, her boyfriend, two brothers, and a sister.

"That would be great, Coach."

"What can I bring you for Christmas?"

"You don't have to bring anything, just come by and say Merry Christmas. That'll be enough."

"Do you guys do a big Christmas thing? Turkey and all that?"

He looked down at the ground and scraped his cleats through the grass. "Nah, we don't do much. It's just another day."

I hugged him again and said, "You take care of yourself. I'll see you soon."

As I walked down the line congratulating the other players and the coaches, I thought to myself, *Things will be different at Julius's house this year. I'll make sure of it.*

I enjoyed the satisfaction of having seen those young boys accomplish something together late into the night. Grace invited me over to spend the night and celebrate. I drank two glasses of wine and told Grace tall tales of the team's heroics on the football field. She smiled and congratulated me and acted as though she was interested. She probably was, too. Grace was too genuine, too honest, to fake anything.

Around midnight, Grace put her head on my shoulder and yawned deeply. I was living with my mother, but I occasionally stayed with Grace. "Are you going home tonight or would you like to come to bed?" she asked.

"I don't think I'll drive after drinking this wine."

"It's good to see you this way, Darren. I know you're proud of the boys, but you seem proud of yourself, too. That makes me happy. It's a good sign."

I squeezed her shoulders and kissed her on the forehead.

"I love you."

"I love you, too." She took a deep breath and closed her eyes.

CHAPTER 3

It had been eighteen months since I'd been released from prison. The Tennessee Board of Professional Responsibility had taken six months to have a hearing to reinstate my license after I was exonerated for a murder I hadn't committed, and for which I'd served two years in jail. During the hearing, I had to prove by "clear and convincing evidence"—a very high standard of proof—that I was no longer "a danger to the community." The entire thing was nothing but a charade. The feds should have apologized to me, written me a check for the two years of my life they'd taken and the torture they'd put me through, and been done with it. And the Board of Professional Responsibility should have simply recognized the federal court's dismissal of my charge and reinstated me on the spot. But that would have made entirely too much sense. I guess I could have sued the feds, but it would have meant reliving the experience over and over, and I just wanted to move on.

It took another month for the opinion to come down that I was no longer dangerous and that my license to practice law should be reinstated. After that, I had to catch up on my continuing legal education hours—classes that lawyers are required to take each year. They're usually held at a fancy resort or hotel somewhere, and most of the lawyers either duck out of the classes or sleep through them. But they're required to take a certain amount of hours. Why? Because they have to *pay* for the hours. The CLE racket is a huge moneymaker for the elite few who organize and host the events. The whole thing reminded me of a prison hustle.

Once I'd been reinstated and caught up on my CLE, I had to set up shop all over again. Rachel, my secretary and paralegal before I went to jail, had taken a job with another lawyer. I still had some of the money I'd earned representing fellow inmates in prison, but I didn't have enough to hire anyone, so I rented a small office in a rough building in a neighborhood known as the Old City, and hung out a shingle.

I was living with my mother on the west side of Knoxville. I made a down payment on a compact car with almost two hundred thousand miles on it and prayed it would start every morning. I was able to see my eight-year-old son, Sean, every other weekend, but his mother, my beloved ex-wife, Katie, had sued me for child support as soon as I was released from prison. She didn't have to sue me. I would have paid child support, and I told her as much. I would have paid more than a court would have ordered me to pay, but she took such pleasure in dragging me into court that she couldn't resist. I was making such a small amount of money at the time that she wound up getting only $400 a month. I knew as soon as I started making more money, she'd drag me back into court. It was something I could look forward to until he turned eighteen.

I was pleasantly surprised by one thing. As soon as I was reinstated, business started coming in the door. I'd built a good reputation as a criminal defense lawyer prior to going to prison, and I'd gotten a ton of free publicity over the past couple of years, both during my trial and after my exoneration. A reporter for the *Knoxville News Sentinel* ran a story on me the day I opened for business in my new office, and by the end of the day I had eight appointments scheduled.

I also took on appointed cases. Rupert Lattimore was, by far, my most notorious case. Lattimore and three accomplices had carjacked and murdered two college kids. The Criminal Court judge who appointed me to Lattimore, a woman named Eleanor Montgomery, actually thought she was doing me a favor. She called me on the phone, was extremely courteous and complimentary, and asked me whether I would take on what she suspected would be a difficult case.

"It'll do you good, Mr. Street," she said. "Lots of free publicity, jumping headlong into a bad murder, representing your client zealously. It'll get you all the way back into the game."

She was right about getting all the way back into the game, but she was wrong about it doing me good. Because I'd never before felt genuine hatred for a client, and I hated Rupert Lattimore.

On the Sunday evening following the football championship, I sat in the interview room at the jail looking at him. For the first time in my career, I genuinely regarded my client as a miserable, worthless piece of garbage. Prior to representing this guy, I had nearly always been capable of maintaining a sense of indifference about my clients. It's simply something defense lawyers have to learn to do—just part of the job. But I loathed Rupert Lattimore. I hated everything about him. I hated the way he looked. I hated the way he smelled. I hated his name, his tattoos, the constant sneer he wore on his face. But more than anything else, I hated what he had done, and by extension, I hated myself for being a part, albeit indirectly, of what he had done.

I guess the name Rupert would have alone been enough to turn him into a jackass. He told me he'd been named after a great-grandfather, but who names a kid Rupert? Life is tough enough without having to deal with the unnecessary shit dished out by bullies who would take exception to the name Rupert. His parents should have been slapped.

Rupert was a strapping twenty-eight-year-old man from an area of Knoxville called Mechanicsville. He'd kidnapped, raped, and murdered a young couple, both of them just college kids. He didn't do it alone—he had three accomplices—but he was, without a doubt, the leader of the group. It was his idea to go out and steal a car. It was his idea to pull out a gun and kidnap Arielle Blevins and her boyfriend, Stephen Whitfield, who just happened to be in the car Rupert decided to steal.

It was his idea to take them to the small house where he and his brother and his cousin and his girlfriend were staying. It was Rupert who hog-tied Stephen Whitfield with a garden hose before he dragged him out back of the house to a set of railroad tracks where he raped Stephen with a broomstick and choked him with a belt before he shot him twice in the back and once in the head.

Then Rupert and his boys went back inside and went to work on Arielle. She'd already been tied up and left in a bedroom. Rupert and his brother and his cousin took turns raping Arielle every possible way a person can rape another person for two days. Then, when Rupert sobered up long enough to realize they might have left some DNA on her or inside her, he decided it would be a good thing to pour bleach down her throat, into every orifice they had raped, and all over her body. Then Rupert put a plastic trash bag over Arielle's head and two more over the rest of her. He then stuffed her headfirst into a trash can in his kitchen while his girlfriend stood by and watched. After about thirty-six hours—according to the medical examiner—Arielle eventually suffocated.

Rupert had actually been stupid enough to tell me he did all those horrible things. He was unapologetic about it, proud even. And his reasons for killing, raping, maiming, and torturing two innocent human beings?

He had a hard life growing up.

His mother was a drunk, and his father wasn't in the picture.

He'd been in prison for robbing people and felt as though he was mistreated by the guards, the administration, and the other inmates.

He needed Stephen Whitfield's car so he could sell it in order to buy drugs.

He was fucked up on alcohol and methamphetamine that night.

Those were the reasons he gave me, but the reality was that he was a sociopath, a pure predator who felt no empathy for anyone. He hated everyone, including me. In fact, he hated me more than I hated him. I could feel the loathing. It oozed from him like a poisonous fog.

I looked across the table at Rupert. I had trouble looking him in the eye, and I was sure he could sense my reluctance. "Are you ready for tomorrow?" I said.

"Are you?"

I nodded my head slowly. "As ready as I can be under the circumstances. The police have actually done a hell of a job locking down this case. The evidence is overwhelming. You can testify in your own defense if you want, but I wouldn't advise it because you've told me you did everything they're accusing you of doing, you have a long criminal history, and the prosecutor will eat you alive if you get on the witness stand. We don't have a single witness who has come forward who wants to help us. The psychological expert we brought in says you're not crazy or mentally challenged, so those defenses are out. We can say you were high, but that isn't going to get us anywhere. All of your codefendants have made deals with the prosecutor and are going to testify against you. But yeah, to answer your question, I'm ready. I'll go in there prepared and cross-examine their witnesses. I'll give you the best defense I can."

"Which ain't gonna be shit."

"You didn't give me much to work with."

"Man, I oughta come across this table and stomp your ass into the floor."

I smiled at him. "I wish you'd try. I really do. I spent a year in the max section of the Knoxville jail, and then a year in a federal maximum security prison, you know. Did I tell you that? No, I guess I didn't. I was falsely accused of a murder, framed by a prosecutor, and did some hard, hard time. Chances are I could kick your ass without those handcuffs and shackles, but if you come at me all cuffed up like that, it isn't going to go well for you."

He leaned toward me as though he was going to lunge, but he didn't. Instead, he spit in my face.

"Motherfucker," he said. "When I escape, I'm gonna look you up late at night."

I wiped my face with my sleeve, stood, and pushed the button on the wall to summon the guard. There was a time in my life when I would have broken his jaw for spitting on me, but instead I just looked at him. Something inside of me was telling me to stay calm for the moment, because I'd get even with him later.

"You're gonna be in a small box for the rest of your life until they execute you," I said. "It'll probably take them about fifteen years, but they'll get around to you eventually. But if you ever manage to escape and come looking for me, you can rest assured I'll be waiting with a pistol in one hand, a beer in the other, and a smile on my face. Have a nice evening, Rupert. I'll see you in court tomorrow."

As I walked down the hall outside the interview room toward the light and freedom outside the jail, I smiled and shook my head.

I went home, got a couple of hours of restless sleep, and went to court the next morning expecting to begin Rupert's trial.

The prosecutors were at their table. I was at my table with my cocounsel, a competent, experienced lawyer named Bret James—defendants get two lawyers in death-penalty cases. There were about a hundred prospective jurors waiting for jury selection to begin. There were several reporters and a few cameras. The judge walked in, sat down, called the case, and said, "Is everyone ready?"

"I got something I want to say," Rupert said.

I cringed as the judge looked at me.

"Your lawyer should be the one speaking for you, Mr. Lattimore," Judge Montgomery said.

"My lawyer threatened to kill me yesterday. I don't want him representing me."

"He threatened to kill you? I find that hard to believe."

"Ask him," Rupert said. "If he ain't a liar, he'll tell you he threatened to kill me."

"Mr. Street?" the judge said.

I stood and cleared my throat. "As I recall, just as we were finishing up our final preparation at the jail yesterday evening, Mr. Lattimore first threatened to stomp my ass into the floor. I believe I told him that probably wouldn't go well for him because I'd spent some time in prison and know how to defend myself. After that, he spit in my face. Then he said when he escaped he was going to look me up late at night. I took that as a threat on my life, and I told him I'd be waiting with a pistol. So yes, I suppose you could say I threatened to kill him. I think it's fair to say emotions were running high. He's about to go on trial for his life, and he doesn't think I've done enough to help him."

The judge looked at me openmouthed as I waited for the inevitable public humiliation I was about to receive. "So Mr. Lattimore, who is accused of murdering two people, first threatened to physically assault you, then spit in your face, then threatened to escape and come to your home late at night? And you told him you'd be waiting with a gun? Is that correct, Mr. Street?"

"Yes, Your Honor. That's pretty much what transpired."

"Well, I don't see how you can represent him under these circumstances. You're relieved, Mr. Street. The trial is postponed. I'll find another lawyer and set another date and notify everyone. Mr. Lattimore, I'm going to appoint another lawyer for you, but let me warn you, if you pull this kind of stunt again, you'll be representing yourself. That's it. Court is adjourned. Everyone can go home."

And with that, we all left. I went through the back to avoid the media and went to my office to fill out the paperwork to bill the state for the 250 hours I'd spent preparing to try Rupert's case. When I was finished, I went to a bar in the Old City and drank too much, which was something I rarely did. I didn't really know why. Maybe it was the PTSD Laura Benton had mentioned, but when I walked out of the courtroom, my chest felt tight and I kept grinding my teeth that afternoon. I guess I just needed to unwind. I called Grace around eight o'clock that night, and she came and picked me up.

"What brought this on?" she said when I got into her car.

"Not sure. I think the Rupert Lattimores of the world may be getting to me."

"You could always do what Laura suggested and find another profession."

"When hell freezes over," I said. "I'm not letting Rupert or any other scumbag run me out of my chosen profession."

"It's your life," Grace said. "I just want you to live it well. Hanging out in bars isn't exactly your style."

"Can we talk about my mental and emotional frailty tomorrow?" I said. "I just don't feel like hearing it right now."

"Fine," Grace said. I looked at her and saw her mouth had drawn into a tight line. "As a matter of fact, why don't you talk with your mother about it, because that's where I'm taking you. You smell like a brewery. I don't think I want you in my bed tonight."

CHAPTER 4

It was pure coincidence that at the same time Rupert Lattimore's case was supposed to be tried in state court, a man named Ben Clancy was going on trial for murder in federal court. Clancy was a former prosecutor, a fire-and-brimstone type who built his reputation on convicting murderers and sending them to prison for life or to their deaths. He'd convicted my Uncle Tommy of murdering my Aunt Linda by falsifying and hiding evidence, but when I got old enough to start practicing law, I vowed to get Tommy out of prison. I did it, too, with the help of a brilliant lawyer and former friend named Richie Fels. Once Tommy was out, I went after Clancy in the next election for district attorney and helped a man named Steve Morris beat him.

Clancy found a way to get me back. After being hired by the United States Attorney, he framed me and convicted me for a murder I hadn't committed. Ben Clancy was the primary reason I spent two years in prison. But when I was exonerated, he was arrested, and now he was standing trial for what he'd done to me.

Since I'd been planning on trying Rupert Lattimore's case during the entire week, my schedule was clear, and I could have taken in some of Clancy's trial. I decided against it because I didn't want to deal with the inevitable questions the media would ask me. I also couldn't bear the thought of looking at Clancy's face. I'd seen him on the television news a couple of times. He looked older and frailer, and he'd lost quite a bit of weight in jail. The thought of seeing him in person, however, nauseated me. I stayed at the office, caught up on paperwork, studied appellate opinions that had come down recently that might impact some of my clients, met with a few new prospects, and agreed to take two cases—a vehicular homicide that had some legitimate issues, and an arson case that appeared so circumstantial I didn't think the client would ever be convicted.

The Clancy trial was moving quickly, and on Wednesday, it appeared to blow up in the prosecution's face. My former friend, Richie Fels, was representing Clancy, which meant Clancy had put up at least $200,000 for Richie's fee. On Wednesday, James Tipton, who had lied through his teeth during my trial but had been coerced and threatened by Clancy to do so, took the stand against Clancy. From everything the television news and the papers said, Richie crushed him on cross-examination. Richie was able to make him admit that nearly every word out of his mouth during my trial was a lie. Once a liar, always a liar, Richie inferred to the jury. If he was willing to lie *then*, why should anyone believe him *now*? Richie was also able to make James admit that he'd been a drug dealer for a long time. James said he'd quit, but juries don't like liars and they like drug dealers even less. Richie took the federal government's case and flipped it on its ear. The case started on Monday, went to the jury on Friday afternoon, and within two hours, the jury was back with a verdict.

Clancy was acquitted. He was free.

As soon as the news broke, I got a call from my mom. "Are you all right, Darren? I just heard about Ben Clancy."

"I'm fine. I expected it."

"It just isn't fair," she said. "What is wrong with this system? It sends my brother to prison for almost twenty years for something he didn't do, and it sends my son to prison for something he didn't do. And now Clancy walks away free, and he's guilty as sin."

"It isn't perfect," I said.

"Perfect? It isn't even adequate. There has to be some reform."

"It'd be impossible to change the American judicial system much, especially the criminal justice system. There's just too much money involved now, too many special interests. Policy makers are bought by lobbyists, and the next thing you know, more and more people are going to jail, and more and more jails are being built. The parole and probation systems are huge rackets, the court costs and fees are out of control. It's a mess."

"I think you should get out," she said. "I agree with that psychiatrist you talked to. Go back to school and become a doctor or pharmacist or an engineer. You're smart. You can do anything you want, and I'll help you every way I can."

"That's very kind of you, Mom, but I think I'll stick it out a little while longer. Somebody has to fight for people who can't fight for themselves."

"Where do you think this hero complex came from?" she asked.

"Probably from having to deal with the man you married a long time ago."

She was quiet for a few seconds. "You're probably right about that. Biggest mistake of my life, but if I hadn't married him, I wouldn't have you. So you take the bad with the good, right?"

"Right."

"Well, I just wanted to let you know I was thinking about you and tell you I love you. You're still planning to take Grace out tonight, right?"

"I am."

"So I'll see you sometime tomorrow?"

"Probably late morning."

"I love you, Darren. Have a good night."

"I love you, too, Mom."

CHAPTER 5

The day Clancy was acquitted was Grace Alexander's birthday. She and I had developed a romantic relationship that had begun very subtly during my trial and incarceration and blossomed over the past year and a half. It was also my weekend with Sean, but his mother had taken him to Dollywood over the fall break. I knew how much Sean loved Dollywood and the Gatlinburg and Pigeon Forge area, so I agreed to forgo my visitation that weekend as long as she would let him stay an extra weekend the following month. They wouldn't be back until Sunday afternoon.

On that Friday, Grace picked me up at my mother's house around 7:00 p.m.—my car was dying a slow and painful death—and we drove downtown to Market Square. I'd made us a reservation at The Oliver Hotel, which I'd heard was quaint, had excellent service, and was a little pricey. There was a restaurant adjacent to the hotel called the Oliver Royale, and I'd also made us a reservation there.

"Did you hit the lottery?" Grace said as we waited for a bottle of champagne to be delivered by our waiter.

"I'm doing a lot better on the financial front," I said. "Besides, this is a special occasion."

"Really?" she said. "Care to share?"

"In a little while," I said. "Let's eat first and then take a walk."

I was looking at her over a candle, and the light caused her green eyes to flicker. She was a lawyer, a criminal defense specialist who worked for the Federal Public Defender. Grace was beautiful no matter what she was wearing and whether or not she was wearing makeup or lipstick. But that night she was absolutely exquisite. I'd asked her to dress up because I was taking her somewhere nice, and she'd taken me seriously—strapless black dress and heels, blonde hair wavy and worn loose, makeup perfect. I had trouble keeping my eyes off her, and I was very much looking forward to helping her out of the dress later on.

"I heard about Clancy," she said. "I'm sorry."

I shrugged. "It was inevitable. I knew Richie would chew James up and spit him out in front of the jury. At least the feds had the nerve to go through with the trial. They had to know they were going to lose."

"How have you been sleeping?" Grace asked. "Still a lot of nightmares?"

"This thing with Clancy hasn't helped."

"I wish you'd go back and see Laura. She asks about you every time I see her. She really thinks she could help."

"No, thanks," I said as a bottle of Dom Pérignon, vintage 2006, was placed on the table in a bucket. "She said I should be anything but a lawyer. I'm a lawyer. I'm not a quitter."

We sat while the waiter went through the ritual of opening the champagne, offering me the cork, pouring a small amount for me to taste, and then filling Grace's flute and mine.

"To PTSD," I said, holding up the flute.

"To overcoming PTSD," she said, and I clinked her glass gently. The champagne was perfect, and I took a moment to enjoy the warmth as it slid down my throat.

"So what are you going to do?" Grace said. "Any strategy or plan for dealing with the PTSD?"

"Nah, I think I'll just tough it out," I said. "Eventually the nightmares will ease off. A lot of guys who have been in the service have overcome it. It just takes time. I'm not a big drinker, so that's a plus, and I don't do drugs. I've read some about it, and I think if I take decent care of myself and don't fall into bad habits, I have a good chance of being okay eventually. Besides, sleep is overrated."

Grace smiled. "You're a nut," she said.

"You're right. I really am a nut, and now I have an official diagnosis to prove it."

"I didn't mean it that way. You know you can call me anytime. If you can't sleep, just call and we'll talk until you're ready to try again."

"Will you talk dirty to me?"

"I'll say anything you want."

She would have, too. She was one of the kindest, most considerate people I'd ever met. And she was fun and mischievous and sexy as hell. She was thoughtful and smart and athletic, and we shared a lot of common interests in things like books and movies and University of Tennessee sports. Music, not so much. She loved classical music. I'd tried to wrap my mind around Mozart and Beethoven and Chopin, but I just couldn't feel it. I was more of a Southern rock and country guy. But outside of that, we were a great match. My mom was crazy about her, and Sean thought she hung the moon. Katie was so jealous of her I could tell she wanted to spit every time Grace's name was mentioned, especially if Sean said something nice about her.

We took an hour and a half, lingering over an excellent gourmet meal, and polished off the bottle of Dom. When we were finished, we went outside and strolled through Market Square. We walked by a bench and I asked her whether she'd like to sit for a second. It was early November, but a warm front had rolled in and it was in the midsixties.

"How's your mother?" she asked.

"She's good except for the cat."

"I hated to hear about Tink," Grace said.

Tink was a tabby my mother had owned for eight years. She'd died suddenly of cancer a couple of weeks earlier, and my mother had taken it pretty hard.

"She's had time to grieve," I said. "I'm going to the shelter tomorrow morning to get a kitten. That'll brighten her up."

"You're sweet," Grace said.

"Can I ask you a question?" I said as we sat down on the bench. "What do your parents really think of me?"

Grace's dad was a law professor, sharp as a tack, and her mom was a physician's assistant. They lived very comfortably in San Diego. I'd visited with Grace twice, and while they seemed to tolerate me, I didn't exactly get the sense that I was what they had in mind for their baby girl.

"They don't really know you, Darren," she said. "But they respect my judgment. I think they worry about you because they know what you went through. But they're open-minded people, and they're not judgmental. Why do you ask?"

I reached into my jacket pocket and pulled out a small wooden box. I dropped to one knee in front of her.

"Because I'm in love with their daughter and would like to marry her," I said as I opened the box. It had a small LED light in it and revealed a one-and-a-half-carat diamond that had cost me a small fortune. Grace's eyes widened.

"I love you, Grace Alexander, and can't imagine living without you," I said. "I know I'm not perfect and I bring some baggage, but I promise I'll work hard to overcome it. Will you marry me? I love you more than I can put into words."

Tears slid down both of her cheeks, and she wrapped her arms around my neck. She pulled back for a second, and then kissed me in a way that was transcendent. I'd never felt that way before.

"Yes," she said. "I love you, too, Darren Street. The answer is yes."

CHAPTER 6

Donnie Frazier and Tommy Beane had been in town for two days, just enough to make sure the information they'd received on Darren Street was accurate and to do a little surveillance. As they drove by the white house on Boyd Station Road at two in the morning, they both felt fortunate. It was on a large piece of property, with the nearest neighbor being at least a half mile away. A railroad track ran down the opposite side of the road, so there were no houses at all on that side of the road for a five-mile stretch.

"I hope there ain't no damned yappy dog inside there," Frazier said.

Frazier was a thirty-three-year-old beanpole of a man with long, sandy-blond hair. Six months earlier, he'd been released from the Northern Correctional Facility in Moundsville, West Virginia, after serving twelve years of a sixteen-year sentence for second-degree attempted murder.

Frazier's brother, Bobby Lee Frazier, had stabbed Darren Street eleven times with an ice pick during an altercation in Street's cell when they were in the same federal maximum security prison in Rosewood, California, a year and a half earlier. Bobby Lee wound up getting his throat cut by Street's cellmate during the fight, but the cellmate later hanged himself. Donnie Frazier yearned for revenge for his brother's death, and Street was the only person left alive.

Frazier looked over at his cohort, Tommy Beane. They'd grown up together in Cowen, West Virginia. Frazier thought Beane was stupid, but he tolerated him, mostly because he just didn't have many friends. Beane was a burglar by trade, a lifelong thief and thug. He was short and thick, barrel-chested and heavily muscled, with black hair that he combed straight back, dark eyes, and muttonchop sideburns. The Frazier boys and Beane were all high school dropouts by the age of sixteen and had partied together, broken into houses and businesses together, and hurt people together. Theirs was a bond of redneck sociopathy—violence, and indifference to the lives of others. Beane had actually had a real job once. He'd worked for Archland Coal in Cowen for two years. It was during his tenure at Archland that he'd learned how to handle explosives. He also knew where Archland kept its dynamite and blasting caps, and just a few days earlier, Donnie had taken advantage of Beane's knowledge and experience. He'd talked Tommy into breaking into Archland's warehouse, and they'd stolen fifty pounds of dynamite—more than a hundred sticks—enough caps to ignite them, and a roll of safety fuse.

Frazier had watched while Beane crimped the fuse into the blasting caps and bound the sticks into two bundles of twenty-five each back at the hotel. They were both sober tonight, and Frazier was dying for a beer. But dealing with high explosives required a steady hand and a clear mind, Beane kept saying. Sobriety actually made Frazier shaky, but he'd agreed to stay sober until the job was done. He figured they would celebrate after Street was dead.

"His car is in the driveway," Frazier said as they passed the house a second time. "He's there. No lights on. Let's park at that church down the road and walk back."

Frazier parked the beat-up, fifteen-year-old green Ford pickup behind the church, and the men pulled two gym bags from behind the seat. They crossed the road and disappeared behind the line of trees that had grown between the railroad tracks and the road. Once they reached the house, they ducked beneath the deck out back, slithered on their bellies up under the crawl space, and placed the dynamite near the center of the house. Beane then rolled out thirty feet of safety fuse and lit it, and the two men took off running. They made it back to their car in a little less than ten minutes. Frazier jumped in, started the truck, and pulled up near the road with the lights off.

"How much longer?" Frazier said.

"About four minutes. Do you want to get the hell out of here, or do you want to watch it blow?"

"I'm watching," Frazier said. "Son of a bitch was responsible for my brother getting killed. I'm gonna sit here and watch him go up in flames."

CHAPTER 7

The night I spent with Grace at the Oliver Hotel was magical.

Until I got a call at four in the morning.

It was from my friend Bob Ridge, the football coach and Knoxville policeman. When the phone woke me up, I looked at the caller ID and wondered, *What the hell?*

"Something wrong, Bob?" I said into the phone.

"Oh, Darren, thank God you're okay. Where are you?"

"I'm at a hotel with Grace. What's up?"

"There's been a . . . there's been . . . Darren, you need to come to your mother's house right away."

I couldn't imagine what was going on, but an internal alarm went off and I immediately felt an incredible sense of anxiety. This was going to be bad. I just *knew* it was going to be bad.

"Why?" I said. "What's happened?"

"I don't want to talk about it over the phone. You just need to get here as soon as you can."

Grace had awakened by the time I hung up.

"I'm sorry," I said, "but we need to leave. That was Bob Ridge. Something has happened at my mom's."

"Any idea what?" Grace said.

"He wouldn't say, but from the tone of his voice, it isn't good."

It took us about twenty minutes to get dressed, get checked out, and get into the car. It took another fifteen to drive to my mom's. I could see red-and-blue lights flashing three-quarters of a mile from her house. A quarter of a mile from her house, we were stopped by a Knoxville police officer and told we couldn't get through. I explained to him who I was and that Bob Ridge had called me, and he let us pass. When we pulled up near the house—we had to stop a couple of hundred yards away because of all the emergency vehicles blocking the road—I got out and started jogging. It didn't take long before I realized that my mother's house, the house she had lived in for decades and that she loved, was nothing but a smoldering pile of ash. It had been completely obliterated. My car was leaning against a tree fifty feet from where it had been parked in the driveway.

I stopped dead in my tracks, staring in disbelief. *How could this possibly be? Was I having one of my nightmares? Would I wake up in a minute drenched in sweat and babbling incoherently? There was a house there. My mom's house. It was built solidly of wood and stone and concrete, and was full of furniture and appliances and photographs and knickknacks. How could it be gone?*

Grace caught up to me a couple of seconds later and I heard her mutter, "Oh my God. No."

Bob Ridge's massive form came into focus a minute later.

"What . . . what happened?" I could barely speak.

"We're not sure yet," he said. "Did your mother have a propane tank?"

"No. Everything in the house is electric. The fucking house is gone, Bob. Where's my mom?"

"We're looking, Darren."

"Is her car around? It was in the garage. That's my car against the tree over there."

"There's a car, well, what's left of a car, buried beneath the rubble at the far end of the house."

"Then she was home. She's dead, isn't she, Bob?"

"It's too early to say. Take it easy. Maybe we'll find her."

I was numb. I felt my legs give, and I dropped to my knees. I wanted to yell at the sky and curse God. I wanted to kill something or someone. I wanted to cry, because at my core, I knew this was somehow related to me. Whoever had done this wanted me dead.

After a minute, I looked up at Bob. He and Grace seemed like apparitions.

"You'll find her," I said, "in pieces."

CHAPTER 8

I was right. Over the next three days, as they sifted through the ash and rubble of what had been my mother's home, they found bits and pieces of her. Part of a leg here. A burned piece of skull there. A couple of fingers. The only comfort I could take from any of it was that she had obviously been killed instantly. She hadn't suffered.

What little was found of her was sent to Neeley's Funeral Home in Farragut, and a memorial service was held a week after her death. I was told later it was well attended and that the preacher did a wonderful job paying tribute to my mom. It was all like a mist-shrouded dream to me. I barely remembered attending and didn't remember any details.

All of my clothes were gone and my car was destroyed, along with mementos from high school and college, and cards and letters I'd received from Sean, my mom, and Grace. Nothing—absolutely nothing—in that house had survived the blast intact. Grace was kind enough to allow me to move into her apartment, but I slept on the couch. She bought me clothes and hovered over me, but I could barely acknowledge her. I purposefully kept her at a distance, emotionally and physically, because I knew something deep inside of me had changed, something had broken, and I knew innately that I had become dangerous. All I could think about was what I was going to do to whoever had killed my mom. Sometimes I fantasized about kidnapping the person and torturing him, cutting off ears and fingers and toes and limbs. Sometimes I thought about burning him alive. I thought about waterboarding him and then shooting him in the head. The thoughts were ugly and vile, and I was almost ashamed of myself.

Almost.

The police came around immediately. Two Knoxville homicide investigators, Dawn Rule and Lawrence Kingman, were assigned to find my mother's murderer. They were, of course, assisted by a slew of arson investigators and forensics investigators. The day after my mother's memorial service, Dawn Rule called me and asked whether I would come to the Knoxville Police Department headquarters the following morning. I agreed. The nondescript brick building was on Howard Baker Jr. Avenue, a couple of miles east of Neyland Stadium. I showed up at eight thirty.

Dawn Rule was a blue-eyed redhead around forty, a little overweight, with pale skin. She wore her hair short and spoke in a chirpy voice. She was wearing a pair of navy-blue pants and a white blouse, open at the neck, with a badge and gun clipped to her belt. Kingman was younger by a few years, maybe thirty-five. His receding hairline had been clipped within a quarter inch of his scalp, and he had chocolate-brown eyes and a nose that looked like it had been broken more than once. I'd already talked to both of them briefly; they'd checked my alibi at the hotel, and I didn't think I was a suspect in my mother's murder.

I was escorted into an interview room by Detective Rule, and she offered me a bottle of water, which I accepted. Kingman came in a couple of seconds later and closed the door.

"Dynamite," Kingman said, his tone matter-of-fact. "Our forensics people have confirmed through the lab that dynamite was used to blow up your mother's home."

"What kind of a coward does something like that?" I asked. It was almost appropriate that dynamite had been used, because I felt as though a fuse had lit inside of me. It had been smoldering for years, since Clancy had framed me and sent me off to prison, and while I'd endured and tried to overcome the things that had happened to me there, now my mother's death had become the spark that ignited the fuse. It was burning hot and fast, and I knew it would soon lead to a violent explosion.

"Any way to trace the dynamite?" I said.

"We've been working on it with the Bureau of Alcohol, Tobacco, Firearms and Explosives. It appears the dynamite was purchased by Archland Coal Company in West Virginia. They blow holes in the mountains and mine coal."

"And why would a coal-mining company in West Virginia want to kill my mother?"

Rule cleared her throat. "We think the question is: why would a coal-mining company want to kill you?"

I nodded my head. "I've thought about that—a lot. I've made a bunch of enemies during my career, dealt with a lot of whack jobs. I didn't really think any of them would do something like this, but I guess I was wrong. I don't recall ever pissing off a coal-mining company, though. What have you found?"

"We think a resident of a little place called Cowen, West Virginia, population about five hundred souls, may be responsible," Rule said.

"I don't know anybody from Cowen, West Virginia," I said.

"Maybe you do, or at least you did."

"Yeah? Who's that?"

"A man named Robert Edward Lee Frazier. Ever heard of him?"

I felt my heart speed up just a tick. She was talking about Bobby Lee Frazier, the man who stabbed me eleven times with a twelve-inch ice pick because I kicked his ass in a prison yard and embarrassed him in front of his friends after he'd tried to intimidate me into doing legal work for him for free.

"I've heard of him," I said, "but he's dead. He didn't do it."

"We know he's dead. Your cellmate killed him, defending you."

"I didn't tell you that." I was still uncomfortable talking about anything that had happened in prison, especially to the police. "But even if I had told you that—which I didn't—what difference would it make?"

"Bobby Lee has a brother," Detective Kingman said. "Name's Donald Jackson Frazier. Everybody calls him Donnie. He was released from prison six months ago. It might have been him looking to get to you."

If it *was* him, he would soon be meeting me face-to-face. I certainly didn't say that to the two police officers sitting in front of me, but that was exactly what went through my mind. "What prison was he in?"

"Why?"

"I don't know, might have run across him."

"I doubt it," Kingman said. "You were in the federal system. He was in the West Virginia state system, a place called The Northern Correctional Facility in Moundsville."

"Moundsville, huh? Sounds like a place I'm glad I didn't get to visit. Listen, I've thought about it a lot, and the more I think about it, the longer the list of suspects gets. It might have been some clown from West Virginia, but it might also have been Ben Clancy, or some friend of Rupert Lattimore, or any one of a dozen other outstanding citizens I've defended over my career."

Frazier's brother made sense. Perfect sense, but I didn't want the police to arrest him. If he had really killed my mom, I wanted to confirm it myself and deal with it in my own way.

"Have you talked to this Frazier guy?"

"We haven't found him yet," Detective Rule replied. "He chose to serve all of his sentence, didn't want to be on parole, so he isn't under any kind of supervision."

"Think he did it alone?"

"Not unless he knows a lot about explosives. The dynamite was placed to do maximum damage, and they made sure they used more than enough to destroy the house and kill anyone inside. Plus, you have to know what you're doing with dynamite. You have to use blasting caps and crimp the safety fuse into the caps. You can blow yourself up in a hurry if you screw up."

"So you have two suspects plus every crazy who was unhappy with my efforts on their behalf in the courtroom," I said. "Is that all?"

"We have one suspect and believe he probably had an accomplice," Rule said, correcting me. "That's it for now. We just wanted to fill you in. Thought you'd want to know."

"I appreciate it." I was suddenly anxious to get out of there and get busy on my own. "Let me know if there's anything I can do to help."

CHAPTER 9

The police didn't know it, but I had a far more reliable source of information than them. His name was Mike "Big Pappy" Donovan, and he was the shot caller of the Independent White Boy car at the federal max prison in Rosewood, California, when I was there. Inmates divide themselves into groups, primarily based on race. They're called cars. Some guys choose to ride in gang cars—Bloods, Crips, Aryans, MS-13—but others choose not to gangbang. Those guys wind up in independent cars, and since I was white, I wound up in the Independent White Boy car. Pappy was the leader, or "shot caller." He negotiated with leaders of other cars for rights to prison hustles like gambling and drug dealing and cigarette selling; he negotiated solutions to disputes between people in his own car and between people in his car who might have a beef with people in another car. He negotiated with the guards and the prison administrators. He was roughly the same size as Bob Ridge—six feet seven inches tall—and he was muscular. If you got out of line, he could, and would, ruin your day.

I had handled an appeal for him and was actually able to get him out of prison. We proved that the cop who had arrested him on a bogus crack cocaine charge was a liar, and Pappy was released after serving twelve years of a thirty-five-year sentence for distributing crack cocaine. Before he was released, though, he helped me escape, and I was subsequently able to prove my own innocence with the help of Grace.

Big Pappy and I had been in touch a few times since we'd been freed. He owned a trucking company that was based in Georgia, and he traveled through Knoxville occasionally, so we'd been able to have a few meals and a few beers and talk about our time at the prison.

The first time we got together was at a bar in the Old City. After he got a few beers in him, he said, "Darren, old buddy, I have a confession to make."

"You shot the governor," I said.

He laughed and said, "Nah, I stay out of politics. But when I told you I hadn't ever messed with cocaine while you were working on my appeal, I wasn't exactly being truthful. The cop that eventually busted me was crooked as hell, and we did the right thing in my appeal. But I moved a bunch of powder coke back in the day. Did some other bad things, too. I sort of deserved all that time they gave me in prison, not that I want to go back."

I shook my head and smiled. I knew Pappy was no angel. You didn't do the things he did in prison without having an extra-hard shell and a healthy dose of crazy predator in you. But I played along. "You're kidding me, right?" I said.

"Afraid not. I played you. I wanted you to believe in my innocence, thought it would make you try harder. I was right, too, wasn't I?"

"Probably," I said.

"Still friends?" he said.

"Friends? You helped me break out of prison and get myself cleared. I'll always be your friend. How's Linda, anyway?"

Linda Lacy was a woman who Pappy claimed as his girlfriend while he was in prison. She continued the trucking company he'd started and ran it for twelve years. She also hid and invested the millions he made in prison from his various hustles. Linda had given me a ride across the country in an eighteen-wheeler when I broke out of prison.

"Linda's not around anymore," Pappy said. "I caught her in bed with a guy who worked for me. Thought he was my friend. I didn't take it well."

"So you sent her packing?"

"In a manner of speaking," he said. "I sent her a long, long ways away. I'm afraid she won't ever be coming back, if you know what I mean."

"I think that's all I want to hear," I said.

"Probably for the best. You can take a little comfort in knowing that she didn't go on her journey alone. Her lover went with her."

Pappy had just told me he'd killed two people. He trusted me, and after what he'd done for me in prison, I trusted him. I knew he had far more contacts within the prison walls than I did, because he'd been in so much longer, been to so many more prisons, and he'd been a shot caller. He'd also told me he missed prison in a strange sort of way, and that he stayed in touch with a lot of guys on the inside. He didn't miss it enough to want to go back, but being a shot caller is the ultimate sign of respect in a prison, and he told me he missed that kind of respect.

I called him within five minutes of leaving the police station. He'd heard what happened to my mother and had even showed up for her memorial service even though he'd never met her. I didn't remember him being there, but Grace had told me he'd come.

"My man, Darren," he said when he answered his cell. "You all right?"

"I need to talk to you," I said, "but not over the phone. Where are you?"

"In Cincinnati, but I'm headed your way. Be rolling through Knoxville in about four hours."

"You know the Flying J truck stop on Watt Road?"

"Been there many times."

"Meet you there around one thirty this afternoon?"

"You got it, brother."

"I'll be waiting in the lot out back. When I see your truck pull in, I'll just come get in the cab."

"Sounds like a plan. See you in a few hours."

Big Pappy showed up right on time in his gleaming, black Kenworth with "Donovan Trucking" emblazoned in gold on the trailer. I'd taken a cab to the truck stop and waved him down when I saw him pull in. He stopped the truck, and I climbed into the cab. I reached over and shook his massive hand.

"Good to see you, my brother," Pappy said.

"Good to see you," I said. "I might as well get right to it. The cops might have a line on who killed my mother, but I want to find them first. I'm going to need your help."

"Who are they looking at?" Pappy said.

"Guy named Donnie Frazier from West Virginia. He was Bobby Lee Frazier's brother. Did you know Bobby Lee was from West Virginia or that he had a brother?"

Pappy shook his head. "No, man, I didn't know that much about him. Didn't want to know."

"Well, this brother was released from a prison in a place called Moundsville, West Virginia, six months back, and they think he might have been looking for revenge."

"Moundsville, huh? Know the name of the joint?"

"Northern Correctional Facility."

"What do you want me to do?" Pappy said.

"Just do your thing. Use your contacts. Find out if anybody's talking, if anybody knows anything about it. You know how it is in prison. If he talked about this before he left, or even after, somebody's going to know. He might have had an accomplice, too. Somebody who knows about explosives."

"And if I find out it was him and that he had a partner?"

"I'd appreciate it if you'd share that information with me."

"And do you mind if I ask what you plan to do with the information?"

"Don't mind at all. If I leave this to the system, they'll probably eventually get around to arresting him and extraditing him back to Knoxville. He'll sit in a cell, he'll get three meals a day, he'll play cards, have sex if he wants to, do drugs, and drink hooch. He'll live a shit life, but he'll be *living*, you know what I mean? Then they'll either try him or he'll make a deal, and he'll get shipped off to a penitentiary, probably for the rest of his miserable life, and the good people of the state of Tennessee will keep him up. They'll house him and feed him and give him medical and dental care. He'll have a better social life in the penitentiary than he'll have in jail. He'll even get to exercise if he wants to. To be entirely honest with you, Pap, I'm kind of over the system right now. This guy probably blew my mother to bits, trying to kill me. If you find out he really did it, I'm going to hunt down the son of a bitch—and his friend, if he has one—and I'm going to blow their brains out."

CHAPTER 10

For the next two days, while I was waiting to hear from Pappy, all I could think about was my mom. Had she been awake when it happened? Had she been afraid? Had she heard someone outside the house? Had she been about to call the police? Had she even heard the explosion? Had she felt anything at all? Had she been in pain when she died? And what if Sean had been there that night? He would have been killed, too. The thought of Sean dying along with my mother was almost too much to bear.

Finally, my cell rang. It was a number I didn't recognize. I answered it, anyway.

"It's me." The voice was Big Pappy Donovan's. "I'm on a throwaway phone. You trust yours?"

"There's no reason for them to suspect me of anything," I said, "but no, I don't trust it."

"Go buy a burner and call me back on this number."

I drove to Walmart—by this time I'd bought another used junker, a compact car—and paid thirty bucks in cash for a prepaid cell. Back in prison, they'd gone for between $500 and $1,000, depending on how many minutes they had on them. The guards brought them in and sold them. It was their most profitable hustle. I walked back to my car, got in, and dialed Pappy's burner phone.

"It was Donnie Frazier," he said.

"Are you sure?"

"Positive. He's been broadcasting that he was going to kill you since Dino whacked Bobby Lee in your cell."

"Anybody with him?"

"Cracker named Tommy Beane. They grew up together in the same town, wound up at the same prison, and were released within two months of each other. Word is Beane used to blow holes in mountainsides for a coal company up in West Virginia, so he knows explosives. They're your guys. I'd bet my life on it."

"Any idea how I find them?"

"They're both staying in a trailer with a woman a couple of miles outside of Cowen, West Virginia. It's on Williams River Road. I'll have the address tomorrow, but I think a better play if you're really going to do this is to catch them outside a little bar called Sammy's, which is on the east end of town on Webster Road. Donnie and Tommy apparently close the place down every Friday and Saturday. The parking lot might be a good spot."

"I'll check it out," I said.

"Do you have a clean gun?"

"No. Everything I owned was destroyed when they blew up the house. Can you get me a gun? And maybe some ID in case I get stopped. I guess I'll end up driving to West Virginia."

"No problem. You need a car?"

"I just bought a junker, but it'd be nice to have something more reliable."

"I'll get you something. How are you doing on money?"

"Okay, but I'd rather not withdraw money or leave any kind of trail when I get ready to go."

"I'll put twenty grand in cash in the trunk of the car. The gun and the ID will be in there, too. You can pay me back later if you want."

"Thanks, Pappy. Do I leave the car where I pick it up?"

"Yeah, leave it in back of the Flying J out where the truckers park overnight. There aren't any cameras out there. When are you going?"

"I'll figure that out as soon as you get me that address. If I can't do them in the parking lot, I'll go to the trailer."

"Dangerous. So many people have dogs. They'll probably have guns at the trailer. A lot can go wrong there. And don't be in a hurry. Take your time and do it right. Make sure you do what you want to do, but don't get caught."

"I'll figure it out."

"Darren, are you sure about this? You haven't ever killed anyone, have you?"

I took a deep breath before I answered. "No, I've never killed anyone."

"Big step to take."

"I can't stop thinking about what they did to my mom. They had to know it was her house and that she was in there. They didn't give a damn about her. And it was pure luck that Sean wasn't there that night. They would have killed him, too."

"You don't think the cops are up to the task?"

"I think my attitude toward Donnie Frazier's and Tommy Beane's constitutional rights has changed. As far as I'm concerned, they don't have any. I'm going to kill them, Pappy, I'm going to get away with it, and I'm not going to regret it. I really only have one concern."

"Yeah? What's that?"

"I'm afraid I might enjoy it."

CHAPTER 11

That night, as I lay in bed with my eyes closed, listening to Grace's rhythmic breathing, I kept seeing my mom's face on the inside of my eyelids. It was as though she was being projected onto a screen. The face would be calm, and then it would smile, and then her mouth would open as if she were screaming, and then it would explode, only to return to the screen, piece by piece, an explosion in reverse. It became haunting after a while, and I opened my eyes and sat up on the side of the bed. I got up and went into the bathroom, drank some water, and tiptoed back into the room. I glanced at the digital clock on the bedside table near Grace. It was two in the morning, but I knew I wasn't going to sleep anytime soon. And even if I did, since my mom's death, the nightmares and the thoughts of killing whoever had bombed her house had increased in frequency and intensity. I'd gotten to the point where I would rather stay awake.

I went into Grace's den and picked up a book I'd bought from Amazon, *Man's Search for Meaning*. It had been written in 1946 by an Austrian of Jewish descent named Viktor Frankl. Frankl was a trained psychologist and had been imprisoned in three different Nazi concentration camps during World War II. It was during his imprisonment that he'd also turned toward philosophy as a means of trying to survive the terrible conditions under which he was being held. His message was largely positive, but there were sections of the book that talked about the depersonalization of inmates who had been liberated and who were so numb they were initially unable to understand what freedom meant or how to emotionally respond to being free again. It was probably the first academic, intellectual approach to Post Traumatic Stress Disorder, although he hadn't used that terminology. I had gone through many of the things he described when I was released from prison, and that's why I'd wound up in the same room with Dr. Benton. It took me a while to get my "free legs," as I called it. I couldn't comprehend pleasure. Everything was so surreal that I was simply unable to enjoy simple pleasures and deal with the lack of constant restriction.

Frankl wrote that a second stage began after the mind initially accepted the person was again free, and it was during that stage that a very real danger of mental illness presented itself. Many former concentration camp prisoners became obsessed with dispensing the same kind of violence that their abusers had dispensed. When I was first released from prison, I'd had some of those thoughts, but I'd been able to put them out of my mind because I had my mom and Sean and Grace. I'd had nightmares constantly, and while I'd occasionally thought about violence and murder, I hadn't been obsessive. But after what happened to my mom, I found myself in a state of mind that I knew wasn't normal and was definitely dangerous. All I could think about was killing the two men who Big Pappy said were responsible for her death. I knew, at some level, that what I was thinking about doing was wrong and could land me right back in jail, but I'd made up my mind that I was going to kill them. If I was caught and they tried to imprison me again, I would find a way to commit suicide.

As I turned a page in Frankl's book, I noticed movement in the hallway. Grace appeared, wearing a sheer, black nightgown that was backless and had spaghetti straps. She looked incredible wearing it, but I hadn't had any desire to touch her since the day my mom was killed. She sat down on the couch next to me and snuggled in. "Can't sleep again?"

"I tried. Didn't work out."

"How's the book?"

"I don't think it's helping much, to be honest. I mean, I'm trying to accept this guy's message that life is about loving others, that love should be the ultimate goal of any meaningful life, and that if I'll just open my heart and give myself to others, my life will have real meaning, and everything else will work itself out. But I'm not feeling it. I mean, the night my mom was murdered I had just offered to give myself to you for the rest of our lives. I told you I loved you, I showed you I loved you, and every bit of it was sincere. And then what happens? Mom is murdered."

She put her hand on my arm. "You're grieving, Darren. You're going through a period of denial and isolation. It's perfectly normal, and it will pass. When it does, you'll probably become angry."

"I'm already angry," I said.

"Okay, then you have every right to be. You've been through a lot over the past few years, and this is completely over the top. But we have to be careful. We have to make sure you don't become self-destructive. You need to go back and see Laura, and you have to be open and honest with me. I'll help you through this, Darren. You still have me, and you still have Sean. I know it just seems like talk right now, but all we really need is time. Time and love will get you through this terrible thing."

"Thank you, Grace," I said. I reached over and caressed her cheek. "I appreciate what you're trying to do."

I wondered what she would think or do if she knew what I was planning. Would she shun me? Try to talk me out of it? Ultimately, it didn't matter. I'd made up my mind.

"Would you like to come back to bed?" she asked. "Are you ready to make love to me?"

"I want to," I said, and I was sincere. "I really, really, want to. But I just don't think I can right now. I don't think I could let myself go."

"It's all right," she said. "You'll be ready soon enough."

"Go back to bed. I feel guilty keeping you up."

She stood, bent over, and kissed me on the forehead. "I love you. I'll see you in the morning."

"I love you, too. Good night."

As soon as she disappeared into the darkness of her bedroom, I closed Frankl's book, leaned my head back, and closed my eyes.

The image of my mother was gone. It was replaced by a faceless man lying on the ground. He was faceless only because I didn't yet know what Donnie Frazier looked like. I was standing over him, straddling him, with a pistol pointed at his forehead.

I pulled the trigger, and the blood sprayed.

CHAPTER 12

I decided to take Big Pappy's advice, so it took me a couple of weeks to get things arranged so I could make the trip to West Virginia. First, I had to pick up the car and the extras I needed. The car was a white Chevy Monte Carlo. Georgia plates. In the trunk was a backpack that contained $20,000 in hundred-dollar bills, a couple of prepaid cells, and two Georgia driver's licenses with my photo on them. One of them had been photoshopped to make it appear as though I wore a beard and glasses. They both said my name was David Wilkes and that I lived in Atlanta. There was a matte-black, Beretta 92FS nine-millimeter pistol with a box of ammunition and two fifteen-round magazines. There were also two eight-by-ten, glossy mug shots of Donnie Frazier and Tommy Beane with the address Big Pappy had told me about written on the back of Donnie's mug shot. I immediately went to a gun store in Maryville and bought ten more boxes of ammo. Then I went to a Walmart in Surgoinsville and bought another ten. I wanted to put at least a thousand rounds through the Beretta before I aimed it at Donnie Frazier and Tommy Beane.

I parked the Monte Carlo in a StorageMax facility not far from my law office. The space was ten feet by thirty feet and cost more than $200 a month, but thanks to Pappy, I had plenty of money. I paid cash and used one of the false IDs Pappy had provided, the one without the bearded face in the photo.

The next thing I did was call an old law school friend of mine, Marty Henley. Marty and I had graduated at the same time, had taken several classes together, and had done some fishing together. I knew Marty was also an avid hunter and his family leased a couple of hundred acres northwest of Knoxville just outside of Petros—not far from the old Brushy Mountain State Penitentiary—on which they hunted deer. I told Marty I'd decided to get into shooting and asked whether he'd let me go up there and practice. He was more than happy to oblige. His family had a shooting range all set up, he said. He gave me directions, and I spent several evenings there over the next ten days. I was getting behind at my law practice, and I could tell Grace was wondering what I was up to and where I'd been each night when I came home. But she didn't push, and I didn't offer any explanations.

In the meantime, I was talking to Pappy. He had a guy on-site in West Virginia, making sure nothing had changed. Frazier and Beane were still living with the woman in the trailer on Williams River Road just outside of Cowen. They were still frequenting the bar called Sammy's. They were sleeping during the day and breaking into cars and houses at night.

As a final touch, and at Pappy's suggestion after seeing the second photo ID he sent me, I went into a costume store in the Old City downtown district and bought a realistic-looking fake beard and some adhesive. I also bought some nonprescription glasses that made me look like Clark Kent.

On the night before I left for West Virginia, a cold drizzle started to fall just as I left the range where I'd shot two hundred rounds through the Berretta. It was a Wednesday, and I showed up at Grace's apartment just after dark and walked in. I could hear classical music playing— probably Beethoven—and smelled garlic sautéing in a pan. I walked into the kitchen, and Grace was standing at the stove, wearing a red apron over her jeans and button-down blouse. There was a half-empty glass of red wine on the counter behind her.

"Hungry?" she asked.

I nodded. I wasn't hungry, but there was no point in hurting her feelings. "What's cooking?"

"Chicken parm."

"The garlic smells fantastic."

"It'll be ready in about forty-five minutes. Would you like some wine?"

I'd stayed away from alcohol since my mom's murder, afraid of how it might affect me, but Grace was smiling and the mood was so pleasant that I accepted. "Sure. Just half a glass, though."

"You should loosen up just a little."

"I'm trying."

She turned down the heat on the garlic, poured a half glass of wine, and walked over to me. She set the wine down on the counter and draped her arms around my neck. "You're the best-looking man I've ever seen, you know that?"

"And you're the most beautiful woman I've ever laid eyes on."

"Do you still want to marry me, Darren? It hasn't come up since . . . well, it hasn't come up."

"Of course I still want to marry you. I just need a little time. I remember the night I proposed to you, while I was kneeling, and told you I know I bring a lot of baggage but I'd work hard to overcome it. I have more baggage now, which means I have to work harder. I'm working, Grace, I swear I am."

"Is that where you've been every evening? Working on your baggage?"

"You could say that."

"Don't be coy with me, Darren. Are you seeing someone on a regular basis? A counselor or psychiatrist?"

"A grief counselor," I lied.

She smiled a smile so genuine it made me feel even more ashamed for lying. Then she kissed me gently on the lips and turned back to the stove. "I'm proud of you."

"Grace, I need to tell you something. I'm going to go away for the weekend."

"What? Where?"

"I'm just going to get out of here for a couple of days. I'll be back by Monday, maybe even Sunday evening. I'll probably fish a little and camp. I just want to try to clear my head."

"You don't want some company?"

"I'd love some company, but the counselor says I need to try to sort a few things out on my own, and that's what I plan to do. You won't be able to reach me. I'm not even going to take my phone."

Grace reached around for her glass of wine and held it up. "To peace of mind."

"To peace of mind," I said, and we both took a drink.

CHAPTER 13

I left Grace's apartment at six in the morning, drove to Walmart, and purchased some inexpensive fishing gear and some camping gear. It was all for show. All for the cameras. It was an alibi, albeit a flimsy one, because if everything went right, not a single living soul on this fishing-camping trip would see or talk to me. The drive through the rain to Cowen was miserable. The roads were winding, narrow, and full of potholes. I took the long way, getting off the interstate at Kingsport, Tennessee, and heading up back roads through Tennessee, Virginia, Kentucky, and West Virginia, because I didn't want to go through any tollbooths, and the shorter routes involved tollbooths. Tollbooths had cameras.

At mile marker 41 on Interstate 81, not far from Greeneville, Tennessee, I pulled into a rest stop. I went into the bathroom and closed myself into a stall, carrying a shaving kit that contained the beard, a small mirror, some adhesive, and the glasses I'd bought. I brushed the adhesive on my face, rubbed it around, let it dry, and then carefully placed the beard around my mouth and up to my sideburns. The color matched my hair almost perfectly, and it actually looked extremely realistic. I put the glasses on and walked out of the stall. I looked in the mirror. All I needed was a cap—which I had in the front seat of the car—and nobody would recognize me.

The drive took almost seven hours, which meant I arrived in the hell-on-earth town known as Cowen, West Virginia, between one thirty and two in the afternoon. The place was full of run-down houses and trailers. There was an auto-parts store, a funeral home, a couple of small convenience stores, several churches, and a smattering of bars and fraternal organizations like the Moose Club and a VFW. It reeked of depression and poverty, and the low, gray skies and drizzling rain only intensified the impression. I drove around, familiarized myself with Sammy's tavern, and drove by the address Pappy had given me. The green Ford truck he said belonged to Donnie Frazier's girlfriend was parked in the driveway of the run-down gray trailer. There were trash bags strewn about the yard, along with an old washer and dryer and a rusted-out car sitting on concrete blocks. The trailer sat on a gentle grade. There were trailers within fifty feet on both sides, probably members of Frazier's girlfriend's family. I saw no fewer than four Doberman Pinschers running free among the three trailers. If I was going to kill Frazier and Beane—and I had every intention of doing so—it would have to be in the parking lot of the bar.

After hanging around Cowen for an hour or so, I drove another twenty minutes to Webster Springs and checked into a small hotel there, wearing the ball cap, the beard, and the glasses. Again, I used the fake ID and paid cash for one night. If I wasn't able to kill Frazier and Beane on Friday night, I'd check in to a different hotel later and kill them on Saturday. The hotel clerk, an elderly woman who I knew would more than likely be shown my photograph—sans the disguise—by the police within a week or so, barely paid attention.

I went to my room, unpacked my things, and began obsessively cleaning the Beretta. Every time I'd used it at the range, I'd cleaned it before I left. I'd become extremely proficient with the Beretta. At ten to fifteen yards, which is where I guessed my targets would be when I cut loose on them, I could pretty much put a bullet wherever I wanted. I'd practiced moving, and I'd practiced in the rain and wind. I'd practiced in low light but not at night. I'd initially used only the traditional factory sights, but I'd later added Crimson Trace laser sights to the pistol because I'd read they would improve accuracy in darkness and awkward shooting positions. And I wanted to be sure I killed both of those sonsofbitches, no matter what the conditions were.

Once I was finished cleaning the pistol, I drove a couple of miles down the road and found a fast food restaurant, where I ordered at the drive-through and took the food back to my room. I flipped on the television and ate the greasy burger and fries, and then, out of the blue, I fell sound asleep. I awoke four hours later without even having dreamed. It was the first time in weeks I'd slept for that long without having a nightmare, and I could only believe that it was because I'd found the peace of mind Grace had mentioned the night before. I'd actually traveled several hundred miles to commit two murders, and knowing I was really going to do it made me feel better.

I stayed in my room all night and until 11:00 a.m., which was checkout time, the next morning. I was extremely careful about what I touched, and I carefully wiped down everything to clear it of fingerprints, just in case. I thought about DNA—hair, sweat, fingernails, flakes of skin—but I decided I'd just have to live with the risk. Even if, by some miracle, the cops managed to track me to that room and got some DNA that matched mine, it still didn't prove I'd killed anyone. It proved only that I was within twenty miles of the crime scene the night before the murders and earlier that day.

I'd slept very little and spent most of the time visualizing how I would handle myself when Frazier and Beane came out of the bar. Would I say anything to them? No need, I decided, because within seconds, they would be dead. I thought about justice quite a bit and whether what I was doing was right or wrong, but ultimately I convinced myself that justice was nothing more than a state-sponsored approach to revenge that used laws drafted by politicians to justify their actions. I was simply acting alone, doing what needed to be done without state sponsorship. They would call me a vigilante. I would think of myself as an avenging angel.

I checked to make sure the beard still looked natural. It was loose in a few spots, so I decided to take it off, shave, and reattach it. When I was finished, it looked perfect. I left the hotel and drove through Cowen two more times that day. It was so small I didn't want to seem conspicuous. I figured out where I was going to park the Monte Carlo—on the street in front of a NAPA auto-parts store a quarter mile from Sammy's bar—and then I decided to go into Sammy's and grab some takeout, just so I could get a look inside the place.

I parked the car a couple of blocks away and walked to the bar. I checked both the outside and inside for security cameras and was relieved to discover there were none. The place was tiny. There were six stools at the bar. Two of the bar stools were occupied by men. There were three booths against the front wall to the right when you entered through the side of the building—all empty—and there was a pool table, a jukebox, an old-style pinball machine, and a dance floor that would accommodate two couples, as long as nobody was obese.

I sat down on one of the bar stools and ordered a cheeseburger to go from Sammy himself. He was wearing a name tag and was the only person working. I wondered why he wore the name tag. A bar like that in such a small town? Everybody had to know who he was. I guess it just made him feel important to wear some kind of badge. Sammy took my order and went back into a tiny kitchen area where there was a flattop grill. He cooked the burger himself and brought it back out.

I paid him in cash and gave him a two-dollar tip, and then I went outside and wandered around the parking lot for a little while. It was gravel, on the right side of the building as you faced it from the road, about fifty feet by seventy feet, and was bordered by the road in the front, an alley to the right, and a creek in the back. There was a drop-off to the creek, and I decided that's where I would wait. I walked down by the creek, sat down, and ate the cheeseburger. It was surprisingly good.

The research I'd done told me that I wasn't up against a quick-reaction force as far as police went. Cowen didn't even have a public police department, although they did have a police "agency" that consisted of five people employed by a private company, two of whom patrolled the town on occasion. There was no jail in Webster County, which was where Cowen was located, and that meant the sheriff's department was also very small. The investigation of the two murders I was about to commit would most likely fall to the West Virginia State Police. They would, no doubt, eventually be contacted by the two Knoxville detectives who had originally told me about Frazier and Beane, and then the heat would come. I had a plan for what I would do when that happened. I was, after all, a criminal defense lawyer. I knew how to handle cops.

After I looked over the parking lot and decided exactly how I would get back to my car after I shot Frazier and Beane, I drove back to Webster Springs and decided to use some of the fishing equipment I'd bought in Knoxville. I passed the afternoon and much of the evening fishing off the bank of the Elk River on the outskirts of the small town. The rain had passed, and while it was chilly, the leaves in the mountains were bright with color, and the sun was shining. It was a good day to exact some revenge.

My mother crossed my mind several times while I was fishing the river. I thought about her attempting to protect me from my drunken and abusive father when I was young, how she would deflect beatings for me onto herself. I thought about how he caused her to lose most of her faith in God, and I thought about the day when I had grown enough to beat him to a bloody pulp and throw him out of the house. My mother was sad that day, but she was proud of me. I thought about how she was with my son, Sean, so patient and kind and understanding. I thought about how she'd sacrificed for me and worked her fingers to the bone so I could go to college and get a law degree. I remembered the look of pride and satisfaction on her face when they hooded me at the law school graduation ceremony. I thought about how she'd stuck by me when I was falsely accused of murdering Jalen Jordan and was held without bail for a year awaiting trial. She stuck by me when they convicted me and carted me off to federal prison. She'd fought for visitation rights with my son, Sean, and was eventually able to see him, which meant I was eventually able to speak with him on the telephone from prison. She helped me keep from losing hope, and when I was released, she helped me get back on my feet.

Her reward?

She was blown to bits while she slept, by two murderous cowards. I kept trying to picture her face, but as time passed, her features had faded. I didn't have a single photograph of her. Everything in the house had been obliterated or burned. The memories were still there, but they were like flames flickering with the passage of time, getting smaller and cooler with each passing day. I wondered several times where she was. One minute, she was lying in her bed asleep, and the next, she was gone. But where? Was her soul floating around somewhere? If so, I hadn't felt it. Was she in another dimension of time and space? Was she in some paradise, playing a harp and floating on a cloud? That seemed as ridiculous as imagining her burning in an eternal fire beneath the surface of the earth. But where was she? She was gone so quickly. It was so surreal and made so little sense. The fact that she'd been blown up in her sleep was so random that I wondered whether anything had any real purpose, whether everything was random, and whether any form of life making it to the natural end of the biological clock was nothing more than pure luck. As darkness fell and I packed up the small tackle box and climbed the bank to get back into my car, I was certain of only one thing.

Donnie Frazier's and Tommy Beane's biological clocks were about to stop ticking.

PART II

PART II

CHAPTER 14

Ninety minutes after the shootings

The rest area was deserted, and I'd done my research and knew there weren't any cameras, but I needed to get out of there quickly. I looked at the blood on my face for a few more seconds, and then I pulled the gloves and the glasses and stocking cap off, removed the beard, and stuck everything into the backpack. I turned on the water and let it run to warm up.

I did it. I killed those bastards.

I stared at myself in the mirror, wondering if I was looking at the same person I'd looked at in the mirror that morning. Of course I wasn't. I couldn't be looking at the same person, because the person I was looking at had recently committed two extremely brutal murders. I was now outside of the law. The question was whether I could remain outside of the penitentiary. I thought about the looks on Donnie Frazier's and Tommy Beane's faces, how they'd changed from redneck-aggressive to genuine surprise to primal fear to lifeless. *Screw those guys,* I thought. I didn't regret a thing.

I wet my hands and began rubbing my face. I rubbed until all the dried blood I could see was gone. I pulled paper towels from the dispenser, dried my face, and stuck the towels in the backpack. As I picked up the backpack and started out of the restroom, all fifteen shots I'd fired played back in my head in slow motion. Explosions roared, bodies jerked, and pink mist floated.

By the time I got back to the car and opened the door, I was smiling.

Three hours after the shootings

Special Agent Will Grimes stifled a yawn as he stood next to Sammy Raft outside Sammy's Bar and Grill and watched as a wood-paneled station wagon sped past him into the parking lot and skidded to a stop in the gravel. Dr. Larry Rogers, otherwise known as "the Crusty Coroner," had arrived.

Grimes had gotten the call pretty quickly. It had been relayed from the bar owner to the county sheriff to the state police detachment in Webster Springs to the state police headquarters in Elkins, West Virginia, which was where Grimes was stationed. Cowen was on the fringe of the large area his troop covered, so Grimes had to drive almost two hours to get to Sammy's bar in the tiny town. Two troopers from Webster Springs had already secured the crime scene. The local sheriff hadn't even bothered to show up.

Grimes was forty, an eighteen-year veteran of the West Virginia State Police. He'd started as a trooper and worked his way up through the patrol ranks, eventually switching over to the Bureau of Criminal Investigation ten years earlier. He was now a sergeant and an experienced criminal investigator. What he'd seen inside Sammy's bar was either an anger killing, a revenge killing, or someone was making an example of those boys. They'd been shot all to hell. Sammy had told him who they were and given him some background information on them. Grimes wasn't really surprised they'd wound up dead. It was the manner in which they'd been killed that bothered him. They'd been executed, pure and simple. Whoever killed them had walked straight up to the booth they were sitting in and just started blasting away. Both of the victims had pistols in their belts, but neither had had a chance to even get a hand on one. It was a killing as cold-blooded as any Grimes had ever witnessed.

Another thing that was bothering him was the story the bar owner, Sammy Raft, was offering. Sammy told Grimes he'd gone into the bathroom around eight o'clock to relieve himself. Donnie Frazier and Tommy Beane, the two victims, had been the only two people in the bar at the time. Sammy said while he was standing at the urinal, all hell broke loose. He said the gunshots were deafening and just kept coming and coming and coming. He couldn't say for sure, but he guessed ten, maybe as many as eighteen or twenty, shots had been fired.

The thing that bothered Grimes was that there weren't any windows in the bar. It was just a concrete block building. You came through the door at the front left side of the building and couldn't see who was there until you got all the way inside. That meant the killer would have had no way of knowing for sure that Sammy wouldn't be standing behind the bar. Was this guy that ballsy, that lucky, or was Sammy lying about the way it had really happened? And if he was lying, why?

A sixtysomething man got out of the 1968 Ford LTD Country Squire station wagon. Grimes recognized him immediately but forced himself not to smile. He'd worked with Rogers many times and knew that he'd driven his "baby girl," which Rogers affectionately called the antique wagon, over from Charleston. Rogers was a gruff, eccentric man, but he was good at what he did. He was small, maybe five feet five inches tall and 130 pounds. He had pale-blue eyes that were always encircled by oval, wire-framed glasses, and the top of his head was bald. The sides and back were covered by long, unruly gray hair, and his chin sported a bushy Vandyke. He covered several counties in West Virginia, just as Grimes did.

"Why ain't your people here yet?" Rogers said to Grimes as he approached. He didn't say hello, didn't offer a hand.

"They're on the way," Grimes said. "Had to gather everybody up, load the gear, and then drive from Elkins. Takes a little while."

"Think this state will ever make it into the twentieth century?" Rogers said.

"I believe this is the twenty-first century, Larry."

"Exactly."

Rogers brushed past Grimes and Sammy Raft and entered the bar. He came out a few minutes later and stood with his hands on his hips a few feet from Grimes. Then he loaded his left jaw with a wad of Red Man chewing tobacco.

"Well," Rogers said as he spit a long stream of tobacco juice into the gravel, "they're dead."

"Yes," Grimes said. "Very astute of you, Larry."

"My guess is that the cause of death is going to be various trauma caused by a shitload of gunshot wounds."

"Appreciate that."

Rogers spit into the gravel again. "Have your boys haul 'em to our lab in Charleston. Got everything I need there for the autopsies. Preliminary report in four, five days. Final in about a month."

"Okay," Grimes said. "We'll bring them up."

"For what it's worth, looks to me like a revenge killing. These boys did something to somebody. They got paid back in spades."

Grimes nodded. "I always respect your opinion."

"Brownnoser," he heard Rogers mutter under his breath as he began to amble back toward his wagon. "Only opinion you respect is yours."

"Quite a guy," Grimes told Sammy as they watched the station wagon tear out of the lot, throwing gravel in its wake.

"Looks a little crazy to me," Sammy offered.

"We're all a little crazy, I suspect," Grimes said. "Listen, Sammy, I have some more work to do, and the forensics team will be inside the bar for most of the night. So you can go on home now. But I'm going to come pick you up at ten in the morning."

"Why?"

"Because I want a written statement from you. We're going to take a ride up to my headquarters in Elkins."

"Do I have to?"

"It'd be best, Sammy. You don't want this to go sideways on you. I just want to make sure you're protected. Go on now. I'll see you in the morning."

"Will this place be cleaned up?" Sammy asked. "Will your guys get all that blood out of there?"

"Sorry. We'll take the bodies, but the rest will be up to you."

CHAPTER 15

"How'd it go?" Big Pappy said into the phone after I'd checked into a hotel off Interstate 64 about thirty miles outside of Lexington, Kentucky. I'd killed Frazier and Beane around eight o'clock and then driven four hours to Lexington. I'd finish the drive into Knoxville the next morning.

"It went," I said.

"They come out early? I didn't expect to hear from you for at least another couple of hours."

"I did it inside the bar. There was nobody else there, and the bartender went to the restroom."

"And nobody saw you?"

"The bartender, but he isn't going to say anything."

"Why not?"

"Because he loved his mother."

"Loved his mother? What are you talking about, Darren? That doesn't make any sense."

"He won't say anything," I said. "Trust me. He hated those two guys. They were ruining his business, and when I told him they'd raped my mother, he pretty much gave me the green light to do whatever I wanted."

"You told him they'd raped your mother?"

"Just to throw the cops off a little."

"He's still a witness. You should have killed him."

"I had no reason to kill him."

"So how did it go down?"

"The bartender went into the bathroom, and I walked up to their booth and did what I went there to do."

"Are you sure they're dead?"

"Positive. I unloaded the whole clip on them, and I shot them both in the head at least three times."

"Damn, Darren. I can't believe you really did it. How do you feel about it now that it's over?"

"I don't regret it, if that's what you're asking."

"That's not what I'm asking. How do you feel after taking somebody's life?"

"Powerful," I said.

"That's some pretty heavy stuff, man. It's the same thing I've felt when I've killed people."

"How many have you killed, Pappy?"

"Does it matter?"

"I guess not, but it doesn't seem like heavy stuff to me. I feel like I've had a huge weight lifted from me. I feel free."

The feeling I was experiencing was something I hadn't expected. I thought I would feel some pangs of guilt or remorse, maybe some horror over the realization that I was capable of committing such a violent act, but I felt none of those things. I felt empowered, relieved, and, like I told Pappy, free of the burden I'd been carrying around, knowing the men who murdered my mother were still breathing.

"So we're sticking to the plan going forward?"

"I'll have the car at the Flying J by noon tomorrow. I'll leave the gun and the ID in the trunk. I'm trusting you to take care of those things. I have the clothes I was wearing, and the disguise, in a gym bag here in the room. I'm going to stop at this piece of property where I've been shooting and burn everything. It's so far in the boonies nobody will ever think to look there."

"What are you going to do when you get back to town?"

"After I drop the car off, I'll take a cab to the storage place where I left mine. Then I'll go to Grace's. I've been neglecting her, and I plan to set that right."

"Neglecting her how?"

"Lots of ways, but I'm going to fix everything."

"What about your law practice? Going back to work?"

"I'm going to act like nothing has happened. Business as usual."

"Congratulations, brother," Pappy said.

"On what?"

"On becoming a member of the fraternity. Not everybody has what it takes to do what you did tonight."

He disconnected the call, and I thought about what he'd said. He'd actually congratulated me for becoming a killer. I shrugged my shoulders and muttered to myself, "Thanks, I guess."

CHAPTER 16

Will Grimes pulled into Donnie Frazier's girlfriend's driveway on Williams River Road a little before midnight. Neither Frazier nor Beane had had identification on them, but Sammy Raft had known them and knew where they lived. He'd also known about Frazier's girlfriend, and had told Grimes about her. As soon as Grimes parked the department-issued Ford Edge in front of a run-down trailer, the car was surrounded by four snarling, barking Dobermans. Grimes began to blow the car's horn. A woman finally came out, wrapped in a thick robe to protect herself from the chilly night air. He flashed his blue lights, lowered the window a little, and yelled at the woman to get control of the dogs. It took her several minutes, but eventually the dogs were herded into a chain-link-fenced pen between her and the trailer to Grimes's right.

As soon as Grimes saw the woman shut the gate, he got out of the car and walked toward her.

"What do you want?" she asked.

"Are you Emma Newland?"

"Who wants to know?"

Grimes produced his shield. "Name's Will Grimes. I'm a special agent with the Criminal Bureau of Investigation. Can we talk inside for a minute?"

On the way over, Grimes had asked for a criminal history on Emma Newland and found only a ten-year-old shoplifting case and some traffic tickets.

"Let's talk right here," Newland said.

"Fine," Grimes said. "I'm sorry to tell you that your boyfriend, Donnie Frazier, and his friend Tommy Beane were killed earlier tonight. They were shot to death at Sammy's."

The woman seemed to stagger backward, and Grimes reached for her arm. "Are you all right?"

"I don't . . . it's just . . . I'm gonna need a minute."

Grimes knew Emma Newland was thirty-two, but she looked twenty years older. Her hair was a dull brown and her face was puffy and pale. Her teeth were ravaged, probably by meth abuse, and her shoulders sagged.

"Can we talk inside, please, Miss Newland?" Grimes said.

She turned toward the trailer without saying a word and climbed the rickety stoop. Grimes walked into a small box of filth and stench that nearly made him gag. The sink was piled high with dirty dishes and cups and silverware, the one trash can he could see was overflowing, the stove top was filthy, and the place smelled like a honky-tonk toilet at two in the morning. The only light that was on was in the kitchen, which was just to the right of the entrance. Emma Newland trudged to a small table and sat down heavily. She looked up at Grimes with sad brown eyes, lit a cigarette, and said, "Any idea who did it?" She wasn't crying, and Grimes wondered whether, at this point in her life, she was even capable of tears. She looked like she'd had it rough.

"I was hoping you could help me with that," he said. "Anything unusual happen lately? Anything that might have brought this on? I don't mean to be cruel to you, Miss Newland, but they were each shot several times. They were ambushed in the bar. Apparently, someone just walked in and started shooting. The owner says he was in the bathroom and didn't get a look at the shooter, but whoever it was, we think he was very angry about something."

"People get angry," Emma pointed out.

"I agree, but it isn't often they get angry enough to do what was done in that bar. Donnie and Tommy didn't have a chance." Grimes watched closely as Emma took a drag off the cigarette and looked down at her shoes. He was looking for something, anything that might give him an in, a way to find out whether this woman knew anything that would help him. "I won't arrest you."

She raised her tired eyes. "For what?"

"For anything. I need to know why this happened, and if you can help me, even if you may have had something to do with a crime they committed, I won't hold you accountable. I'm after the person who committed two vicious murders tonight."

"I didn't have nothing to do with what they did," Emma said.

"Who is they, and what did they do?"

"Donnie and Tommy. I knew they shouldn't a done it," she said.

"Done what?"

"Blew up that house."

"They blew up a house? Where?"

Emma snuffed the cigarette out in an ashtray already filled with butts and folded her arms across her chest. "Knoxville. Belonged to some lawyer's momma. I don't know the whole story, but I heard them talking about it. A little over a month ago, Donnie and Tommy stole a bunch of dynamite, went down to Knoxville, and blew up this lawyer's momma's house. The lawyer was supposed to be there, only he wasn't. They killed his momma, but they missed him. I'm guessing that could be the man you're looking for."

Grimes had heard of the bombing in Knoxville. It had been all over the news for a couple of days. "So you knew all about this dynamite thing in Tennessee before it happened and didn't tell anybody?"

"I heard them talking about it, but I wasn't sure they would actually *do* it," she said. "They were always talking crazy shit. Besides, I wasn't looking to wind up at the bottom of one of these old coal-mining shafts around here with my head blown off. That's exactly what would've happened if I'd told anybody."

"Is there anything around here from the bombing in Tennessee? They leave anything lying around?"

"I don't think so. To hear them tell it, they used everything. Donnie said the explosion looked like a nuclear blast. He said it shook the earth, blew his mind."

"Will you give us permission to search your property?"

"I reckon, as long as you ain't gonna charge me with nothing."

"I already told you I won't charge you with anything."

"You might find some meth and some pipes, shit like that. Maybe a little bit of stolen property from houses they broke into."

"I'll need you to sign a statement."

"Fine."

"Okay, sit tight. I'm going to go outside and make a couple of calls. Looks like we're going to be up all night."

CHAPTER 17

Will Grimes walked into the interview room at his headquarters in Elkins and set a piece of paper in front of Sammy Raft. Grimes had slept for only two hours in his car and was exhausted. Grimes had made Raft follow him from Cowen to Elkins, and had then put Raft in an interview room by himself. He'd been stewing for half an hour.

Raft was fidgeting with a Styrofoam coffee cup when Grimes walked in. "I need you to sign this."

"What is it?" Raft asked.

"It's a Miranda waiver. It says you're willing to give up your right to remain silent and talk to me. You need to know that anything you say can be used against you in court later if you wind up getting charged with a crime."

"Are you planning to charge me with a crime?" Raft said.

"Depends," Grimes said. "Sign it."

Raft signed the paper and said, "Depends on what? I didn't do anything."

"It depends on whether you lie to me. I don't think you killed those boys, but I think you know who did."

"You're wrong," Raft said. "I didn't know him."

Grimes raised his eyebrows. He knew the story Raft told him wasn't entirely true. "So you saw him."

Grimes watched Raft's shoulders slump. He'd been reluctant to come to Elkins, and now Grimes knew why.

"I don't want to get involved," Raft said. "I ain't got no idea who the man was. I only saw him for a second, didn't hardly look at him."

"But you saw him shoot Donnie and Tommy, right?"

"No. I'm telling the truth about that. I went to the bathroom. He was sitting at the bar when I went in the bathroom, and all of a sudden the damn place sounded like a war zone. I was scared outta my mind. There wasn't no way I was walking back out of that bathroom until I was sure he was gone. Matter of fact, I expected him to come in there and shoot me rather than leave a witness behind."

"Okay, we're doing better, Sammy." Grimes took a sip from his own cup of steaming coffee. He felt tired and lethargic and needed the caffeine to give him a boost. What they said about murder investigations was true: the first forty-eight hours were the most important. He didn't need to be wasting time. "Now I want you to start from the beginning. Don't leave anything out. And remember, lying to me will only cause you problems down the road."

"I saw him twice," Raft said reluctantly.

"Twice?"

"Yeah. He came in the afternoon and ordered takeout. Then he came back around eight."

"Did he order anything the second time?"

"Longneck Budweiser."

"What'd you do with the bottle?"

"I emptied it and threw it away. He didn't even touch it."

"He ordered a beer and didn't touch it?"

"Right."

"Why would he do that?"

"You'd have to ask him."

"Did he touch the bar, a glass, a knife, fork, anything?"

"I don't think so. He was wearing gloves, anyway."

"What about when he came in the afternoon? Touch anything?"

"Don't know."

"Drink anything then?"

"A can of Pepsi, but he took it with him."

"Did he say anything when he came back later?"

"He told me to go into the bathroom. Said he had a problem with the two boys in the booth, and there was going to be trouble. Said I could go into the bathroom or die with them."

"You didn't have a cell? Why didn't you call the police from the bathroom?"

"You're kidding, right? We're talking about Cowen here. Besides, my cell was under the bar. I don't carry it in my pocket when I'm working."

"Describe him," Grimes said.

"I don't know," Raft said. "He was normal height and build, I guess. I mean, he wasn't real tall or real short or real skinny or fat. He was wearing dark clothes and a black toboggan, already told you about the gloves. Didn't see his hair, but he had a brown beard and was wearing black-rimmed glasses."

"I learned a couple of things last night that caused me to call the Tennessee Highway Patrol and the Knoxville, Tennessee, Police Department," Grimes said. He reached into a folder and pulled out two photographs. "One of these is a booking photo from a few years ago, and the other is a much more recent driver's license photo. I want you take a look and see if this could be the man who was in your bar. His name is Darren Street, and Donnie Frazier and Tommy Beane were suspected of murdering his mother."

Grimes slid the photos across the table, and Raft stared at them.

"Take your time," Grimes said.

Raft shook his head. "It isn't him. I told you, the man had a beard and wore glasses."

"Imagine this man with a beard and glasses," Grimes said.

"It's not him."

"You're sure?"

"Yep."

"You're absolutely positive."

"I'm telling you, it isn't him. You trying to get me to tell you something that isn't true?"

"I don't think you're telling me the truth about much of anything," Grimes said.

Raft shrugged his shoulders. "I don't know what you want from me."

"I want you to tell me that the man in those photographs is the same man that walked into your bar and murdered Frazier and Beane last night."

"That isn't gonna happen because it just isn't so," Raft said.

"We can protect you, if that's what you're worried about," Grimes said.

"You already threatened to arrest me, and now you're trying to put words in my mouth. I don't think I want any protection from you. Are we done? Can I go now?"

"Go on. Get the hell out of here," Grimes said. "I'm tired, and I don't have time to fool with the likes of you right now. But don't think for one second this is over. I'll be back, and when I come back, I'll have a warrant for your arrest."

CHAPTER 18

When I left Lexington the next morning, I drove to Marty Henley's leased property near Petros and built a huge fire from deadfall that I found not far from their shooting range. I burned the clothing I was wearing when I shot Frazier and Beane, along with the beard and the glasses. The spirit gum glue I used to secure the beard and the fake ID also went into the fire. I'd tossed one of the burner phones off a bridge near the interstate in Lexington; the others I put back in the backpack in the trunk, along with $10,000 in cash. I'd spent only a few hundred of the $20,000 Pappy had given me, and I kept around $9,000, just in case I needed cash for anything I hadn't thought about. I didn't think Pappy would mind.

I parked the car at the Flying J in Knoxville around two in the afternoon, went inside the truck stop, and used a pay phone to call a cab. The truck stops were one of the few places that still had pay phones. The cab picked me up ten minutes later, and I had the driver take me to the storage facility where I'd picked up the Monte Carlo and left my car. I got the car out and headed to Grace's.

She wasn't home, so I picked up my cell phone that I'd left in the kitchen and called her. She was surprised that I was back so soon and said she was at the grocery store and would be home in about half an hour.

She walked in a little while later, carrying several plastic bags in each hand. She was wearing black jeans and a tight red sweater and was suddenly the sexiest woman I'd ever seen in my life. I couldn't wait to get my hands on her. I reached down and took the bags from her, set them on the kitchen table, and lifted her off the floor. I carried her into the bedroom and laid her on the bed.

She looked up at me seductively and smiled. "I take it you got some things worked out."

I pulled my shirt over my head and got into bed next to her. "I did." I kissed her on the lips. The touch of her sparked an animalistic lust, and we spent the next twenty minutes making love as though it would be the last time.

"Wow," Grace said when we were finished. "Did you spend the night eating oysters?"

"Not exactly."

"Where did you go?"

"Fishing."

"Fishing? Really? Did you catch anything?"

"I caught a couple of big ones."

"Did you bring them home?"

"No, I left them where I caught them."

"You look different," she said. "You look like you've managed to lift this tremendous burden you've been carrying around. There's some light in your eyes." She reached out and ran her fingers down my cheek. "I'm proud of you, Darren. You're so strong."

"I don't know about that," I said, "but I think you're right about one thing: I got rid of a burden."

CHAPTER 19

They came at seven o'clock the very next morning. The two Knoxville detectives, Dawn Rule and Lawrence Kingman, started beating on Grace's door. I was already awake, sitting at the counter in the kitchen, drinking a cup of coffee. Grace was sound asleep. I'd kept her awake most of the night. I would never have guessed that cold-blooded murder would stimulate hot-blooded virility so intensely.

I knew it was them before I went to the door. Only cops come banging at that time of the day. I walked down the hall, grabbed my robe from the door in Grace's bedroom, and closed the door so Grace wouldn't hear what was being said. Then I walked to the entrance and opened the door.

"Good morning," I said to Rule and Kingman.

"We'd like to ask you some questions," Rule said. "Mind taking a ride?"

"Am I under arrest? Do you have a warrant?"

"No, you're not under arrest," she said.

"Then I'm not going anywhere. What's this about?"

"The man we told you about, Donnie Frazier? Somebody murdered him along with a friend of his named Tommy Beane."

"Really? What a shame."

"Mind telling us where you were on Friday?"

"So I'm a suspect in a double murder?" I asked her.

"Where were you on Friday?"

"You know damned good and well that I've been a criminal defense lawyer for ten years," I said. "I don't have to tell you anything."

"Seems to me you'd like to have yourself eliminated as a suspect as quickly as possible," Kingman pointed out.

"If you want to suspect me, then go ahead and suspect me. Do that thing you do. Investigate. You're going to wind up chasing your tails if you think it was me."

"Did you kill them?" Rule pressed. "They were shot to pieces at close range. Whoever did it was angry."

"If Frazier was anything like his brother, then he had plenty of enemies." I shrugged. "He probably pushed one of them too far."

"You didn't answer my question," Rule said. "Did you kill them?"

"I didn't kill them," I said. Lying was becoming easy for me. The words rolled off my tongue smoothly and evenly. "But I can't say I'm sorry they're dead if they really killed my mom."

"We'll never know for sure now, will we?" Rule said.

"I suppose not."

"You might as well talk to us, give us a statement, so we can check it out," Kingman said. "Otherwise we're going to look up your ass with a spotlight. If you did it, we'll nail you for it."

I smiled. Talking about looking up my ass made me think of the dozens of times I'd had to spread my cheeks for guards in jails all over the country when Ben Clancy put me through an experience called diesel therapy. The feds had put me on a bus in tight handcuffs and shackles and rode me all over the country. I spent roughly eighteen hours a day on a bus for three months, and then, each night, I'd be herded into some county or city jail or some state pen, and the guards at each stop would strip-search me and make me spread my cheeks.

"You think this is funny?" Kingman said. I was making him angry, which gave me a sense of satisfaction.

"Do you think I haven't had cops look up my ass before?" I said. "Go ahead. Look as far up there as you want. You won't find a thing."

And with that, I shut the door in their faces.

As I turned and started back into the house, I saw Grace moving slowly toward me in the hallway. She was sleepy-eyed and wearing a sheer, red-silk negligee.

"Who was that?" she mumbled. "I heard you talking to someone."

"A couple of Jehovah's Witnesses," I said. "Nice kids. C'mon. Let's go back to bed."

"Again?" she said, almost bewildered.

"I want you."

I did. I wasn't sure why, but I wanted her desperately. Maybe it was plunging myself inside of her the same way the bullets plunged into Frazier and Beane. Maybe bringing her to orgasm gave me a warped sense of dominance that paralleled in some small way what I'd felt when I ended Frazier's and Beane's lives. Maybe it was simply the act of letting myself go that made me so insistent.

"Please?" I said, yearning for that feeling of power.

"Let me brush my teeth," she said. "I'll be right there."

CHAPTER 20

I got back out of bed an hour later and told Grace I was going to visit my mother's grave. She mumbled something and went right back to sleep. It was a cold Sunday morning, and the sky was bleak. Dark-gray clouds hung low over the mountains. I drove over to Woodlawn Cemetery, which was a place I'd heard my mother say she wanted to be buried many times in the past. There was very little left of her after the blast, so I'd had the remains cremated and the ashes placed in a lacquered mahogany box. The box was buried at Woodlawn in a plot on the west end of the property near a maple tree. Grace had helped me pick out a headstone, and Mom had purchased enough life insurance to cover the expenses and have a little left over.

She'd also been to see a lawyer and had him draft a will that I'd known nothing about. It left her estate to me, and I was also the executor. The estate was going through probate, but when it was all said and done in about three months, I was going to wind up with about $400,000. I'd had no idea she'd stashed that kind of money. Her homeowner's insurance company, on the advice of their adjuster and their lawyer, had refused to pay the claim I filed for the destruction of her home. They classified the bombing as a "terrorist act," and there was an exclusion in the contract on which they were relying. I'd considered hiring a lawyer and taking them to court, but had ultimately decided against it. I'd thought about building a house on her property someday, but I knew I'd more than likely just wind up selling it at some point.

I parked my car just a little ways from her grave and walked over. The wind was blowing, and I pulled my coat up tight around my neck. As I stood there in front of the stone, I tried to feel her presence.

"I need to know you're okay with what I did," I said. "I killed the men who killed you. I did it in a public place. It was messy and bloody, and I suppose it was awful, but I don't regret it one single bit. After what they did to you, they deserved what they got."

I stood there looking at the stone. Tears began to well in my eyes as I thought of the magnitude of both the act I'd committed and the fact that it didn't change anything. She was still gone, still dead. The stone went out of focus for a minute. I fought the tears back and went on.

"I've changed, Mom. Something snapped in me when they killed you, and I don't think I'll ever be the same. All I know is that the rules seem to have changed for me. I didn't deserve what happened to me when Ben Clancy railroaded me into prison. He just went on trial and got acquitted, so once again, he's managed to dodge justice.

"I didn't deserve the things that happened to me while I was in prison. I didn't deserve losing all that time with you and with Sean. The only good thing that came out of it was my relationship with Grace, and now I'm not so sure where we're going to wind up. You didn't deserve to die, and I didn't deserve losing you. You died because of me, because of something that happened while I was in prison, and I'm so very sorry for that. But I tried to make it right, and I hope I have. From now on, I'm going to rely on myself. I'm not going to rely on the police or the courts for justice. I'll see to it myself that justice is done."

I looked up at the dark clouds rolling by like angry monsters. They reflected the way I'd been feeling, full of anger and destructive force and being blown by the winds of destiny to some unknown destination.

"Where are you?" I yelled. *"Where are you? Am I standing out here in the cold, talking to a stone? Are you just gone? Give me some kind of sign!"*

I looked back at the marker and sighed. I shoved my hands deep into my pockets and tried, once again, to imagine her face. I missed her smile, her laugh, her advice. I missed the feeling of knowing I had someone in my life who shared my blood and knew me better than anyone else in the world. I missed her love.

"I hope you're not gone, but I've never seen any real evidence that there's life or existence beyond the one we have here," I said. "Maybe I'm wrong. I *want* to be wrong, but I don't think I am. I'm going to go now. I just wanted to tell you that I killed them. I killed the men who killed you. I set things right. I'd do it again tomorrow."

I walked back to my car and got in. Just before I started the engine, a bolt of lightning ripped across the sky in front of me, earthshaking thunder exploded like a cannon, and the skies opened up.

CHAPTER 21

Grace Alexander awoke to the chirping of her cell phone. She didn't recognize the number, but the caller ID said "Knoxville Police Department." She answered the phone.

"Miss Alexander, this is Dawn Rule. I'm a detective with the Knoxville PD, and we're investigating a homicide. We were at your home earlier and spoke to Darren. Did he tell you we were there?"

Grace was still half-asleep.

"Miss Alexander? Are you there?"

"I'm here," Grace said. "You woke me up. What did you say about Darren?"

"Is he there right now?"

"No. Why are you asking about Darren?"

"He's a suspect in a double murder that was committed in Cowen, West Virginia, Friday night. The two men who were killed were our primary suspects in his mother's murder. Do you have any idea where he was Friday night?"

Grace sat up in bed, suddenly on alert. Darren a suspect in a double murder? Could it be possible? He said he'd gone fishing, but he'd come back so . . . so . . . *different*. His sexual appetite was suddenly off the charts, and he seemed almost strangely empowered. Could those two phenomena be related to his having killed two men? No, it wasn't possible. He was getting better, and now the police were, once again, trying to ruin Darren's life. Hadn't he been through enough?

"I'm going to hang up now," Grace said.

"Don't do that," Detective Rule said. "You're not a suspect. All I'm asking is whether you know where Darren was on Friday night."

"I don't have to tell you anything about Darren."

"I'll subpoena you and put you in front of a grand jury and make you answer under oath," Rule said.

Grace needed more time to digest this news. She wasn't going to be pressured by a cop. Besides, she knew the local cops didn't use the grand jury as an investigative tool. Only the feds did that. "No, you won't. You can't intimidate me."

"Would you mind coming down to the police station and giving us a written statement to that effect?"

"I'm not going anywhere, and I'm not giving you anything," Grace said. "You are aware that I'm a defense attorney, correct?"

"Then we'll come to you. When would be most convenient?"

"I don't want you here. Leave me alone. Whatever you suspect Darren of doing, he didn't do it. He's been falsely accused before, you know. I'm not going to help you frame him again. He was with me Friday. All night."

"If you aren't being truthful with me, you're committing a felony."

"That's a load of crap, and you know it," Grace said. "I know the law, Detective Rule. If I make a false statement to you concerning a material fact in an investigation and it prevents you from apprehending or locating a suspect, then I've committed a felony. I'm not preventing you from apprehending or locating anyone. You probably know exactly where Darren is."

"As a matter of fact, we do. He's visiting his mother's grave. Does he do that often?"

"Go piss up a rope," Grace said, and she hung up the phone.

She went into the kitchen and fixed herself a cup of hot tea. Her hands were shaking. She thought back over everything. Darren had left early Thursday and had come back Saturday afternoon. She had no idea where he'd gone. He said he'd gone fishing, but he hadn't said where. She remembered asking him whether he caught anything, and he'd said, "Two big ones." He also said he'd left them where he caught them.

Could Darren possibly have killed two people? Grace didn't think him capable of such a horrific act, but he'd been under such tremendous mental and emotional strain that perhaps he'd done something she couldn't imagine. And the sudden change in him after he'd returned— the seemingly brighter outlook, the voracious sexual appetite—made her wonder what had really gone on over those two days. And he'd lied to her earlier about the police showing up at her house. He'd said he was talking to Jehovah's Witnesses. Something significant had occurred, but murder? Surely not murder.

She picked up her phone and punched in Darren's number.

"Where are you?" she said when he answered.

"On the way. I stopped and picked us up some breakfast."

"A detective named Dawn Rule just called me."

There was silence for ten full seconds. "Okay, what did she want?"

"You know exactly what she wanted since she talked to you earlier this morning. She wanted to know where you were on Friday."

"Maybe we shouldn't talk over the phone," Darren said.

"Maybe not. You're coming straight here?"

"Yes."

"Good. I'll see you in a few minutes."

CHAPTER 22

"I just lied to a police officer," Grace said as soon as I walked in the door.

I'd never seen her angry, at least not angry with me. Her cheeks were pink, and her eyes were narrow and intense. Her mouth was a tight line.

"What do you mean?" I said.

"I told her you were here with me Friday night."

"Thank you."

"Thank you? Thank you? Is that all you have to say? Where in the hell were you Friday night?"

"I told you, I went fishing."

"Where?"

"At Abrams Creek near Cades Cove."

"Did you stay at the campground?"

"No, I slept on the bank by the creek."

"It was cold Friday night, Darren."

"I made a fire and a shelter, and I had a tent and sleeping bag. They're in my car. Would you like me to go and get them? In fact, I bought quite a bit of gear. It's all in the trunk if you'd like to come out and take a look."

"As a matter of fact, I think I would," she said.

We walked together to the parking lot of her apartment complex, and I popped the trunk on my car. The fishing gear, sleeping bag, small tent, and light I'd purchased were all there. I'd had the foresight to remove the price tags and wrinkle some things. There were even a couple of bags of Outfitter's Choice dehydrated camping entrées. I patted myself on the back mentally. It was a pretty convincing show.

"Satisfied?" I said as she looked over the gear.

"You've never told me you were a camper," she said, still looking down at the trunk.

"You know I like to fish."

"So?"

"Fishing and camping go hand in hand. I've camped a bunch of times in my life."

"Why haven't you ever mentioned it?"

"I guess it's just never come up. You never talk about camping."

"I've never been camping," Grace said. "I've never spent a night in the woods. A lot of people around San Diego camped, but my parents weren't among them and neither were any of my friends. The closest I've ever come to camping was a sleepover at my girlfriend's when I was a teenager. We pitched a tent in the backyard, but we went into the house around midnight."

"I guess I'll have to take you and introduce you to the wonders of the great outdoors," I said.

"Swear to me on your mother's life that you didn't go anywhere near West Virginia on Friday night."

My mother was dead. There was no life on which to swear. And I needed Grace on my side. "I swear on my mother's life that I wasn't anywhere near West Virginia on Friday night."

"The police think otherwise."

"I know. But they have this little problem. It's called proof."

We turned and walked back toward her apartment.

"Have they told you that two men suspected of killing your mom were murdered Friday night?" she asked.

"Yes. Do you know what else they told me?"

"What's that?"

"Last week, they told me they had a suspect in Mom's murder. They told me his name and where he was from."

"Why would they do that?" Grace said.

"I think they were just trying to make me feel better, letting me know they were working the case and that they had what they thought was a solid suspect."

"Cops don't usually do that, do they?"

"I don't know. I've never been the son of a murder victim before. You would think they'd keep that kind of information to themselves, though, unless, at some level, they wanted me to go up there and do something about it."

"You think they were trying to set you up?"

"I don't know what to think," I said. "After what I went through a couple of years ago, I wouldn't put anything past a cop or a prosecutor. But I didn't kill them, Grace. I swear it. Do you believe me?"

She nodded her head slowly and looked up into my eyes. "Be careful, Darren. They're after you. I don't want them to take you again."

CHAPTER 23

I was leaving Criminal Court Monday afternoon after having my vehicular assault client arraigned when my cell phone rang. Luanne "Granny" Tipton was calling. Granny was the matriarch of the Tipton family, the grandmother of the same James Tipton, who had been both my friend and enemy in the past.

"Hi, Granny," I said when I answered the phone.

"We have a problem, Darren," she said. "A serious problem. Could you come up here and try to help?"

"Of course," I said. "What's going on?"

"It's James. He wants to kill himself, and I'm afraid he might do it."

I jumped in my car and headed toward Gatlinburg. The Tiptons lived in the mountains a few miles outside the resort town in the Smokies. It took me about forty minutes to get there. I called Grace on my way and left her a message that I was going to visit the Tiptons. I didn't tell her why. When I pulled up in front of Granny's white frame house, her son Eugene was sitting on a four-wheeler. He motioned for me to get on behind him. I did so, and we headed up a mountain trail. Ten minutes later, we topped a small ridge and Eugene stopped the four-wheeler and cut the engine.

"He's not far from here," Eugene said. "I don't want to shake him up any more than he already is. Let's walk."

"Granny said he wants to kill himself," I said.

"Looks that way," Eugene said. "He's smoking dope and drinking moonshine. My boy was squirrel hunting up here a couple of hours ago and heard him talking to himself. He has a pistol with him."

"Is this because of what happened at Clancy's trial?" I said.

James had been the federal government's star witness against Ben Clancy. But he had been destroyed on cross-examination, and Clancy had walked away free and clear.

"It's a lot of things, but I think that was the last straw."

We rounded a curve, and there they were. Granny and Eugene's brother, Ronnie, were standing about fifteen feet from James. James was sitting sidesaddle on a four-wheeler. He had a joint in his left hand and a chrome revolver in his right. A mason jar of clear liquid—three-quarters empty—sat on a fender.

When he recognized me, James said, "Counselor! Welcome to the party."

"Doesn't look like my idea of a party with that gun in your hand," I said.

"Oh, it's a party all right, but it's about to end."

"What's going on, man?" I said. "Surely this isn't about Ben Clancy. You're not going to let that miserable bastard be the cause of you killing yourself, are you?"

"You don't know nothing about me, Darren," James said as he took a deep drag off the joint. "I'll give you an example. My real name ain't Tipton. It's James Crawford. I was dumped on the Tiptons by my mother when I was five years old. She shot and killed my daddy because he raped her two or three times a day, every day. He was a piece of work, my daddy. Me and my brothers and sisters all used to close our eyes or get out of the house when he'd start on her. He'd just rip her clothes off and go at it. Didn't care who was watching or how she was feeling. She'd cry, and he'd beat her. We were too young to do anything about it.

"He hated me," James said. "Don't really know why other than he was just a miserable, hateful son of a bitch. Used to punch me in the head, kick me. He even shot me one time. I was walking in the woods one morning when I was four. It was a Sunday. When I came out of the tree line, I heard a loud crack and a buzz or a shock wave, and then I realized something had peeled the skin off the side of my head just above my right ear. I walked up to the house to get Momma to take care of the wound, and Daddy was sitting on the porch with a rifle. He looked at me and said, 'Damn, boy, I thought you was a deer.'"

"I had a lot of problems with my father, too, James," I said. "You just get past it and move on."

"I don't think I really belong here, you know what I mean?" James said. His eyes were glassy, and his voice was becoming monotone. I felt like I needed to do something before he went past the point of no return, so I took a step toward him. The pistol, which was a massive .357 Magnum, immediately came up and was aimed directly at my chest. I noticed it was steady.

"My momma shot him," James said. "She finally shot him one night. We lived about a mile down the mountain from here. She packed all us kids up in the truck and she dropped me off in Granny's driveway. I remember crying and telling her I wanted to stay with her, but she pushed me out of the truck and told me Joe and Luanne would take good care of me. They caught her in Nashville and brought her back here for a trial. She died in prison, and my brothers and sister wound up in foster homes. I ain't seen them since that night."

"Don't do this," Eugene said. "Granny and Granddaddy took good care of you, didn't they? And me and Ronnie, we lost our momma and daddy in the car wreck, but we ain't killing ourselves. We lost Granddaddy Joe, but we ain't killing ourselves. We've always treated you like a brother, haven't we? Please don't make us watch this."

"I didn't ask you to come up here," James said. "If you don't want to watch, then go back down the mountain." He looked at Granny and a tear slipped from his eye. "You've been good to me, and I thank you. And I'm sorry I've never been nothing but a pain in the ass."

"This is a coward's way out, James," Granny said.

"I know. All I've ever been is a drunk and a drug addict. I've always been a coward, and now you won't have to deal with me anymore. And now I won't have to think about what a fool I let Ben Clancy make me out to be. I let the man help him put Darren in jail, and then I couldn't hold up on the witness stand well enough to hold him accountable for what he did. I think about it every day, you know. All the time. I'm tired of it."

I watched as the pistol changed position from being pointed at my chest to being shoved into James's mouth.

"No!" I yelled as the pistol discharged with a deafening crack, and James Tipton's brains and skull sprayed onto a mountain laurel bush behind him.

CHAPTER 24

Granny Tipton didn't even bother with a church funeral for James. They just buried him in a small family cemetery about a quarter of a mile from her house on the mountain. A lanky, bespectacled man whom I suspected was probably a preacher said a few words, but he kept it secular and he kept it short.

Grace came along with me to pay our respects. When it was over, we stopped by Granny's house. Eugene and Ronnie and their families were there, along with a small group of people I didn't know. There were fewer than twenty in all. Granny's kitchen table was covered in food that had been dropped off by friends and neighbors and, I suspected, former business associates. There were flowers all over the house. It smelled like a rose garden.

Grace and I were standing in the kitchen talking with Eugene when I spotted Granny in the den alone. I excused myself and walked in and stood next to her. She was looking at some framed photos on the wall, old family photos that were hanging above an upright piano.

"That's my husband, there," she said, pointing to a lean, handsome man with an angular face. He was sitting in the seat of a Ford tractor. "That's also the tractor that killed him," she said.

"I'm sorry, Granny," I said.

"Oh, no, I wasn't looking for sympathy," she said. "Just stating a fact."

Granny was a brown-eyed, silver-haired woman who was solidly built, even at her age, which I guessed to be around seventy-five. There was no roundness to her shoulders; she stood straight, as though a piece of steel rebar ran through her spine. From everything I'd learned about her, all she'd ever known was hard work. She was a no-nonsense woman most of the time, but I'd also found her to be charming and mischievous when the mood struck her. She also had a dangerous air about her at times, and this was one of those times.

"Are you all right?" I said. "I mean about James?"

"The boy was so miserable he almost blew his own head off, and I had to stand there and watch it. So, no, I'm not all right about James."

"Forgive me. That was insensitive."

"Stop apologizing, Darren. It makes you sound weak. That's what James's real problem was. He was weak. Too much liquor. Too many drugs. Weakens the mind and the spirit."

I wasn't sure whether I should broach the subject, but I decided to, anyway. "And what about Ben Clancy? How are you feeling about him?"

I heard her take in a quick breath at the mention of Clancy's name. She turned and looked at me. "What do you mean, Darren?"

I'd been thinking about Clancy obsessively since James's suicide, very much the way I'd thought about Frazier and Beane before I killed them. I couldn't bear the thought that Clancy was getting up in the morning, eating meals, reading, listening to music, and living his life as though nothing had happened, while James was being consumed by worms.

"James may have done too many drugs and he may have drunk too much, but you and I both know Clancy was the cause of this. I'm wondering whether we should do something about him. Maybe *I* should do something about him."

"There was a lot more going on in James's mind than Ben Clancy," Granny said, "but you're right. Clancy made things much worse than they might have been. What do you propose to do about him?"

"You know my mother was killed a little while back, right?"

"I heard, and I'm sorry I didn't make it to the funeral. I don't really have an excuse. I just don't like funerals."

"It's all right," I said. "I barely remember it. But the reason I ask is that I was told by the police that they had a suspect in my mother's murder. I asked some old prison friends of mine to confirm it because they have more reliable sources than the police, and it turned out the police were right. This guy named Donnie Frazier and a friend of his, Tommy Beane, put a bunch of dynamite underneath my mother's house and blew it up and killed her. They thought I was there, but I wasn't. So I set things right."

She raised her eyebrows and said, "You set things right? How?"

"I went to West Virginia. Those two men won't be bothering anybody else."

She nodded her head slowly and looked back at the wall. "And how are you sleeping?"

"I haven't slept well since I went to prison. That hasn't changed much, but even if I'd been sleeping like a baby all this time, I'd still be sleeping like a baby."

"You're a complicated man, Darren," she said.

"You have no idea. But back to Clancy. He sent my uncle to prison for twenty years for a crime he didn't commit. God knows how many others he convicted by lying and cheating. He set me up using James, and I wound up in prison for two years. He tried to kill James and burned his trailer to the ground. And now he's gotten away with everything again, and James has committed suicide. Clancy is walking around free as a bird. Something just isn't right about that. I think I'd like to fix it."

"And how would you go about fixing it?"

"Leave that to me. But I would like to ask you a couple of things."

She didn't take her eyes off the wall. "I'm listening."

"Do you still have hogs in the pen by the barn? And if you do, can I bring him there?"

She turned her face back toward mine and nodded almost imperceptibly.

"Would you like to be there?" I asked.

"I think I would," she said quietly, and she turned and walked out of the room.

CHAPTER 25

When we got back to Grace's after the funeral, she said she needed to run a couple of errands. As soon as she left, I called Big Pappy on one of my throwaway phones.

"I'm going to do Ben Clancy," I said. "An old friend of mine committed suicide because of him a few days ago. He didn't have to answer for what he did to me or for what he did to my uncle or for what he did to anyone else. It's time for him to pay up."

"I knew it," Pappy said. "You've developed a taste for it."

"Maybe. Do you have a laptop with you?"

"Sure, I've got one right here in front of me."

"Will you look up Clancy's home address for me? I don't want to do it from here in case the cops get their hands on my laptop somehow."

"Sure, just one second." He found the address, and I committed it to memory.

"Do you need some help?" Pappy said.

"I'm not sure yet. Let me do some surveillance and I'll let you know."

"Be careful, brother," he said, and we hung up.

I put the throwaway back in my closet and went back into the kitchen. I checked my regular cell and noticed there was a call from

Katie. She'd left me a voice mail that said she needed to talk to me about Sean, that it was important, and asked me to call her back.

"Can we meet somewhere?" she said when I got her on the phone.

"When?"

"Now? I'm off work today. Are you working?"

"Had to go to a funeral."

"Are you going to be able to pay your child support?"

I felt heat rising in my chest. Money. With Katie, it was always about money.

"I can pay my child support, Katie. What do you want to talk about?"

"I'd rather talk in person. How about we meet at Dead End BBQ in an hour? You know the place, right?"

"I know the place. I'll see you there."

I called Grace and told her Katie wanted to meet, and I drove to the restaurant an hour later and sat in a corner in the bar. It was midafternoon, and there were fewer than ten people in the dining area. Katie walked in, wearing casual clothing—jeans and a simple, pink, button-down blouse, but I knew it was all designer and expensive. And she made everything she wore look even better than the designer intended. She could easily have been a fashion runway model. She was five feet eleven inches tall—two inches taller than I was—and had a lean, athletic build. Her sandy-blonde hair was long and wavy, her face perfectly structured, and her eyes emerald green. I'd always felt like she was far too good-looking for me, but when we'd been in college we'd had a certain sexual chemistry that had kept us together for a good while, and then Sean came along. I'd discovered she was having an affair with an older man just before I was arrested and sent off to prison, and she'd wasted no time divorcing me.

I said hello, and she sat down. She ordered a salad and a glass of water, and I ordered a beer.

"Drinking a lot these days, are we?" she said.

I was hoping the conversation would at least be civil, but that wasn't apparently in the cards. "Drinking very rarely, actually. But then I'm not around you very often."

She snorted in that snotty little way of hers. "There's no point in making small talk with you because I just don't like you. But I thought I should tell you in person. Leonard and I are getting married."

Leonard was Leonard Bright, a man from Lexington who was fifteen years older than Katie and the man she'd been having an affair with prior to my arrest and conviction.

"Congratulations," I said, "but I fail to see why you felt the need to tell me that in person."

"Leonard has sold his Mercedes dealership and his development company," Katie said. "We'll be moving to Honolulu, Hawaii, in a month."

It took me a second to process the information. Hawaii? Thousands of miles and half a Pacific Ocean away? The waiter set my beer and her salad on the table as I pondered the implications of what she'd just said.

"What about Sean?" I said stupidly.

"What do you mean, what about Sean? He's coming with us."

"You can't take my son and pack up and move to Hawaii," I said. "I won't let you."

"Why, Darren? You rarely spend time with him, and when you do, you're distracted, and from what he says, you pretty much dump him on Grace."

"That isn't . . . he didn't—"

"Yes, he did. Besides, I've already talked to my lawyer about it. There isn't anything you can do. It'll be in Sean's best interests. He'll be going to the Punahou School. It's one of the best private schools in the world. When we first started talking about this last year, I called the school and asked about admission. His test scores are off the charts, his teachers all wrote him glowing recommendations, and he did great in the interview. He's in, starting in January."

I knew they'd been to Hawaii on vacation, but Sean hadn't said anything to me about interviewing at a school. He hadn't said a word to me about Katie considering a move to Honolulu.

"He'll have opportunities that he would never have here, Darren. Don't be selfish about this."

"Did you tell him to hide this from me?"

"I told him there wasn't any reason to upset you until we were certain it was going to happen. Now that we're certain, I'm telling you in person." She reached into her purse and pulled out a document. She shoved it across the table at me. "This is the written notice that's required by law. You have thirty days to file a petition in court if you want to oppose, but I hope you won't waste your time or money, because you'll lose."

"But he won't be with his father. He needs me. I need him."

"He wasn't with his father when you were in jail. And from what I'm hearing, you might be on your way back. You're a suspect in a double murder. How do you think the judge who decides whether Sean can go—if you try to stop me—will feel about that?"

"Who told you I'm a suspect in a double murder?"

"A couple of cops. Rule and Kingman? I believe you know them. Very nice people. They came and talked to me, just wanted to know if maybe you'd let something slip to Sean or to me. I was surprised when you didn't give me more trouble when I kept Sean in Gatlinburg that weekend. Now I know why. You went off to West Virginia and killed the two men who killed your mother."

"That's a damn lie," I said, immediately expecting that she was wearing a wire. "I didn't kill anybody."

"Well, they think you did, and they're doing everything they can to prove it."

"Where's the wire?" I said.

"I beg your pardon?"

"The wire. The bug. The listening device. The transmitter the cops gave you before you walked in here."

"I have no idea what you're talking about."

I stood, reached in my wallet, pulled out a ten-dollar bill, and set it on the table. "You can go fuck yourself. Try to take my son away from me and see what happens."

"Was that a threat, Darren? Did you just threaten to hurt me or kill me?"

"Take it any way you want," I said. "Sean isn't going anywhere."

As I turned and stalked out of the restaurant, Katie stood up and yelled, "That man just threatened to kill me! He threatened to kill me!"

CHAPTER 26

I was in the law office of Gwendolyn Taylor at 8:00 a.m. the next morning. She was the same lawyer who had helped my mother gain visitation rights with Sean when I was in prison. In her midfifties, Gwen had long mouse-colored hair streaked with silver. The outfit of the day was faded blue jeans and a light-blue button-down blouse. She wore the tired, cynical look of a divorce lawyer, a person who fought vicious battles all day, every day, on behalf of her clients, often with children caught in the middle of the combatants.

I told her about the conversation Katie and I had had at the restaurant the previous day, although I left out the parts about threatening Katie and being a suspect in the murders in West Virginia.

"How rich is this guy?" Gwen asked me after we'd talked for a little while.

"Mega, I think. Sean has told me about his place in Kentucky. He has thoroughbreds and a bunch of land, apparently. Owned a Mercedes-Benz dealership and some kind of commercial real estate development company. Katie mentioned that he was one of the biggest donors at the University of Kentucky, and I looked it up on the Internet. He's given them nearly ten million through his charitable trust."

"And she said Sean has been accepted to the Punahou School? What's so special about that?"

I'd printed out some information about the school and set it on her desk. "Very exclusive. A bunch of famous people have gone to school there, including a former president of the United States."

"How much time have you been spending with Sean?"

"I get him most weekends, but since my mom was killed, I haven't seen a lot of him, to be honest. I've been pretty disconnected, and I didn't want him to think it was because of him."

"He loved his grandmother," Gwen said.

"Yes," I said. "He loved her very much."

"A court could very easily conclude that being around you is a constant reminder of her, and that moving away could ultimately be good for him. As I'm sure you know, it will all come down to what the judge thinks is in the best interests of the child."

"I thought about this all night, Gwen," I said. "And honestly, I just don't think I have much of a chance of keeping her from taking him. I'm not in a great place mentally. I'm living with my fiancée, but we haven't set a date for a wedding. I don't have anywhere near the money Katie's husband has. I certainly can't offer Sean the opportunity to go to some famous private school. He'll experience things in Hawaii that he could never experience here, and if I'm honest about it, I just don't have a lot of room for him emotionally right now. This is the worst possible time she could have pulled something like this. Well, the best time for her. Worst time for me. And there's one more thing I guess I should tell you about, because she brought it up yesterday and will try to use it if we go to court: I'm a suspect in a double murder in West Virginia."

"I know," Gwen said.

"You what? How could you know that?"

"I'm a lawyer. Lawyers are gossips. Everybody knows, Darren. At least everybody in the legal community."

"Can she use that if I fight her?"

"You weren't listening to what I just said."

"I beg your pardon? I don't understand."

"I just said everybody in the legal community knows you're a suspect in a double murder in West Virginia. Everybody knows that the two men you're suspected of murdering probably murdered your mother. The judge who will hear your case is Tom Rambo. He's a part of the legal community, Darren. He knows. He won't need to hear it from the witness stand."

"So you think I'll lose," I said.

She nodded her head. "Given my experience in these matters, which, unfortunately, is quite extensive, I think the judge will allow Katie to move your son to Hawaii and will grant you visitation when he isn't in school."

"Which will be about two months a year if I'm lucky."

"That's probably about right. You'll get him in the summer."

"What if he doesn't want to come? What if he loves Hawaii and doesn't want to come back here in the summer?"

"He'll want to see his father. I can't sugarcoat this for you, Darren. It's going to be extremely hard for you, but you're going to have to make an extra effort to stay in touch with him. You'll have to call him a lot. FaceTime with him. Do whatever you can to keep your relationship loving and viable. Write him letters. Send him gifts. You're going to have to show him how much you love him, how much you really care."

I put my head in my hands and leaned forward with my elbows on my knees.

"I can't believe this," I said. "I can't believe that snooty, spoiled rotten, belligerent bitch is going to take my son from me."

"She can take him out of the state, but she can't take you out of his heart," Gwen said. "You're the only person that can allow that to happen. Now promise me you won't do anything rash."

"Like what?"

"Just don't do anything to get yourself in trouble."

"Are you insinuating I might harm Katie?"

"Her lawyer called me yesterday afternoon after the two of you met. He knew you'd come to me. He said you threatened to kill her."

"I didn't threaten to kill her," I said.

"Stay away from her," Gwen said. "I'll call her lawyer and work out the custody details and make sure you get a chance to say goodbye when the time comes."

I got up and walked out of Gwen's office in a daze. She could say whatever she wanted about keeping my relationship with Sean alive while he was thousands of miles away on a beautiful island. I knew it would be next to impossible.

First Mom, and now Sean. Grace would be all I had left.

CHAPTER 27

I put the situation with Sean out of my mind by focusing my anger on Ben Clancy. I suspected that Clancy was a creature of habit, and I was right. Each morning at around 7:00 a.m., he left his house and drove a short distance to Charlie's Cove Road. It ran along a steep ridge above the Tennessee River. Some developer with more money than brains had apparently believed he or she could sell vacant lots along the road, but the slope leading down to the river was so steep, so rocky, and so long that not a single lot had been sold, not a single house had been built. I watched Clancy for two days from my car, and then I watched him from a perch above the road, lying flat on my belly, in the gray light of the morning for three more. He would park at the beginning of the road where it cut off from Somerset Road, which was the street on which he lived, and walk to the end of Charlie's Cove Road. It was just under half a mile to the end where it formed an oval cul-de-sac. Clancy would walk around the cul-de-sac, return to his vehicle, and drive back home. He carried a walking stick and was alone. I'd read in the newspaper or heard on television less than a year earlier that his wife had died while he was in jail awaiting trial. As I watched him from above, I thought the walks were a metaphor for his life. No dog, no friend, no wife. He was alone. It was appropriate for a man like him.

On the third day, after watching him, I decided I needed some help. It would just be too difficult and too risky to grab him by myself. I called Big Pappy.

"Going to need some help with that thing I was telling you about," I said.

"Yeah? What do you need?"

"A one-inch, manila hemp rope, fifteen feet long, and I need you to soak it and stretch it. Then I need you to wax about five feet on one end."

"Say that again?"

"Do you need to write it down?"

"Yeah, let me grab a piece of paper. One sec." He came back on the line shortly thereafter and I repeated the instructions. "So you're going to hang the man?"

I'd decided to hang him while obsessing about what he'd done to my uncle, to me, to James, and to the others I didn't know about. Shooting him or stabbing him would be too quick and too messy. I figured we could grab him off the street and then take him to a contained, concealed spot. That spot was Granny Tipton's barn. I'd driven up and spoken to her about it, and she was in agreement. We could hang him there, but before we did it, we'd have a little time to allow him to reflect on his behavior.

"That's the plan. I also need some hand and wrist restraints, a gag, a van, and a willing assistant."

"When?"

"When can you come?"

"Three days."

"Perfect."

"So I'll see you Tuesday," Pappy said. "I think I'll just drive the van up. You're sure you don't want a gun this time?"

"Shouldn't need one."

The next three days seemed like three months. I got up early the next two days—which was no problem since I barely slept, anyway—and made the trip out near Clancy's. He didn't vary from his routine. In fact, he was downright anal about it. You could set your watch by the guy.

I was extremely careful about cops. I was careful to the point of paranoia. I read everything I could get my hands on about modern surveillance and countersurveillance techniques. What I learned was fairly simple. They couldn't track me electronically if I left my phone at home, and they couldn't track me physically if I did plenty of walking, used public transportation, and went to as many crowded places as I could and melted in among the people. Then I'd simply slip out a door, grab a cab or a bus, and move to the next destination. I knew that even though I was a suspect in two murders, those crimes had been committed in West Virginia. The Knoxville guys might be bird-dogging me some, but it wasn't really their case and the department wasn't going to commit a huge amount of resources. I hadn't heard from anyone in West Virginia, and unless they were getting really close, I probably wouldn't. I'd crossed state lines to commit two murders, which meant the feds could have gotten involved, but I hadn't heard from them and hadn't noticed anyone that even resembled a fed anywhere near me. And finally, I'd killed two merciless scumbags who had deserved killing. Most cops don't like vigilantes, but they like cowards who bomb the homes of defenseless women even less.

The plan was for Pappy to stay in a small hotel near Maryville on the second night and then meet me three blocks from Grace's apartment at five on the third morning. Grace usually slept until 6:30 a.m., had to be at the office at eight, and got home between 5:30 and 6:00 p.m. She and I hadn't been talking much, and my libido had cooled considerably since that first night after I'd killed Frazier and Beane. Still, I tried to keep up the impression that I was trying, both at home and at work. I hired a middle-aged secretary named Brenda Brown, who was experienced and smart. I left in the mornings and went to the office. I worked my cases. I went to court.

I also told Grace I was continuing to see a grief counselor, and I would occasionally make up things we had discussed. She believed me, but I could tell she was growing a bit impatient, maybe even distant.

On the day I planned to kill Ben Clancy, I told Grace I had an early meeting with a client so I would be leaving at 4:30 a.m. I also told her I wanted to go to the gym, which I'd been doing occasionally, and that I would shower and dress there after I worked out. I walked out the door as though I was going jogging before my workout, and that's exactly what I did, making sure there were no cops around. I got in my car, drove to the gym, and parked in a corner of the lot. Pappy pulled up in a brown van with tinted windows right on time. I got in and we pulled out. Clancy's house was thirty minutes away, so we went to a Waffle House about fifteen minutes from Grace's apartment and ate breakfast. Both of us were wearing fake beards and hats. I'd glued my beard on during the drive to the Waffle House, and Pappy was already wearing his when he showed up.

We lingered over the breakfast and coffee until six and then headed toward Clancy's. At 6:50 a.m., we turned onto Charlie's Cove and went to the cul-de-sac at the end. I drove. We'd decided that Pappy would grab Clancy because Pappy was just so damned big and strong. I put the van in park, and Pappy climbed into the back. The van had a sliding side door, and very soon, he would be jumping out.

At precisely 7:10 a.m., I saw Clancy top a slight ridge about a hundred yards from the end of the cul-de-sac.

"Here we go," I said, and Pappy put his hand on the door handle. I put the van in drive and started out slowly, but as I moved toward Clancy, I stomped on the gas and the van leaped forward. I skidded to a stop next to Clancy. He was wearing a long, gray overcoat and a goofy-looking fur cap that covered his ears. I saw his gray eyes widen as Pappy slid the door open and leaped out of the van. Clancy tried to raise his walking stick, but Pappy grabbed the old man in a bear hug and flung him into the van like a sack of flour. Clancy tried to yell, but Pappy had him on his stomach and thrust his knee into his back so hard Clancy couldn't even breathe. He stuffed a bandana he'd brought into his mouth and covered it with duct tape. Then he bound Clancy's hands and feet with plastic restraints. He picked Clancy's walking stick up off the floor and handed it to me.

"Souvenir," he said. "I'm keeping it."

I'd started moving as soon as Pappy had thrown Clancy in the van and shut the door. By the time Clancy was gagged and fully restrained, we had passed his car and were on our way to Granny Tipton's mountain home.

CHAPTER 28

Granny, Eugene, and Ronnie were all waiting for us when we pulled up. The barn door opened, and Eugene waved us in. I drove the van inside and the door closed behind us. It was just after eight in the morning. I'd driven up the mountain and spoken to Granny a couple of times since James's funeral, just to make sure she was still all right with what I was going to do. The last time I'd visited was the day before. She seemed more eager than ever to gain some revenge for what Clancy had done to James.

One of the things we had talked about during our first discussion was how Clancy should die. Granny was the one who'd mentioned hanging him. Her barn, like many barns on small farms in the South, was set up for multiple uses. People kept livestock in stalls, stored hay and straw and feed, parked their tractors out of the weather, et cetera. Many of them also used their barns for curing tobacco in the fall, and Granny's barn was set up for that. The Tiptons, like many small farmers in Tennessee, hadn't grown tobacco in many years, but the posts that crisscrossed the barn starting about ten feet off the ground and continuing to the top of the gabled roof were still in place. Granny had had Eugene and Ronnie cut two fresh posts from large oak branches they'd found on the property, each about twelve feet long, and those had been bolted together and then lashed to two thick support beams in the center of the barn.

I waited for Ronnie and Eugene to help Pappy pull Clancy out of the van, and then I backed it out of the building. Ronnie and Eugene closed the large door, and I walked back in through the small door a few feet to the right of the large one, carrying the fifteen-foot length of hemp rope Pappy had brought. I looked around before I walked back in. I knew Eugene and Ronnie's children were in school, and I was certain their wives had learned long ago to look the other way and never ask questions. When I got inside, Clancy was lying on the ground on his side in the middle of the barn floor. I looked at him and didn't feel the slightest pang of mercy or regret.

"Put him in a chair and take that gag out of his mouth," Granny said to Ronnie and Eugene as I started fashioning the waxed end of the rope into a hangman's noose. It was a fairly simple knot that one of my friends had shown me when I was a kid. I never thought I'd use it for the real thing.

Once Clancy was seated, Eugene walked over by the wall and picked up a stepladder. He set it down directly behind Clancy. I handed him the rope and he climbed up to the two oak posts and started wrapping and tying until the other end of the rope was secured around the posts. When he climbed back down, the noose hung about seven feet off the ground.

I don't think what was about to really happen dawned on Clancy until I took my fake beard, my glasses, and my hat off. I walked over and pulled the fur hat from his head. His red hair had thinned and faded to gray, and he'd lost some weight in jail. His gray eyes looked at me with utter contempt.

"You," he said. "I should have killed you years ago."

"Let's not talk about me," I said. "We're all here to talk about you. This is Luanne Tipton here to my right. She's a lovely lady, but I'm sure you've never met her and wouldn't give a damn if you had. James Tipton was her grandson. You remember James, don't you? He was the guy you used to frame me for a murder you coerced him into committing. I'm sure I don't have to go into all of it. You know what you did. You do know that James blew his brains out with a hand cannon, right? Did you hear about that? I'll bet you did, and I'll bet you smiled.

"The problem we're all having—oh, and these two gentlemen are Eugene and Ronnie, James's brothers, and this big guy here is Michael, but everybody calls him Big Pappy. He's a close friend of mine and is going to enjoy watching you hang. Like I was saying, the problem we're all having is that you were supposed to do the right thing. You were supposedly one of the good guys. A career prosecutor. But you might be the biggest hypocrite and the worst criminal I've ever known. As a matter of fact, I've decided you're a damned psychopath. And your precious judicial system has been letting you get away with lying and cheating and killing for years and years and years. How many innocent people did you send to death row, Ben? You don't have to give me an exact number, just a ballpark figure will do. Five? Ten? You don't want to say? That's all right. Let's be conservative and say seven. That makes you a serial killer, as far as all of us are concerned. You do know that's why you're here, right? We had a trial before we came and picked you up. We were the prosecutors and the jury and the judge. We decided not to allow you to have a defense. Sound familiar? You're being awfully quiet. Anyway, we convicted you of being a miserable son of a bitch who deserves to die, and we sentenced you to getting what you deserve. And now we're going to hang you. Do you hear those pigs snorting over there? After we hang you, we're going to feed you to them. Do you have anything to say before we carry out your sentence, Ben?"

I was hoping he'd cry and beg for his life, but I knew he was too proud. He wasn't getting out of this, and he knew it. He looked at each one of us through those beady gray eyes and said, "You're all just pimples on my ass. You'll be burning in hell while I'm walking with the Father."

"We had a choice when we were planning this out, you know," I said. "We could've dropped you in a humanitarian way. There are tables for body weight and the length of the rope. We could have measured it all out and dropped you so that your neck would break and you wouldn't feel much at all, if anything. But since you've never had an ounce of humanity in you, we decided to short-drop you. You're going to strangle slowly. It could take as long as five or six minutes for you to die. I hope you suffer, but sadly, I think you'll probably pass out in about twenty or thirty seconds."

I turned and looked at Eugene, Ronnie, and Pappy.

"Gentlemen," I said, "I think it's time for Mr. Clancy to go meet this maker he's talked about for so long."

All four of us grabbed him at the same time. I dragged him up the ladder by the collar of his coat while the others pushed from the bottom. Big Pappy and Eugene each used one of their hands to steady the ladder while Granny held it with both hands from the back side. Clancy tried to kick and squirm at first, but he knew it was hopeless, and after a few seconds accepted his fate. I slipped the noose around his neck and tightened it snugly around his throat while Ronnie held his feet on one of the rungs. I jumped off the ladder and backed away a couple of steps. Pappy, Eugene, and Ronnie stood with me. Granny stayed behind Clancy.

"We're waiting," I said.

Clancy looked down at me. His eyes had taken on a far-off look. "For what?" he mumbled.

"For you to be a man and step off on your own."

His legs were shaking as he stood, awkwardly balanced, on the third rung of the ladder.

"Fuck you," he said. "Fuck all of you. Enjoy hell."

He stood there defiantly for another ten seconds. Suddenly, the ladder was jerked backward. It clattered to the floor while he began to writhe as the rope tightened and he slowly strangled. We watched the same way a crowd would have watched back in the days when the government was hanging people in the town square—with prurient fascination. His eyes bugged, his face contorted and turned pink, then purple, then it began to fade to a pale white. He passed out within a couple of minutes, and I took a great deal of satisfaction in knowing that he knew I was largely responsible for ending his life. I felt no sorrow, no remorse at all. It was very much like the feeling I'd experienced after shooting Frazier and Beane. I felt empowered.

Granny walked into a stall and came back with a bottle of Tipton's Mountain Moonshine, a brand the family was now producing legally. She said, "To killing a son of a bitch that needed killing," and took a long swig from the bottle. "None of us will ever speak of this to anyone."

We passed it around while Clancy dangled from the end of the rope. Twenty minutes later, we cut him down and dragged him to the pigpen. Granny hadn't fed them in three days, and they tore into him. I turned away, not really wanting to watch that particular brand of gore, and walked to the van.

"It's done. Time to move on," I said to Pappy, and we walked outside, climbed in the van, and drove away.

CHAPTER 29

There was a large gun show in Knoxville the day after we took care of Ben Clancy. I don't know exactly why I felt the need to buy a gun, but I did. I think I just wanted something I could use without having to get Big Pappy involved. Tennessee has virtually no gun laws on the books, so I knew I could go to a show and find something in the parking lot. I could just buy from an individual, and there would be no paper trail.

I told Grace I was going to go fishing for a little while at Volunteer Landing Park and headed out. My first stop, after the usual doubling back and pulling into and out of parking lots to make sure I wasn't being followed, was at the same costume shop in the Old City where I'd bought the disguise before I went to West Virginia. I bought a beard, some glasses, and some adhesive and put the disguise on in the parking garage a couple of blocks from the store. Next, I went to an ATM and withdrew $500 in cash.

The gun show was at the Chilhowee Park & Exposition Center off Magnolia Avenue in East Knoxville. I showed up at eleven in the morning and just sat in the parking lot and watched for a while. It was a decent morning, sunny but chilly with a light breeze. I was surprised at how many people were there. From what I'd read on the Internet, it cost ten bucks just to get in, and most of the guns they sold were more expensive than if you went to a local gun shop. But the Second Amendment supporters were out in force. I was also surprised that there were no police vehicles, at least none that were identifiable. As I sat in my car for about thirty minutes, watching, I saw at least two hundred people walk up to the Jacob Center and go inside. Finally, I'd seen enough to identify at least two people who were dealing out of their vehicles.

About fifty feet to my right was a green Honda CR-V. I'd noticed the occupant get out of his vehicle a couple of times and have conversations with people. He opened his trunk once and retrieved a box, and then he and the man he was talking with got into his car. The man got out of the passenger side a few minutes later carrying the box. I suspected he wasn't doing anything illegal—he was simply selling a gun or two out of his private collection. I walked up in front of his vehicle and gave him a small wave. He rolled his window down.

"Looking for anything in particular?" he said in a thick Southern drawl. He looked around forty, had bright-green eyes, was wearing a University of Tennessee baseball cap, and had a perfectly waxed, brown handlebar mustache.

"Handgun. Probably a twenty-two, and I'd like a silencer if you have one."

"Got a Walther P22 and a Gemtech Seahunter," he said. "Last year's model but there ain't been a round through either one of them. They're still in the box."

I assumed the Walther was a pistol. I had no idea what a Gemtech Seahunter was. "Mind if I take a look?"

"Come on around and hop in."

I walked around to the passenger side, and he went to the back of the CR-V as the rear hatch opened. He reached inside and pulled out a couple of boxes, then walked back around and got in on the driver's side.

"Nice little combo," he said as he took the pistol out of the box. "Do you know a lot about this particular gun?"

"Probably not as much as I should," I said.

"Well, as you can see, this is a semiautomatic. The pistol has a prethreaded barrel for the suppressor mount. The magazine holds ten rounds. You use this little wrench, insert it right here near the end of the barrel, and remove the thread protector. Then you put the suppressor mount on that, and then click the suppressor into place."

"How loud is it with the suppressor?"

"Like a whisper," he said. "It's extremely quiet."

"How much?" I said.

"Cash, correct?"

"Of course."

"Three hundred for the Walther and seventy-five for the suppressor."

I figured he was gouging me a little, but under the circumstances, I was willing to pay it. There was no way this gun could ever be traced to me unless I was stupid enough to leave it at a crime scene with my fingerprints all over it.

"I'll take it," I said as I reached into my pocket and pulled out some cash.

"Just as a formality, I have to ask. You're not planning to use this pistol for any illegal purpose, are you?"

"No, sir. I'm just taking it up as a hobby. Bored with the wife."

"And you're not a convicted felon?"

"Never been convicted of a thing."

He smiled, took the money I handed him, counted it, boxed everything back up, and handed the boxes to me.

"Good luck to you, friend," he said. "Don't shoot yourself in the foot."

I got out and walked back to my car with a little smile on my face. I'd just bought a pistol and a silencer without even having to tell the guy my name. What a damned country.

CHAPTER 30

Will Grimes picked up the phone. Sammy Raft was calling, and Grimes hoped he might have some information that would help. The double-murder case in Cowen had stalled, and Grimes needed a break.

"I been thinking about what you said," Raft said.

"And?" Grimes hadn't heard anything from Raft and wondered why he was getting this call out of the blue. Had Raft grown a conscience?

"I might want to take one more look at those pictures you showed me. I'm thinking that might be the same man that was in the bar that night."

"Are you sure?"

"I can't say for positive, I really can't," Raft said.

"Then you're no good to me," Grimes said. "I need a positive identification, not some wishy-washy 'maybe.'"

"It was him," Raft said

"You're sure," Grimes said.

"I'm sure."

"You're positive."

"I'm positive."

"You'd take an oath in court and swear to it in front of a jury?"

"Yes."

"Where are you?" Grimes asked.

"I'm at work. At the bar."

"I'll be there in two hours."

* * *

Grimes showed up right when he said he would, almost two hours on the nose after he and Sammy Raft had hung up the phone. It was three o'clock in the afternoon, and the bar was empty.

Grimes walked in wearing the forest-green uniform of the West Virginia State Police. A "Smoky the Bear"—or campaign—hat sat atop his head. He'd worn the uniform because he thought it might both impress and intimidate Raft. As he looked into the mirror behind the bar, he concluded that he'd made the right choice. Grimes was six feet tall and lean, with a square jaw, dimpled cheeks, and intelligent brown eyes. The uniform made him look bigger, and it was definitely intimidating. Grimes removed his hat and sat down on a bar stool.

"You look scared," Grimes said.

"You look different."

"It's the uniform. Makes me look taller than I am. Where are your customers? How do you keep the place open?"

"I made them leave because you were coming," Raft said. "It's no big deal. The building was paid for a long time ago. I don't make a lot, but it pays the bills and gives me something to do. Business has been a whole lot better since those two boys got shot in here. I thought people would stay away, but just the opposite happened. People are strange. They're curious about it. Ask me all sorts of questions."

"Speaking of questions," Grimes said. "Let's start all over. Why don't you come around and we'll sit in a booth."

Sammy walked around and sat down in the first booth across from Grimes while Grimes pulled out a pad.

"This is a form we use for witness statements," Grimes said. "You talk, I'll write. When we're finished, you can go back over everything and then sign it. Fair enough?"

Sammy nodded.

"You said a man came into your bar the afternoon of the murders and ordered takeout, is that right?"

"That's right."

"What did he order?"

"Just a cheeseburger and a can of Pepsi."

"Did you talk to him at all?"

"Not other than to take his order."

"Was there anyone else in the bar at the time?"

"Nope. Just me."

"Okay, so this man came in around two in the afternoon, is that what you told me?" Grimes asked.

"Right. Around two."

"And then he left and came back later."

"That's right. He walked in right around eight o'clock that Friday evening. Sat down on the first bar stool, right there. Donnie and Tommy were in the booth right . . . well, you saw them. You know where they were."

"What did the man say when he came in?"

"Best of my recollection, he said something about it being awful slow for a Friday night, and I told him it was because of Donnie and Tommy. Told him they'd run all my weekend business off, which was true. They were mean as snakes and loud to boot. If anybody said anything to them, they'd beat hell out of them. They wanted a place where they could come and drink and listen to the jukebox all by themselves, and that's what they'd turned my bar into. They'd turned it into their own private little club. So I told this man he probably shouldn't stay long, that they'd give him trouble if he stayed, and he said thanks for the warning and ordered a longneck Budweiser."

"Which you told me he didn't touch."

"That's right," Sammy said. "He didn't."

"What else did he say?"

"He asked me if I loved my mother."

Grimes's head came up, and he raised his eyebrows. "Is that right?" he said. "Now why would he ask you a thing like that?"

"I thought the same thing, and I asked him the same thing. He said I'd understand in a minute, to please just answer the question. So I told him I loved my mother very much, that she was a wonderful person. And he said something about loving his mother, too, and that Donnie and Tommy had raped her. He called them insects. Then he said he was here to kill them, and I could either go to the bathroom or die right along with them."

"So he threatened to kill you?" Grimes said.

"Yes, sir, he did. And from the look in his eye, I had no doubt he'd do it."

"And you went to the bathroom?"

"I did, and I locked the door. I know he could've kicked the damned door down and killed me if he wanted to, but I didn't get the message from him that he really *wanted* to kill me, you know? He wanted Donnie and Tommy, and by God, he got 'em."

"And the man who came into your bar, asked you about your mother, talked about killing Donnie and Tommy, and was still sitting on that stool when you walked into the bathroom is the same man in the photographs I showed you, but you say he was wearing a disguise."

"He was wearing a beard and glasses and a hat."

"But you're certain the man in the photos is the same man who was in the bar that night?"

"I'm positive."

"A hundred percent positive?"

"You just don't stop, do you?" Raft said.

"A hundred percent positive?" Grimes said.

"A hundred percent."

Grimes finished writing up the statement and after a few minutes, he slid it across the table.

"Read it, then sign right here and initial at the bottom of each page," Grimes said.

Raft did it. Grimes gathered the statement, placed it in a folder, put the folder in a larger folder, and stood up.

"That's it?" Raft said.

"For now," Grimes said. "I'm headed to Webster Springs to talk to the district attorney. It's time to start rattling this Street fella's chain."

CHAPTER 31

Grimes called District Attorney James Hellerman from his cell phone, then drove to Hellerman's private law office in Webster Springs. Grimes knew that it was in this office that Hellerman did the bulk of his work—estate cases, personal injury, and divorce. He was a part-time district attorney because the legislature in West Virginia had deemed that there wasn't a large enough population—and therefore enough crime—in his part of the state to warrant a full-time DA.

Grimes walked into the office—a remodeled colonial-style house just off Main Street in downtown Webster Springs—and said hello to Hellerman's wife, Bonnie, who served as his receptionist, secretary, and paralegal. Bonnie showed Grimes into Hellerman's office.

"Nice to see you again, Will," Hellerman said as he stood and offered his hand.

Grimes returned the greeting and sat down. Hellerman was in his midforties, a bit geeky-looking in a red bow tie and white shirt. He was medium height and pasty, with pale skin and a shock of blond hair that he wore long and had to push back from his eyes on a regular basis.

"So what can I do for you, Will?"

"I have a suspect in the double murder in Cowen. I'm here to ask whether you think I have enough to arrest him."

Grimes recounted the murder of Darren Street's mother in Tennessee, the subsequent investigation that led to Donnie Frazier and

Tommy Beane, the tie-in between Donnie Frazier's brother, Bobby Lee, and Darren Street, and then the murders of Frazier and Beane in Sammy's bar.

"They were trying to kill Street and killed his mother instead?" Hellerman asked.

"Right. Street was at a hotel proposing to his girlfriend, from what the Knoxville police told me."

"But even if Street had been there, they would have killed his mother, too."

Grimes nodded. "They were cold-blooded about it."

He told Hellerman about Frazier's girlfriend, Emma Newland, and that she had told him Frazier and Beane had killed Street's mother. His most important witness, he said, would be the bar owner, Sammy Raft, who had positively identified Darren Street as being in the bar on the night of the shootings and threatening Sammy's life if Sammy didn't go into the bathroom while he killed Frazier and Beane.

"How did he identify this Darren Street?" Hellerman asked.

"I had an old booking photograph and a new driver's license photo sent from Tennessee," Grimes said.

"Booking photo? So he has a record?"

"He was charged with first-degree murder, convicted, and then the conviction was reversed by the trial court. He was apparently framed by a federal prosecutor named Ben Clancy, but Clancy was tried and acquitted a few weeks ago. I was notified by the Knoxville police this morning that Clancy has gone missing. His car was found five days ago, but nobody has seen him since. This Darren Street is a suspect in his disappearance. It looks like Street may have gone full-blown vigilante."

"Did you show him a photo lineup, include other people, or just Darren Street?"

"I just showed him the photos of Street."

"That's a problem. Outside of that, how solid is your witness?" Hellerman said.

"Sammy Raft? To be honest, I don't know. He isn't the brightest crayon in the box."

"Did you influence his identification at all, Will? Be honest, because it'll come out later if you did."

Grimes shrugged. "I may have leaned on him a little. He flip-flopped on the ID. First he said he didn't recognize the guy in the photo, and then, after I threatened to arrest him, he called me this morning and told me he'd changed his mind. The guy in the photo is the same guy that was in his bar, but he had a beard and was wearing glasses and a hat."

"And you think he's right?" Hellerman said.

"I can't be positive, but it makes sense. The owner said this guy came in and asked him whether he loved his mother. Then the guy told him Frazier and Beane raped his mother and he was there to kill them. He told the owner he could either go into the bathroom or die with them. The owner went into the bathroom and the shooting started."

"Do you have any forensics?"

"Just a bunch of nine-millimeter shell casings. No gun to match them to."

"Nothing else?"

"Nothing. We went over the bar thoroughly and didn't get so much as a partial print. We've canvassed, we've checked every hotel in a fifty-mile radius, we've looked at security camera footage from dozens of places and have come up empty."

"So the bar owner, what's his name?"

"Sammy Raft."

"So Sammy Raft, is it? He's pretty much our entire case?"

"Pretty much, depending on whether you can get other evidence of Street's mother being murdered in front of a jury."

"Let's say I'm able to do that, which, to be honest, would be difficult. But let's say I'm able to say that this man is accused of killing two convicted felons with long records who blew up his mother's house and murdered her. This is a classic jury nullification case, Will. His lawyer would use the 'sumbitch needed killing' defense. The jury would let him go because the sumbitches he killed needed killing. And if that doesn't seem to be working, the defense will say Sammy killed them himself. I don't know what his motive would be, but a good defense lawyer will find one."

"What do you want me to do, James?" Grimes said. "Tank it? We have a double murder here, a nasty one. It was an execution, pure and simple. My job is to find the killer and bring him to justice. Do you want me to just let it go?"

"Just keep grinding," Hellerman said. "That's your reputation. Keep grinding, and maybe eventually something will break. For now, though, I wouldn't feel comfortable arresting him. I could take it to a grand jury and probably get an indictment just based on what the bartender told you, but if we wind up going to trial, he's going to face cross-examination, and from what you've told me, I don't think he'll hold up. Let's just wait and see if something else comes up."

Grimes shook his head in frustration. He understood to a degree, but he hated it when lawyers, especially prosecutors, were being overly cautious. If they could indict Street, arrest him, and get him in jail, they'd have a lot better chance of the case breaking open.

"And if he killed that federal prosecutor in Knoxville, too?"

"That's not our problem, is it, Will?"

"Guess not."

The district attorney stood, indicating to Grimes he'd made his decision and the meeting was over.

"Come back when you have more," Hellerman said. "And if you don't get more, don't worry about it too much. From everything I've heard about the Frazier and Beane clans around here, I don't think the community lost a whole lot."

CHAPTER 32

Two days after Ben Clancy went missing, I received a call from Marty Henley, the old friend and lawyer who had allowed me to use his family's property in Petros to target-shoot.

"I'm hearing some bad things about you, Darren," he said.

"Like what?"

"Like the police think you killed a couple of guys in West Virginia."

"Don't believe everything you hear, Marty."

"Pretty strange coincidence, don't you think? You call me up out of the blue and ask me if you can shoot on our land, and then a couple of weeks later these two guys get blown away. Two guys who just so happen to be suspected of bombing your mother's house in an attempt to kill you."

"You've been talking to a lot of people," I said.

"I've been *listening* to a lot of people. Haven't done much talking."

"Have any of these people you've been listening to been wearing badges and carrying guns?"

"No, this is just shoptalk. Lawyer gossip."

"Why are you calling me, Marty?"

"To tell you that I don't care one way or another about what you may or may not have done."

"I haven't done anything."

"Good. Just do me one favor, okay? If the worst happens, and you wind up getting arrested, please don't mention to the police or anyone else that I gave you permission to shoot on my family's property. Lawsuits could be filed. I could be harassed by an overzealous police officer, who might accuse me of being some kind of accomplice."

"I'm not going to get arrested, Marty, because I didn't do anything. But if, by some bizarre twist of fate, I do wind up being arrested, I promise your name will never be mentioned. Fair enough?"

"Fair enough, and one more thing: probably best if you don't go back up there."

"It's your property."

"Thanks, Darren. Good luck."

I was getting used to hearing about the gossip at this point. I'd even heard from a couple of journalists who said they were contemplating writing a story about the police's suspicions that I was involved in the West Virginia murders and perhaps the disappearance of Ben Clancy. I, of course, responded by telling them that I'd own their newspapers if they printed that kind of malicious gossip without any proof. So far they'd held off, but even if they did print a story at some point, I just figured it would be more publicity for me, and publicity, good or bad, always seemed to generate business.

I laid my phone on my desk and mused at the irony. Most lawyers who wanted publicity spent thousands on advertising. All they really had to do was kill a few people, and they'd get all the attention they could stand.

CHAPTER 33

The young woman was flawless.

She came into my office a week after we'd dispatched Ben Clancy. I stood when she walked in, although I have to admit my knees went a little weak. She was about an inch shorter than I was, and she had gleaming black hair and sapphire eyes. Her nose was petite and perfect, her jawline fine and sharp, her teeth bright white, and her lips full and pink. All of this sat above a body that could only be described as centerfold-worthy. She was a truly stunning physical specimen, a trophy in every sense of the word, but she seemed oblivious to the vibe she put out. She radiated sensuality like a cell-phone tower radiated a signal, but she wore conservative clothes and little if any makeup. She was wearing a navy-blue business suit with a knee-length skirt, a button-up blouse that was tight on her breasts, and black shoes with spiked, maybe two-inch heels.

I offered my hand, introduced myself, and invited her to sit down. She told me her name was Katherine Davis.

"I'm embarrassed to be here," she said.

"Why is that?"

"Because I've been charged with a crime, and I'm anything but a criminal."

"What's the charge?" I said.

"Driving under the influence."

"First offense?"

She nodded. "Yes, but I rarely drink, and I didn't have a drop that night."

"Drugs?" I asked.

"I guess. I actually have absolutely no memory of what happened. I woke up in jail and had no idea how I got there."

I'd handled a couple of hundred DUI cases over the years. They had become one of my specialties. I'd had clients who told me they didn't remember anything, but all of them had blood-alcohol counts that were nearly triple the legal limit. This beautiful young lady must have taken a heavy dose of drugs.

"You said, 'I guess,' when I asked you about drugs. What do you mean by that?"

"I don't use drugs, but I'm a graduate student at UT in the criminal-justice program, and we were in finals week. I'd been up studying all night for a couple of nights, but I couldn't turn my mind off and get any real sleep. I was talking to one of my friends about it because I had an important test two days later, and she said, 'I have something that I guarantee will help you sleep. I'll bring it by your place later.' She came by later and dropped off one little pill. I guess I was pretty desperate, because I took it."

"Ambien?" I said.

"Right," she said. "I took the pill, went to bed, and the next thing I know I'm in jail, in my pajamas. Bare feet. The police report says I was weaving on Paper Mill Road at 1:30 a.m. and that I failed the field sobriety tests the officer gave me. I don't remember a single bit of it. Not a bit. Do you think you can help me? I've already been accepted to the UT law school in the fall. I want to be a prosecutor. If I get convicted of DUI, it's going to cause me a lot of problems. I'm twenty-five years old, and I've never been in any kind of trouble before, I swear it. Nothing. No juvenile record. I've never been arrested, never even had a speeding ticket. I guess I shouldn't have taken that pill, but I had no idea something like this would happen."

"Did you read the label on the bottle?" I said.

"She didn't give me the bottle. She just brought me the pill in a plastic baggie."

"I think I can help you," I said. "I can't guarantee it, but I think I can talk the prosecutor and the cop out of this one after they hear the circumstances."

I'd been pleasantly surprised by the attitude shown toward me by the local prosecutors and police officers. Many of them had to know I was a suspect in the West Virginia murders, but if they did—with the exception of Dawn Rule and Lawrence Kingman—they didn't seem to care. None of them had stopped speaking to me, and I hadn't gotten the sense that they were treating me any differently than before. I'd become somewhat of a celebrity after Grace helped me get my conviction for murder reversed, and I'd become a sympathetic figure after my mom was killed. As far as I could tell, the respect and the sympathy they had showed me in the past hadn't changed.

"The biggest problem we have is that driving under the influence is what they call a 'strict liability crime' in Tennessee," I said to Katherine. "That means the state doesn't have to prove criminal intent. It's similar to speeding. If they catch you speeding, they don't have to prove you intended to speed. In a DUI case, all they have to prove is that you were operating a vehicle on a public road and you were under the influence. Can you get me transcripts of your grades and a copy of your acceptance letter to law school?"

"I can do that." She reached into her purse and brought out a tissue. A tear slid down her lovely left cheek. "I'd be so grateful if you can help me get out of this."

"Please don't cry," I said. "I think you're going to be all right. Did they do a blood draw at the jail or take you to the hospital, or do you even know?"

"I have no clue," she said. "I've been so worried and so terrified that everything I've worked for would be ruined because I took a stupid pill. I can promise you one thing. I'll never do it again."

"It helps a lot that you didn't hurt anybody," I said. "Or yourself. I'm really glad you didn't hurt yourself."

She looked at me curiously, and I felt my cheeks warm. I'd just given her the impression that I was attracted to her. It was unprofessional, and I immediately regretted it. "I'm sorry. I didn't mean that the way it sounded."

She smiled easily. "No problem. I like you, too. So tell me, do you enjoy what you do? I want to work for the DA's office, but I hear a lot of stories about defense lawyers being drunks and drug addicts and hating themselves and what they do."

"I'm not a drunk or a drug addict," I said, "but to be honest, what I do can be difficult sometimes. I look at my job as nothing more than being the guy that ensures the government and all the people it employs play by their own rules. They make the rules, so I think they should have to follow them. All the time. No shortcuts, no cheating, no lying. If you become one of them, I'll expect you to play fair."

It was strange hearing myself say those things, because I still genuinely felt that way, with one very important exception. The exception was that if a crime was committed against me or someone in my family, then I would take care of it myself. Screw the government, its employees, and its rules.

"Do a lot of police officers lie?" she said.

"I wouldn't say a lot, but some of them do. Once they make an arrest, they want a conviction, and some of them will do anything to get that conviction. It becomes a game to them. Some prosecutors are the same way. Once they have an indictment, they think they have to have a conviction. But like I said, those people are in the minority, and I hope you won't be one of them. My clients? Different story. About ninety percent of them lie to me. I expect them to lie. I was expecting you to lie, but I don't think you are. That's refreshing."

"Everything I've told you is the absolute truth," she said.

"That's rare around here," I said. "You said you read the report. Did you bring it with you?"

"I did," and she went back into her purse. She handed it to me, and I read it.

"You caught a break," I said. "The arresting officer is Earl Anderson. He's one of the good guys. He won't want to jam you up after I talk to him and tell him what happened."

"You know him?"

"I've been doing this a long time," I said. "I know a lot of the officers. When do you have to go to court again?"

"Three weeks."

"Maybe we'll get lucky and Earl will be there that day and we can get it taken care of so you won't have to worry anymore. Sometimes the officers don't show up. They're working an accident or there might be a scheduling problem or they're sick. If he doesn't show up, we'll have to move it a few more weeks down the road. If, for whatever reason, Earl and the prosecutor won't back off and insist on pushing this, we'll take it to Criminal Court and try it in front of a jury. You'll make a very presentable and sympathetic witness."

"I almost hope he doesn't show up," Katherine said.

"Why's that?"

"Because if he doesn't show up, I'll get to see you again." She smiled broadly and stood.

My stomach fluttered. "I'm a little old for you, don't you think? I'm also sort of semi-engaged."

"You're not that old. What does semi-engaged mean?"

"It means I have a girlfriend I don't talk to very much."

"Well, a girl can always hope," she said. "Do I make arrangements to pay you with your secretary?"

I nodded and reached for the stack of business cards that was sitting on my desk. I wrote my cell phone number on the back and handed it to her. "Nice to meet you."

"Do you give your cell number to all your clients?"

"No."

She reached out to shake my hand and I took it. As she pulled her hand away, she grazed my palm with her fingernails, and I felt a shudder of electricity run through me.

"Nice to meet you, too," she said. "I look forward to seeing you again."

She turned and walked slowly—very slowly—out of the room. I was practically drooling by the time she was out of sight.

CHAPTER 34

Will Grimes was living up to the reputation District Attorney James Hellerman had spoken of. He was still grinding, still thinking, still investigating. He didn't think Darren Street would have been able to simply drive to West Virginia, shoot Frazier and Beane, and drive back to Tennessee. He would have done some surveillance. He would have followed Frazier and Beane, stalked them, and picked his time to strike, which meant he would have had to stay in or around Cowen for at least a day or two. Grimes also wondered whether Street had had some help, someone in West Virginia who was feeding him information.

On a breezy Friday morning, Grimes walked into a small brick home on the west end of Cowen. Lester Routh, a longtime burglar, drug dealer, drug addict, and informant for the West Virginia State Police, lived in the home along with five cats and a woman named Lucille. Lucille worked at a convenience store about a mile down the road and wasn't home. Lester had wanted to meet when she wouldn't be there, and he'd asked Grimes to wear civilian clothes and park at least a half mile away.

"I know what you want," Routh said as he poured Grimes a cup of coffee. "Cream or sugar?"

Grimes shook his head. He was surprised at how clean and orderly the place was. Lester Routh might be a thief, but at least he was a clean thief.

"How could you possibly know what I want?" Grimes said. "Have you become a mind reader?"

Lester sat down heavily in a chair across the kitchen table from Grimes. He had a scruffy three-day beard that was salt and pepper. Grimes knew Routh kept his head shaved, but there was stubble across the dome this morning. His face was pockmarked from acne, and his cheeks were sunken. When he smiled, which wasn't often, his teeth were gapped and yellow.

"You want to know if I know anything about that shooting at Sammy's a while back," Routh said. "You ain't arrested nobody, which means you either ain't got nothing or you ain't got enough. You want my help."

"Well, you're a damned psychic, Lester," Grimes said. "So? Have you heard anything?"

"Maybe."

"Then let's hear it."

"How much?"

"Depends on what you tell me and how much it helps me."

"I want five hundred."

"For five hundred, you better hand me the killer's ass on a platter," Grimes said.

"That'd cost you five thousand."

"What do you have?" Grimes said.

Routh laid his hand down on the table, palm up, and started wiggling his fingers. "Five hundred," he said.

"Not a chance until I hear what you have to say."

"Let me see the money," Routh said. "Put it on the table."

Grimes had known what he was getting into before he came. He'd had to argue for an hour to get approval from his supervisor for $1,000 in cash for the informant. He didn't know whether Routh would have any information, but he'd used Routh in the past, and he'd always been reliable. He seemed to know everyone and everything that was going on in the criminal underworld in and around Cowen. Grimes reached into his wallet and laid five hundred-dollar bills on the table. He put his hand over them and held them in place. "Talk."

"There was a guy asking around a few weeks before your boys got popped," Routh said.

"What guy?"

"He was a messenger boy, a representative of another guy who was representing a third guy."

"You're off to a terrible start," Grimes said as he peeled two of the hundreds off and stuck them in his pocket.

"He was asking about Frazier on behalf of this other guy. He wanted to know if Frazier had made any noise about killing this dude in Knoxville, Tennessee, because the dude had something to do with Frazier's brother getting his throat cut in prison."

"Names, Lester. I need names."

"The guy that was doing all the asking was a biker named Jimmy Baker. Known him his whole life. Young and cocky, a punk, did a two-year bit on a burglary charge and thinks he's a badass. He was asking on behalf of this dude named Rex Fairchild out of Charleston. Baker said Fairchild moved some blow back in the day, and Fairchild and Baker's stepdaddy knew each other. That's how Baker and Fairchild hooked up, through Baker's stepdaddy. Fairchild wanted the information for a friend of his that he was in the coke business with, some heavyweight they call Big Pappy Donovan. Fairchild and Big Pappy both got busted, but neither of them would roll on anybody so they both went to prison. Fairchild wound up doing about seven years, I believe. But Big Pappy got a lot more time. The word I got was that Big Pappy was a shot caller at the same prison where this Darren Street was serving his time. You know what a shot caller is, right?"

"Yeah, I know what a shot caller is."

"So Big Pappy was one of the most respected shot callers in the federal system. Hurt some guards pretty bad, did a bunch of time in the hole, even wound up at Marion for a while from what people say. So when Baker comes asking and mentioning Big Pappy's name, people start talking. And what he was asking about was whether Donnie Frazier may have blown up a house in Tennessee and whether he had any help. And the answer he got was yeah, Frazier and Tommy Beane stole some dynamite from Archland Coal Company and went down to Knoxville, Tennessee, and blew up a house. He was trying to kill Darren Street, but Street wasn't there. When I first heard about it, all I did was shake my head. Donnie and Tommy were two of the meanest, dumbest crackers I ever knew. So once Baker finds out they were the ones that killed Street's mother, he starts wanting addresses and what kind of vehicle they drive and where they hang out and all that."

"How did you find all of this out?" Grimes said.

"Baker comes by here once in a while. We sit out back and burn wood and drink liquor. He flaps his gums when he's drinking."

"Who killed Frazier and Beane?" Grimes said.

"I don't know," Routh said. "I swear I don't know. Nobody's said a word. Information flowed out of here, but apparently none has flowed back. Maybe Big Pappy came in and did it, or maybe he had somebody else do it, or maybe he just passed the information on to Street and Street did it himself or hired somebody. No way to know for sure."

"Where is Big Pappy Donovan now?" Grimes said. "He still in prison?"

"No. He's out. Street's a lawyer, right? The word is that while they were in prison, Street won Pappy's appeal and got him out. But during the time between Street winning the appeal and Pappy actually being released, Pappy helped Street escape, and Street ended up going back to Tennessee and getting his case dismissed. Those two dudes are legends inside the walls all over the country."

"That's great, good for them," Grimes said. "Do you know where Big Pappy is?"

"Runs a trucking company out of Dalton, Georgia."

"And this Rex Fairchild, you say he's in Charleston?"

"Charleston, West Virginia. He owns a used car lot there, from what I hear."

"You hear a lot," Grimes said.

"I don't talk much unless I'm getting paid for it," Routh said. "Learn a lot more that way."

Grimes took the hundreds back out of his pocket and put them on the table.

"I'll probably be back," he said.

"Be sure to call before you come so I can get the wife out of here," Routh said. "She talks a lot. Wouldn't want to ruin my reputation."

CHAPTER 35

I hadn't seen Dan Reid since I was tried and convicted of murder, but I knew the former Special Agent in Charge of the FBI's Knoxville office had retired shortly after Ben Clancy was arrested and had opened his own private investigative agency. I called and asked whether he would come to my office to talk about doing some work for me, and to my surprise, he agreed. He walked in the day after I spoke with Katherine Davis, and I went to the lobby to greet him.

Reid was fifty-two, an inch taller than I was, and had thick, short, salt-and-pepper hair and penetrating robin-egg-blue eyes. He was trim and appeared to be fit, one of those guys who was so lean you could see the muscles in his jaws.

"Is this awkward?" I said when he walked into my office and sat down across from me.

He shook his head. "No reason for it to be awkward. I did my job back then. I didn't think you were guilty, but there wasn't anything I could do."

"Did you know Clancy was framing me?"

"I suspected. What do you think about him disappearing?"

"I think he hurt a lot of people during his career, which means there are a lot of possibilities."

"Some people think you're one of those possibilities, from what I understand."

Again, the rumors. I seemed to be a constant topic of conversation among law enforcement agencies, lawyers, judges, clerks, and reporters. I smiled and shook my head. "You're talking about your former colleagues at the FBI, I assume."

Reid nodded. "Along with some Knoxville cops and the United States Attorney."

"They're mistaken," I said. "I haven't done a thing."

"The feds don't really matter," Reid said. "It isn't their case. No jurisdiction."

"Did you call Grace the night before my trial started and tell her I wasn't guilty?" I asked.

"I'm going to take the Fifth on that one."

"I knew it was you. Well, for what it's worth, thank you."

"Didn't do much good, did it?"

"No, but thanks just the same. So how is the private-eye thing going?"

"I like it," Reid said. "I get to cherry-pick because I don't really need money, and I get to do investigative work, which is something I've always enjoyed. And it gets me out of the house."

"What do you charge?"

"A hundred and fifty an hour plus expenses."

"You pay yourself a little better than the FBI paid you."

"A lot better."

"Staying busy?"

"I've got all I want."

"Interested in taking a look at a case for me?"

"Maybe. What do you have?"

Katherine Davis had been bothering me. It all just seemed somehow contrived. And the fact that she was in the criminal justice program and wanted to be a prosecutor meant she might be close to some cops. The more I thought about it, the way she'd hit on me didn't make sense. She was too young and too gorgeous to be interested in a semisuccessful, hack criminal defense lawyer like me. The thing that bothered me the most, though, was that she hadn't mentioned my conviction and exoneration, and she hadn't said a word about my mother. Perhaps it was just paranoia, but I wanted to be sure she was what she said she was.

"Beautiful young girl who says she took an Ambien and did some sleep-driving. Wound up getting arrested for DUI. She came in yesterday and told me about the case, but by the time she left, she was hitting on me. I told her I was too old for her and I was engaged, but she kept on."

"Maybe you're just irresistible," Reid said.

"I'd love to think so, but this woman could have anybody she wants. I think I smell a rat. It might just be paranoia because I'm constantly hearing rumors about being suspected of murder, but then again, it might not."

"A rat? You think she's working for the cops?"

"They think I killed two guys in West Virginia, and now they think I may have had something to do with Clancy going missing. I guess they think I'm some kind of serial killer now. I wouldn't put it past them to send some pretty young thing in here to try and get an admission out of me."

"Do you have anything to admit?" Reid said.

"Like I said, I haven't done a thing. Haven't killed anybody. I just don't have it in me."

"Do you have her date of birth and Social Security number?"

"Everything you need is on the intake form she filled out yesterday. Got her driver's license number, too, if you need it."

"Every little bit helps," Reid said. "So what exactly do you want me to do?"

"I want you to be discreet and find out everything there is to know about her. Where she grew up, her circumstances. Follow her. She says she's a grad student in criminal justice at UT and has been accepted to the law school here in the fall. I'd like to know if that's really true."

"And what if it turns out she's working for the Knoxville PD?"

"I hope she isn't. I really do. I'd like to think she's just a beautiful young woman who finds me attractive. But if she's working for them, I'll tell her to go play rat somewhere else. I hate informants."

"Do you have a time frame?" Reid said.

"As soon as possible. Can you get on it immediately?"

"I need to tie a couple of things up first. Give me three days, and then I'll get started."

"Excellent. Thank you."

"For what it's worth, I'm really sorry about your mother," Reid said.

"Thank you. It's been tough."

"I'll tell you something else," he said. "If somebody murdered my mother, you can bet your ass I'd be looking to put a bullet in them."

"The law frowns on vigilantes," I said. Once again, paranoia began to overtake me. Was Reid trying to get me to admit something? He'd been an FBI agent his entire adult life. If I admitted something to him, his instinct would have probably been to go straight to the Knoxville PD.

"Right," Reid said, "and sometimes that's just a damned shame. Are you still with Grace Alexander?"

"I am."

"Tell her I said hello. And tell her I had a little too much to drink that night I called her."

"Will do," I said.

As Reid got up and walked out of the room, I leaned back in my chair and let out a deep breath. Reid seemed okay, but I couldn't help but wonder whether he'd stab me in the back if I gave him half a chance. I'd have to be careful around him.

It was getting to the point where I couldn't trust anyone.

CHAPTER 36

That same afternoon, I had to go to Criminal Court for a motion hearing on an arson case I was handling. In the motion, I was asking the judge to disqualify the prosecution's "expert" fire investigator on the grounds that his education, training, and experience did not meet the legal criteria for an expert under the current, controlling case law in Tennessee. My client, a thirty-five-year-old sleazebag named Eddie Burton, had more likely than not burned his girlfriend's house down so he could bleed her for the insurance money, but the prosecution's case was thin and their expert simply wasn't qualified. I had no idea why they had chosen to use this particular expert, but he had very little training, very little experience, a limited education, and he simply wasn't very bright.

While I was sitting at the defense table waiting for my case to be called, I looked up, and in walked my old client Rupert Lattimore, the man who had engineered the kidnapping, rapes, and murders of two college kids. I'd been appointed to represent Rupert, but the judge had taken me off the case after Rupert and I took turns threatening to kill each other.

Rupert, who was handcuffed, chained at the waist, and shackled, shuffled straight to the defense table accompanied by two sheriff's deputies. I looked up and smirked at him.

"Well, if it ain't the murdering, motherfucking lawyer," Rupert said quietly.

"Go fuck yourself, Rupert," I said.

"Man, I been hearing what you did up there in West Virginia. I hope they catch you and give you the damned death penalty. From what I hear, you walked into a bar and ambushed them two boys, shot the shit out of them. It was a coward killing from what I hear."

"Really? Kind of like how you stuck a broomstick up Stephen Whitfield's ass after you and your boys had him hog-tied? And didn't you eventually shoot him in the back? And then you went in and raped that poor defenseless girl for two days and then poured bleach down her throat before you covered her in trash bags, stuffed her in a trash can, and let her suffocate? That took a real man, Rupert."

"Damn shame about your momma," Rupert said. "How much of her did they find? A couple of little pieces? I'm surprised she wasn't fucking somebody and got him blown up, too. All I've heard about her was that she was a whore."

I felt heat rise in my stomach, and every muscle in my body tensed. I had a pretty thick skin when it came to the courtroom and clients and some of the things they'd say. But I hated Rupert, and hearing him call my dead mother a whore pushed me over the edge. My vision tunneled. I stood up and looked him dead in the eye.

"You're gonna pay for that," I said.

"Yeah? What are you gonna do?"

I turned my back on him and walked out the side door into the hallway. I was seething. I paced up and down the hall for a few minutes and then went outside. I'd gotten into the habit of carrying two phones with me—my regular cell and a throwaway. The throwaway was in my car, and I jogged to the parking garage and retrieved it from the glove compartment. Big Pappy had texted me his most recent burner number, and I dialed it.

"What's up, my man?" he said cheerfully.

"I have a problem. How much would it cost me to reach out and touch somebody in jail?" I said.

All I could hear was Lattimore's voice: *"All I've ever heard about her was that she was a whore."* The indignity of what had happened to her was bad enough, but for Lattimore to remind me of it so blatantly and in such a vulgar manner had thrown me once again into a mental and emotional rage. And he'd been so smug about it. He genuinely didn't think there was anything I could do about what he'd said, so I could tell he took great pleasure in taunting me. I didn't just want to fuck him up, I wanted to fuck him up badly. I knew what I was planning could be risky, that it could cause me problems, especially with everything else that was going on, but at that point, with the taunts still burning in my ears, I just didn't give a shit.

"Depends on which jail and what you mean by touch," Pappy said. "You want the person dead or beaten or what?"

"The jail is right here in Knoxville," I said. "The city jail. And I want him oiled up. I don't want him to have a face."

"Damn, this dude must have really pissed you off."

"How much?" I said.

"I can probably get it done for about two thousand."

"Set it up for me, will you? Just put it on my tab. And make sure you get somebody who will do it right."

"What did the guy do?"

I told Pappy of my history with Rupert Lattimore, and then I told him what he'd said about my mom.

"Disrespecting a man's dead mother is not a good idea," he said. "I can handle it. Take a few days."

"As soon as possible," I said, "but do it right. I don't need any more heat on me."

I put the phone back in the car and went back into the courtroom. Judge Montgomery was just finishing up introducing Rupert Lattimore to the appointed attorney who would replace me. She set a new trial date, and Rupert shuffled out of the courtroom.

I went back to the defense table, and the judge called my case. We went through the hearing, and I won. The prosecution's expert witness was disqualified, and since they didn't have time to get another one before the trial date and the judge wouldn't give them a continuance, they moved to dismiss the case.

My sleazebag client was thrilled.

Three days later, I heard on the news that an inmate at the Knoxville City Jail had sneaked into Rupert Lattimore's cell while Rupert was napping and dumped a large bowl of baby oil that had been superheated in a microwave oven onto Rupert's face. Rupert was in a local hospital in critical condition. The report said that all the skin on his face had melted off into his hands as he screamed and tried to wipe off the baby oil.

Nobody knew—or at least nobody was saying—who the oil-throwing inmate was, and nobody knew why Rupert Lattimore no longer had a face.

Except for me, of course. And a man named Big Pappy.

CHAPTER 37

I'd put Sean out of my mind, primarily because if I allowed myself to think about him and how much I loved him and would miss him, I was afraid I would actually feel something besides anger and rage, and it was those two emotions that had largely taken over my psyche. When it came to Sean, it was almost as though I was in a perpetual state of what Pink Floyd had once called "comfortably numb," although my numbness wasn't induced by drugs or alcohol. It was induced by a sub-conscious choice I'd made to protect myself from emotional trauma. I wanted to kill Katie and her fiancé. I'd thought about it many times, but I knew killing her would be the end for me. There were limits to what I could do, and I knew I was already pushing them.

To keep myself from thinking about Sean, I spent a lot of time in the woods outside of Petros, which was less than an hour away, pumping rounds through the 0.22 pistol I'd bought. Marty had asked me to stop going there, but I chose to ignore him. Target-shooting was mindless, it kept me occupied, and in the state I was in, I never knew when it might come in handy.

When the time came for Sean to leave, I decided it would be best to say goodbye over the phone. I could have—and should have—taken him fishing or camping or to a movie or to the mall or on a hike. I could have done something that, as Gwen had suggested, would show him how much I loved him and how much I was going to miss him. But instead, I called him the day before they were supposed to leave. It was five o'clock, and my office had just closed.

"You're really going to like Hawaii, buddy," I said when he came on the phone.

"I hope so," he said.

"I've never been there, but I've heard it's a beautiful place. You'll be surrounded by the Pacific Ocean, there are mountains and hills just like there are here, but the weather is a lot better. You'll see a lot of palm trees, and you'll get to do a lot of cool stuff in and around the ocean. Maybe you can take up scuba diving and deep-sea fishing, do some parasailing or learn to surf."

"I'll miss you, Dad," he said, and I heard him start to sniffle.

"Don't even think about me," I said. "Your mom thinks this is best for you, and as much as I hate to agree with her on anything, she's probably right. You're going to go to a great school, and you're going to have a great life over there. So like I said, don't even think about me. Just live your life and be happy all the time."

"Mom says you killed two men. She says you're going back to jail."

"Your mom says a lot of things. Don't worry about it. I didn't kill anybody, and I'm not going to jail."

"Why would she say that if it isn't true?"

"She always says terrible things, Sean. She has ever since we split up. You know that. She just doesn't like me."

"She hates you."

"I know she does. Maybe once you get to Hawaii and she doesn't have to see me or deal with me, she'll stop hating me so much. Maybe that will be another good thing that comes out of all this. My lawyer says you get out of school the last week in May, and I'll fly you here the first week of June. You can stay here until the first of August if you want."

"That's a long time away, Dad."

"No, it isn't. A little over six months. It'll pass before you know it, and then you'll be back here. So I'll see you the first of June, and I'll call you a lot in between. We can FaceTime."

"Okay," he said in a small voice.

"I have to go now, buddy. I'll talk to you soon. Have a good flight to Hawaii, and I'll be in touch."

"I love you, Dad," he said.

I couldn't bring myself to say it. I was too far gone by that time to tell him I loved him. I knew I had to still love him at some level, but I just couldn't *feel* it.

"I know you do," I said. "I'll think about you all the time. Bye, Sean."

I disconnected the call, and as soon as I hung up, I put him out of my mind. I went outside, got into my car, drove to Petros, and started firing away at the targets. I kept on until it was too dark to see.

CHAPTER 38

Will Grimes wore plain clothes as he pulled into the used car lot on MacCorkle Avenue Southeast in Charleston, West Virginia. The lot was relatively small, with about fifty cars in the inventory. A white trailer sat in the middle of the lot, and as soon as Grimes got out of his car, a tall, extremely thin, redheaded man walked through the door of the trailer and started toward him.

"Welcome," the redhead said. His wide smile revealed teeth that were yellow and deteriorating. His complexion was muddy and he had a slight tic when he spoke. The photographs Grimes had seen of this man—booking photos from when he was arrested on drug charges a decade earlier—reflected someone with nearly perfect teeth and a healthy complexion. Grimes wondered whether Rex Fairchild had fallen victim to the plight of so many drug dealers—sampling his own wares.

"What are we in the market for today?" the salesman said.

"Some answers," Grimes said as he pulled his badge from the sport coat he was wearing and held it out. "I'm looking for Rex Fairchild, and from the booking photographs I've seen, you appear to be him."

The smile disappeared from the salesman's face, and he backed up a couple of steps. "Who are you and what do you want?"

"Name's Grimes. Will Grimes. I'm with the Bureau of Criminal Investigation, West Virginia State Police. And like I just said, I want some answers."

"I don't have any answers," Fairchild said. His manner had changed completely, from friendly and accommodating to hostile.

"How can you tell me you don't have any answers when you haven't even heard the questions?"

"I don't want to hear any questions," Fairchild said. "Why don't you just get back in your car and get off my property?"

Grimes looked at Fairchild's hands, both of which were covered in tattoos. "You convicts are all the same. Just can't resist the peer pressure, I guess. My understanding is that you asked an old friend of yours to do some recon work in Cowen for an ex-con named Big Pappy Donovan. You asked him to check out a boy named Donnie Frazier, who happened to have a friend named Tommy Beane. They're both dead now. Am I bringing back any fond memories for you?"

"Got no idea what you're talking about," Fairchild said.

"This Big Pappy Donovan was in prison with a lawyer named Darren Street. Darren Street won an appeal for Big Pappy and got him out of prison, and then Street got out, too. They're big buddies, from what I understand. Real tight. What happened was that those two boys you had your buddy asking about, Donnie Frazier and Tommy Beane, they went down to Tennessee and blew up Darren Street's momma's house. She was in the house, and she got killed. Street wasn't there. Then a couple of detectives in Knoxville screwed up and told Street that Donnie was a suspect because Donnie's brother got killed in prison after he had a beef with Street. So what I figure is that Street went to Big Pappy, who was his old shot caller and is his friend, for help. Pappy came to you because you're in West Virginia, not too far from where those boys lived. You got somebody—and I know who that somebody is—to gather the information. He passed it along to you, and you passed it along to Pappy. Pappy then passed it on to Street. Then Street came into my state and shot those two boys to pieces."

"That's some story," Fairchild said, "but I've never heard of anyone named Big Pappy or Darren Street, and I don't know anybody in Cowen."

"Right now, as far as I'm concerned, you could be looking at two counts of conspiracy to commit murder," Grimes said, "but what I'm really after is Street."

"Can't help you," Fairchild said. "Like I said, I got no idea what you're talking about."

"I just can't tell you how much I hate it when somebody lies to me," Grimes said. "You just stood there and lied right to my face. You were in the cocaine business with Big Pappy Donovan. I have the records from the federal district court to prove it. I have a copy of your indictment. Do you think I'm some kind of idiot that you can just blow off? Because if you think you can just blow me off, you're going to wind up right back in the penitentiary, my friend. As matter of fact, at this point, I'm probably the only person who can keep you out of the penitentiary. Talk to me, and I'll tell the district attorney to cut you some slack. I know you didn't kill anybody. Street did the killing. I have a witness who can identify him. He's the one I want. You just did a favor for an old friend, right? You just asked another old friend to ask around a little, got the information Big Pappy asked you to get, and passed it on. You didn't have any idea those boys were going to get gunned down, did you? How could you possibly have known that?"

"Did I hear you say you have some records from federal court?" Fairchild said.

"That's right, and they say you know Michael Donovan."

"They never proved a damned thing about me and this Donovan you keep talking about. It doesn't matter what that indictment says.

But if you check into it a little more, you'll find out one real important thing about me. I don't rat on anybody. I don't talk about anybody to fucking cops. So like I said a few minutes ago, get back in your car and get off my property."

"You're making a big mistake," Grimes said.

"Fuck off," Fairchild said, and he turned and walked back to the trailer.

CHAPTER 39

Grimes did exactly what Fairchild told him to do. He got in his car and he left. But rather than driving back to Elkins, he decided to pay a visit to the Charleston Police Department headquarters. He walked in unannounced fifteen minutes after he left Rex Fairchild's, and within another five minutes, was sitting in the office of Sergeant Eric Young. Young was in his late twenties, one of only five black officers in the department. He was the supervisor of the Special Enforcement Unit, a group of four detectives who worked primarily vice and narcotics cases and coordinated with the Metropolitan Drug Unit. Grimes introduced himself to Young, gave him some background on the murder investigation he was conducting, and asked whether Young had ever heard of Rex Fairchild.

"Everybody that works drugs has heard of Fairchild," Young said. "He went to prison before I even started working here, but when he came back and set up shop in the used car business, we took a look at him. You don't just put fifty cars on a lot straight out of prison without some money. We thought he might have jumped right back into it."

"What did you find?"

"The money is coming from his father, or at least part of it. His father is in the insurance business, has been forever, and is pretty well off. He apparently went to his bank and cosigned to have the bank finance the cars. My understanding is that he also put up a substantial amount of his own money."

"So you guys don't suspect Fairchild of dealing?"

Young shook his head. "Nah. We moved on. Haven't looked at him in a while."

"He may not be dealing, but he's using," Grimes said. "Probably coke, maybe meth. I just talked to him, and I've seen enough addicts to know that he's using a lot. His teeth are a mess, and he looks like he's starving. Do you think you might be able to help me out?"

"What do you have in mind?" Young said.

"If I'm going to break this murder case open, I'm going to have to do it from the bottom up," Grimes said. "Fairchild is somebody I could lean on, but he's also somebody that I could offer a deal to because he had minimal involvement. He's a coconspirator in a double murder, but I'm not sure he knew that when he got involved. If you guys can pop him on a drug charge, especially if you can catch him with felony weight, I can come in and testify at a bond hearing that he's a suspect in a double murder. If we can get his bond set high enough that he can't get out, or get him held without bond, I think he'll start talking because he'll desperately want to get out and get more drugs. Think you could do that for me?"

Young leaned forward and put his arms on his desk. "You say this guy in Tennessee that's suspected of the murders is a lawyer?"

Grimes nodded. "Criminal defense lawyer. He's also suspected of kidnapping and murdering a former federal prosecutor, but from what I understand, they have next to nothing on him in that case."

"I hate lawyers," Young said. "I maybe hate them more than murderers."

"That makes you a part of a pretty large group, my friend," Grimes said.

"Okay, we'll get on Fairchild for you. If he's using a lot, probably all we'll have to do is a little surveillance. We'll just follow him to his dealer and then pop him on a traffic violation after he picks up his coke. We'll ask if we can search his car, and if he says no, we'll bring in a dog."

"The old tried-and-true traffic stop," Grimes said. "What will you stop him for? Speeding?"

Young smiled. "We'll figure something out. We always do. I'll let you know as soon as he's in custody."

CHAPTER 40

Ten days after my meeting with Katherine Davis, and only three days before Christmas, I got a text from Grace around 5:30 p.m., asking me what time I would be home. It was Saturday, I'd finished up some Christmas shopping, and I told her I'd be there in about an hour. I drove to her apartment around 6:30 p.m. When I walked into the apartment, all my things were piled in the kitchen. Grace was standing with her back to the refrigerator. Her arms were folded across her chest.

"The ring you gave me is on the counter," she said. "I think you should leave. Be sure you don't forget your prepaid cell phones."

I set my briefcase on the floor and looked at her. I put on my best dumbfounded face. "What the hell? What's the matter with you?"

"I got another visit from those two detectives today. They came to my office. Do you know what they wanted this time? They wanted to know where you were the day Ben Clancy disappeared, and do you know what? I couldn't tell them where you were because I didn't know. What I do know is that you left at four thirty in the morning that day. You told me you had an early meeting with a client and that you were going to the gym early."

"That's exactly what I did," I said.

"Stop lying, Darren. I go to the same gym, and you know it. You should also know that I have some good friends who work there. I called one of them after the detectives left and asked whether you punched your member number into the registry that morning. They keep track of everybody that goes in and out of that building. You didn't punch in your number, and you can't get through the security gate that early in the morning if you don't enter the number."

"Your friend is mistaken," I said. "I went to the gym that morning."

"Why do you have three prepaid cell phones, Darren? Why do you have a pistol with a silencer?"

"I'm paranoid about my phone. I'd think you would understand that after what I've been through. And the gun is just for protection. If you'll recall, someone blew up my mom's house trying to kill me not long ago."

"That doesn't explain the silencer."

"It came with the gun when I bought it. I got it at a gun show in a parking lot. It was a package deal. I haven't even fired the damned thing, Grace."

That last statement was a blatant lie, too. I'd already put hundreds of rounds through the Walther. It was a sweet little pistol.

"Who do you call on your prepaid phones? What kind of business do you conduct? I've never once seen you on a prepaid cell phone. I think you started using them when you went on your so-called fishing trip to work some things out. I thought it was strange that you left your cell phone here that weekend. You didn't want it pinging off any towers in West Virginia, did you?"

"You're talking crazy," I said.

"Who was your early-morning meeting with? The one you didn't go to after you didn't go to the gym."

"It was with a client."

"Which client?"

"You know I can't tell you that. It's privileged."

"Bullshit," Grace said. She rarely cursed. She'd moved off the refrigerator and was standing only a few feet from me. "Take your ring, take your things, and get out."

"Grace, please. You're overreacting. Listen to yourself. Do you really think I'm a murderer?"

"At this point, I don't know what to think," she said. "You went through a great deal when Clancy put you in prison. I was so proud of you when you started to come back to life, and I was so happy when you asked me to marry you. But then your mother was killed, and you changed. I already lied to the police once for you, Darren. That weekend those two men were killed in West Virginia, I told them you were here with me. You told me you were fishing. But you weren't, were you? You weren't camping. You were killing people. You said you caught two big ones and you left them where you found them. And then you came back here, and all you wanted to do was have sex after you hadn't touched me in weeks. Do you know how creepy that makes me feel? You go and commit two murders and then come back here and practically rape me?

"And now Ben Clancy is gone, and the police think you killed him, too. Why didn't you want to have sex with me after you killed *him*, Darren?"

She was freaking me out by that point. She knew it all. My primary concern was that she was going to pick up her phone and start dialing the police. Had she done that, she would have witnessed my suicide, the same way I'd witnessed James Tipton's. But she didn't call the police, and I simply thought about the criminal defense lawyer's mantra: *Deny everything.*

"I didn't kill him. I haven't killed anyone."

"You're lying. I'm not going to help the police. I'm not going to tell them a thing, because at some level, I understand why you've done what you've done. But I can't live with a murderer. I can't love a killer. I'm going into my bedroom now. When I come back out, I expect you to be gone."

She turned away from me and walked down the hall. I heard her bedroom door close, and I started gathering my things.

CHAPTER 41

A light snow was falling as Big Pappy Donovan pulled off the interstate and into the parking lot of the TravelCenters of America truck stop in Hurricane, West Virginia. The trip had been facilitated by a cryptic phone call from an old friend and business partner, Rex Fairchild. Fairchild had said it was urgent that they talk in person, as soon as possible. Pappy was running a load of windows from a plant in Chattanooga, Tennessee, to Chicago, Illinois, and decided to take a detour and meet Fairchild in Hurricane.

Pappy had known Fairchild for about fifteen years but hadn't seen him in more than a decade. They'd been introduced by a mutual friend who knew Pappy was moving large amounts of powder cocaine up and down the eastern part of the United States, that Fairchild had plenty of connections in and around Charleston, West Virginia, and that he was looking to get into the business, albeit on a far smaller scale than Pappy. Pappy would supply Fairchild with five ounces a month, either through the mail, a courier, or in person, and Fairchild would triple the volume by cutting it with vitamin B12 or baby laxative. He'd then sell grams and eight balls—or occasionally a half ounce—mostly in the bars around Charleston, and he made a good deal of money. When the feds finally lowered the boom, Pappy refused to acknowledge that he even knew Fairchild, and Fairchild did the same. The feds couldn't prove they'd done business together, because their snitches had never actually seen

Pappy, or heard Pappy and Fairchild do business. They were mentioned in the same indictment, but ultimately Fairchild pleaded to a distribution charge and agreed to a seven-year sentence. Pappy went to trial in Georgia on charges of selling crack, was found guilty, and wound up with thirty-five years, but Darren Street had gotten his case overturned on appeal while they were both at the same maximum security federal pen in California.

Pappy rolled to a stop a couple of hundred yards from the gas pumps out back of the truck stop, and Fairchild climbed in. Pappy put the truck in neutral and pulled the emergency brake. He left the engine running and the heater on. The man sitting in the passenger seat looked far different from the man he'd known earlier.

"What the hell, Rex?" Pappy said as Fairchild reached out to shake his hand. "You sick?"

"No, man. I'm not sick. I'm just scared."

"You sounded pretty upset on the phone," Pappy said.

"A West Virginia state trooper, an investigator named Grimes, came to see me," Fairchild said. He spoke in a quick, choppy manner, and Pappy noticed immediately that the pupils of Fairchild's eyes were dilated and his nose was running.

"You high?" Pappy said.

"What? Me? No, man."

"Bullshit," Pappy said. "I know a geeker when I see one. Your teeth are rotten. When did you start using?"

Fairchild looked down at the floor and then out the window.

"After I got out, man. I don't know why. I never used before I went in, but after I got out I was drinking too much, and then I started trying it out some, and before I knew it I was using all the time."

"You better get off that shit in a hurry. Every cokehead I've ever known has died a miserable death or wound up in prison for a long time. Now pull your shit together and tell me about this cop."

"He knew all about me getting my man to ask about those crackers in Cowen. I don't know how he knew, but he did. He also knew about you. He said I was gathering information for you and passing it on to you, and he said you passed it on to Street and that Street did the killing. I'm not sure what he can really prove, but he said he had a witness who can identify Street. He was also talking about charging me with conspiracy to commit murder, and if he charges me, he'll charge you. I'm not sure what we need to do, if anything, but I gotta admit I'm scared shitless right now."

"Staying high won't help anything," Pappy said. "It has to be the bartender."

"Bartender?"

"The guy who owns that little bar where Darren shot those boys, Sammy whatever his name is. He let Darren do it. He walked into the bathroom and stayed in there while Darren blew them away. I told Darren he should have killed the dude. You don't leave a witness like that hanging after you've just committed a double murder."

"So what do we do?"

"I'm afraid Darren might be hanging by a pretty thin thread right now," Pappy said. "I talked to him on my way here, and he said his girlfriend kicked him out yesterday. He said she thinks he did the killings up here plus another one down there."

"Shit," Fairchild said. "Woman scorned. That's a bad deal. Is she going to rat him out to the cops?"

"He doesn't think so."

"Maybe he needs to off her, too."

Pappy shook his massive head. "Not gonna happen. Who did you talk to up there that might have gone to the police?"

"Nobody. I only talked to one guy, and he's rock solid. He asked around for me, or at least he said he did. Maybe he got somebody else to do it, I just don't know. I'll get in touch with him and see if he has any idea who's talking to the cops about us."

"Do it today," Pappy said. "If I go up there and take care of this bartender, which I think I'll probably wind up doing, then I want to take care of the rat at the same time. Find out who he is, and I'll shut his mouth permanently. And stay away from that nose candy. I can't trust you if you're doing that shit."

"You're not planning to kill me, too, are you?" Fairchild said.

"We're good for now," Pappy said. "But I'm serious about you getting off the coke. People run their mouths when they're doing that stuff. Now get on out of here and find out about the rat in Cowen. I need to get back on the road."

CHAPTER 42

Rocky Skidmore popped the top off a can of Keystone Light beer and rolled his wheelchair into the living room of the trailer he'd been living in for ten years just outside Cowen, West Virginia. The place was a wreck: holes in the interior walls, one toilet that didn't work, and no hot water, but Skidmore didn't care. He had a roof over his head, and he wasn't paying the rent.

At one time, Skidmore had been a bad dude. He'd been the president of the Grave Diggers, an outlaw motorcycle gang that drew its membership from all over northern and central West Virginia and that dealt primarily in drugs and guns. The club's headquarters was a bar called Snake Eyes on the outskirts of Charleston. It was in that bar that Skidmore had first met Rex Fairchild and had nearly killed him.

Fairchild had been early in his cocaine-selling days and had wandered into the Grave Diggers' headquarters, not knowing what he was getting himself into. Skidmore remembered it well. Fairchild had sat at the bar for a little while, and then had walked around, past the jukebox and over to the pinball machines and pool tables. Before long, he started passing the word that he had some coke to sell if anybody was interested. At first Skidmore thought Fairchild must be crazy, then he thought he might just be ballsy. Either way, an outsider coming into a Grave Digger bar and trying to move coke was a huge insult. Within ten minutes of learning what Fairchild was trying to do, he had him on his knees in the walk-in cooler off the kitchen with a gun to his head. Fairchild pissed himself and begged for his life, but what saved him was that he blurted out that he had a source who could get Skidmore all the coke he could move. High-quality coke. Large quantities.

Skidmore bit, and within a week, he was introduced to a huge trucker they called Big Pappy Donovan. For the next several years, until Fairchild and Big Pappy were both busted, Skidmore and his gang had moved hundreds of kilos of coke through West Virginia, Virginia, and Pennsylvania that he had obtained from Big Pappy.

A year after Fairchild and Big Pappy were busted, Skidmore had been paralyzed from the waist down when he crashed his motorcycle into a guardrail on a rainy night and was thrown into a rocky hillside. The gang eventually pushed him out. He was paralyzed and without means, so he wound up moving to Cowen to stay with his sister and her husband, who was a coal miner. They kicked him out after a year because of his drinking and belligerence, but not before he had managed to win the heart of a lonely woman named Bea Baker. Baker had an illegitimate teenage son named Jimmy, and the three of them became a family. Skidmore was often drunk and abusive, but he would also tell the boy stories about his glory days as president of the biker gang and the various crimes they committed. He even told the kid about a couple of murders of rival gang members. Jimmy idolized him.

When he received word through a couple of old gang members that Rex Fairchild was wanting to talk to him, he gave them his phone number. A day later, Fairchild called him and told him Big Pappy needed some information on a guy who had recently been released from prison. His name was Donnie Frazier. Fairchild wanted to know whether Frazier had anything to do with a bombing that happened in Knoxville, Tennessee. Skidmore was too proud to tell Fairchild that he wasn't really capable of getting out and gathering the information, so he'd farmed the task out to his stepson, Jimmy Baker. Jimmy had actually done a pretty good job, too. He'd found out everything Fairchild wanted to know, and Skidmore passed the information along.

But Fairchild had called him that morning, obviously upset, and said that somebody in Cowen was a rat. He said the state police knew everything, even the name of the person who had gathered the information, and that everybody could be looking at conspiracy-to-commit-murder charges. Skidmore called his stepson as soon as he got off the phone with Fairchild and told him to come to the trailer at four in the afternoon. Bea wouldn't be home from her job as a bookkeeper at a sawmill, and they could talk in private.

Skidmore heard Jimmy's motorcycle pull up outside and waited for him to walk in. Jimmy had a trailer of his own about two miles away, but he didn't have a job. He lived primarily off his girlfriend's income as a hair stylist, but he also stole car stereos and broke into houses in and around Webster Springs and Elkins. He'd been caught a few times and sent off to prison once, but he kept on stealing. He just didn't know any other way to get by. Jimmy walked in and mumbled a greeting. He went straight to the refrigerator and grabbed a Keystone Light, then walked back and sat on the couch near Skidmore. He was wearing a black leather jacket, leather chaps, boots, and had taken off his leather gloves. He had a bushy, brown beard and had a wide, black bandana tied around his head. His cheeks were pink and puffy.

"Little cold to be on that hog, ain't it?" Skidmore said.

"Got nothing else to drive," Jimmy said. "The Toyota threw a rod two days ago. Gonna be a while before I can get it fixed."

"We got a little problem," Skidmore said. "Actually, it's a big problem, and I got a feeling you're the cause of it."

"What are you talking about?"

"You know that information I had you gather a little while back?"

"Yeah, what about it?"

"You told somebody about it, and that somebody told the state police. Now the state police are talking about coming at us with conspiracy-to-commit-murder charges. So don't bullshit me. Who in the hell did you tell?"

"I ain't told nobody, I swear it," Jimmy said.

Skidmore lifted a .38-caliber revolver and pointed it at his stepson's head. "Say that again and I'm gonna splatter your brains all over the wall."

"Jesus, Rocky! Take it easy!"

"You been hanging around Lester Routh any? You know that worthless son of a bitch is a paid informant for the state police, don't you?"

"Nah, Lester's all right."

"You don't know he's an informant? Because everybody else in this cracker-box town knows it."

"If he's an informant, I didn't know it," Jimmy said. "I swear it."

Skidmore cocked the pistol. "What did you tell him?"

Jimmy put his hands up. "Please don't kill me, Rocky. Please put that gun down."

"Not until you tell me what you told Lester."

"We were drinkin'. I may have told him about it."

"About what?"

"Everything, I reckon. I think maybe I told him about you asking me to gather up some information on Donnie Frazier for you, and how everybody I talked to opened right up and told me Donnie and Tommy had bombed that lawyer's momma's house and killed her."

"And you told him you passed it along to me?"

Jimmy was nodding. "I'm sorry."

"Did you mention Fairchild or Big Pappy?"

"I may have," Jimmy said. "Please, please don't kill me. I didn't know about Lester. I swear I didn't know. And I was drunk."

"You're dumber than a damn bag of hammers," Rocky said as he lowered the pistol. "And if it weren't for your momma, you'd be a dead bag of hammers right now. Get out of here. I need to start trying to see if we can fix what you fucked up."

CHAPTER 43

I rented a motel room off Interstate 40 and started looking for apartments after Grace kicked me out. I called her at least a dozen times the next day, left her messages, but she wouldn't talk to me. I probably should have been feeling things like sorrow and pain and panic and confusion, but I was pretty much just numb, almost zombielike. I told Pappy about Grace giving me the boot. His primary concern was whether she would tell the police. I told him she'd told the police I was home with her the night I killed Frazier and Beane, and that I didn't think she would betray me. He seemed to accept it, but Pappy was hard to read sometimes.

It was strange, though. My mind kept flashing back to standing in her kitchen, listening to her tell me she couldn't live with a murderer, couldn't love a killer. I hadn't really thought of myself in those terms, but I knew if I got down to the core of what I'd done and didn't try to whitewash the facts with emotion, she was exactly right. I'd put fifteen hollow-point bullets into Donnie Frazier and Tommy Beane and then didn't want to wash their blood from my face. I'd drunk moonshine while Ben Clancy was swinging from a rope in Granny Tipton's barn. I'd arranged to have scalding baby oil poured onto a man's face. And I didn't feel a bit of remorse for any of those things. I had no plans to kill or maim anyone else, but I knew I was certainly capable. I supposed many people would find that kind of self-awareness unhealthy, even terrifying, but I found it liberating. Did that make me a psychopath, I wondered? Had what Ben Clancy and the criminal justice system had done to me, combined with the murder of my mother, and Katie taking my son half a world away, turned me from a troubled but relatively healthy person into a psychopath? I didn't think so, but I didn't know for sure.

On Christmas Eve, just after noon, I called Dan Reid.

"Have you found out anything about Katherine Davis?" I said when he answered his cell.

"Merry Christmas, Darren."

"Sorry. Merry Christmas to you."

"I haven't really had enough time to check her out completely, but she seems to be what she says she is," Dan said. "She lives in an apartment about three blocks from the UT campus. They're on Christmas break so I haven't actually seen her go into a classroom, but I have a couple of friends on the faculty in the criminal justice department, and they tell me she's a grad student, and a damned good one. One of them told me she's been accepted to law school, so she's telling the truth about that. I went to the Sessions Court clerk's office and the affidavit is on file from her DUI arrest, so that's legitimate unless they're going to a great deal of trouble to try to sting you. I've followed her a couple of times, and she hasn't met with anybody that appears to be a cop. She went to lunch and to the grocery store the first time I followed her. The second time she went to the West Towne Mall and did some Christmas shopping."

"Any boyfriends? Seen any men around?"

"Haven't seen any. Why?"

"Just wondering. If she has a boyfriend, I'd be concerned because of the way she hit on me at the office."

"You're not thinking about calling her or going out with her, are you?" Dan said.

I *was* thinking about calling her. I'd thought about it a dozen times since Grace had booted me, but I wasn't about to tell Reid. "No, of course not. I'm still with Grace."

"I'll let you know if anything changes, but from what I've seen so far, she doesn't appear to be working for the police."

"Thanks, Dan," I said. "Have a nice Christmas."

CHAPTER 44

As soon as I hung up, I left the motel and drove to the office, which was closed for the holidays, and found Katherine Davis's file. In it was her cell phone number. I'd had trouble getting her off my mind, I was lonely, and since Grace had made it clear she didn't want me around and Dan Reid said Katherine wasn't a rat, I decided to call her.

"I can't believe you're calling me," she said when she picked up the phone. "I put your cell number in my contacts and when I looked at my phone and saw your name, my heart almost jumped out of my chest."

"I'm no longer engaged," I said, "but I'm still old."

"Men are in their prime at your age," she said. "At least that's what I've heard. Are you in your prime?"

"I don't know. I guess we'll have to see about that. Would you like to get together?"

"Absolutely. When?"

"How about around five o'clock? I have to do some last-minute shopping and could use a little help. It's Christmas Eve, so I'll understand completely if you're already booked."

"I have a family thing at my parents' house at eight," she said. "Would you like to come along?"

"Thanks, but I think I'd be pretty uncomfortable. Not to mention your parents."

"My parents are easygoing," she said.

"Thanks again, but I think I'll pass. Another time, maybe."

"No, no, come and pick me up at five. We'll do your shopping, and you can drop me back at my place before eight."

"Okay," I said. "I'll see you in a few hours."

* * *

I wasn't enough of a psychopath to forget the promise I'd made to myself about Julius Antone, the linebacker on our championship football team. On Christmas Eve around seven o'clock, Katherine and I walked up to the door of a duplex in a government-subsidized housing project in East Knoxville. I was carrying a large box that contained a turkey, a ham, several different kinds of vegetables, bread, desserts, butter, and a couple of gallons of milk. Katherine had her arms full of gifts for Julius, his ten-year-old brother, his eight-year-old brother, his six-year-old sister, his mother, and her boyfriend. I'd bought gift cards for the mother and the boyfriend, but I'd bought gifts for the kids and had them wrapped. I bought one card, signed it "Merry Christmas, Santa Claus," and put it on top of the box containing the food. My car was running, parked by the curb on the street. As we stood outside the door, I could hear voices and a television inside, so I knew they were home.

We set the boxes down, I knocked on the door, and then we turned and ran to my car. It was already dark, and in that part of town there weren't many streetlights. Julius had no idea what kind of car I was driving since I hadn't seen him since my mother's house was bombed and my car was destroyed. Katherine and I sat in my car with the lights off and watched as Julius's mother opened the door, looked down, and saw the boxes. Gradually, the doorway filled with members of the family. They looked at my car, but they couldn't see who was inside.

"Merry Christmas, buddy," I said out loud as I put the car in drive and pulled away from the curb.

"That was sweet," Katherine said as we rode back toward her apartment. I'd filled her in on Julius and his family's situation while we were driving to the grocery store. "Are you always this kind?"

"I try to do what I think is right whenever I can," I said.

"Well, that was one of the nicest things I've ever seen anyone do," she said. "Thank you for allowing me to be a part of it."

"Thanks for helping me out," I said. "Can I ask you a question?"

"Sure. Fire away."

"Why didn't you say anything about what happened to my mother when you were in the office? And you haven't mentioned it this evening. I know you know about it. Everybody knows about it."

"I just didn't think it was appropriate," she said. "I came to your office for help on my DUI charge. I had no idea anything personal would come of it. I mean, I had no idea I'd be so attracted to you. And from what I read in the paper, what happened to her was such a horrible thing. I didn't think it was my place to bring it up. Do you want to talk about it?"

"No, no, it's not that," I said as I turned into the parking lot of her apartment complex. "It just seems like everybody brings it up. I was a little surprised when you didn't."

"It's none of my business," she said, "unless you want it to be. If you ever want to talk about it, all you have to do is start talking. I'm a good listener."

I pulled into a parking space near where I'd picked her up and put the car in park. I didn't want to leave her because she smelled like lemon musk, she looked like a Victoria's Secret model, and she touched me a lot. They were just little pats on the arm and thigh, but they were electric. She also laughed a lot—light and airy laughter that filled the inside of the car and made me smile. The thought of going back to the motel alone was becoming more and more unsavory.

"One more question," I said. "Why don't you have a boyfriend or a husband? As pretty and as smart as you are, I can't believe someone hasn't snapped you up."

She smiled at me and winked. "I'm picky," she said. "Haven't found the right guy up to this point, but things seem to be looking up."

"Have a nice Christmas," I said.

"What are you doing tomorrow?"

I looked down at the dashboard. "My mom's gone, and she was the only family I had except my son. My ex-wife moved to Hawaii and took him with her a couple of weeks ago. Since my fiancée broke up with me, I guess I'll be on my own. I know that sounds pitiful, but I'm okay about it. I'll be fine."

"Where are you staying, Darren?" she said.

"At the Days Inn at Exit 388. I'm looking for an apartment."

"I can't stand the thought of you being alone on Christmas," she said. "My family always has a big meal together at lunchtime, but I can break free tomorrow around six. Would you like to have dinner together somewhere?"

"That would be nice," I said.

"I'll call you tomorrow afternoon. Merry Christmas, Darren."

She got out of the car, and I watched her walk up the steps toward her apartment. The time we'd spent together made me want to spend more time with her, and I realized that probably wasn't such a good thing. Still, there was chemistry there. A lot of chemistry. If she was a rat for the cops, she was damned good at it.

I drove slowly back to the motel. I'd bought a bottle of bourbon the day before, figuring I would be spending Christmas Eve alone. It was sitting on the nightstand by the bed in my room. I opened it as soon as I walked in, turned on the television, and drank until I passed out.

CHAPTER 45

Will Grimes was microwaving a bag of popcorn, getting ready to watch *It's a Wonderful Life* on television in his small house in Elkins.

Grimes's father, William "Billy" Grimes, had also been a West Virginia state trooper. He'd been gunned down during what he thought was a routine traffic stop near the family's home in Ranger, West Virginia, when Will was eight years old. The shooter turned out to be a parole violator who didn't want to go back to jail. Will's father managed to kill the man before he died.

Will believed his father was as fine a man as had ever lived, and he'd resolved to follow in his father's footsteps. Will's mother, who had loved her husband deeply, was unable to handle his death. She'd gone into a deep depression that had lasted for years, and she'd begun to drink heavily. Will and his sister had become more parents than children when they were in high school and college. Eventually, when Will was twenty-five and after he had become a trooper, his mother got drunk and drove her car across the center line of a state highway within a mile of the spot where her husband was killed and hit another car head-on. She died instantly. Two people in the other car, a woman and her fourteen-year-old daughter, were also killed.

After seeing the effect of his father's death on his mother, Will decided he would never marry. He didn't want to subject a woman or children to the same kind of devastation he and his sister and mother had endured if he was killed in the line of duty. He'd met a few women during his life that he felt he could love and marry, but he'd always turned away from them.

He was thinking about the differences between himself and Darren Street as the microwave buzzed and the popcorn crackled. Will had suffered terrible losses, both his father and his mother, but he hadn't turned to the dark side. He hadn't begun murdering people. There was no one for him to murder, of course, since his father had shot and killed the man who had mortally wounded him, but he could have just as easily become bitter and angry and turned to violence as a way to vent his anger and frustration. But he'd chosen another path. He chose to enforce the laws drafted by the duly elected representatives of the state of West Virginia and the United States of America. He believed in law and order. He eschewed the anarchy and vigilantism that Street had embraced. Grimes was certain Street had killed Frazier and Beane, but he still couldn't prove it. He would, though. Eventually, he would gather enough evidence and find enough witnesses to put Street behind bars for the rest of his life.

Grimes was accustomed to being alone on Christmas Eve. His sister had moved to Wisconsin with her husband years ago. They kept in touch, but neither of them felt the need to get together during the holidays. Grimes wasn't maudlin or depressed. He actually enjoyed the solitude.

The microwave beeped, indicating his popcorn was finished, and he retrieved it and let it vent. He pulled a can of Pepsi from the refrigerator and filled a glass with ice. Just as he was about to walk into his den and turn on the television, his cell phone rang. The caller ID indicated Sergeant Eric Young, the detective from the Special Enforcement Unit in Charleston, was calling.

"Merry Christmas, Sergeant Young," Grimes said when he answered the phone.

"I have a gift for you," Young said.

"Is that right?"

"We popped your boy Rex Fairchild about an hour ago as soon as he left his dealer. He had an ounce of powder on him. It's resale weight, so you should be able to lean on him."

"That's the best gift I could have hoped for," Grimes said. "You have what, seventy-two hours to get him arraigned?"

"Right. We'll do it on the twenty-seventh."

"What's the judge like? Is he tough on drug offenders?"

"Not really. They've loosened up a lot in the past couple of years. I mean, Fairchild has a previous conviction and has done some time, and you can come in and testify that he's a suspect in a murder conspiracy, but I don't think the bond will be something he can't make. His old man is loaded."

"Maybe Daddy won't be so hot to make this bond since Sonny Boy has been popped for cocaine again," Grimes said.

"Maybe," Young said, "but you know how parents are. They stick their heads in the sand."

"I think I'll come on down and see him in the morning," Grimes said.

"In the morning? Tomorrow is Christmas."

"Yeah, well, this case is important to me. Tell the guys at the jail I'll be there midmorning, okay?"

"I'll do it," Young said. "Good luck."

CHAPTER 46

Rex Fairchild was craving cocaine and worrying about what was going to happen to him when a guard came and knocked on his cell door on Christmas morning.

"Back up to the pie hole and give me your hands," the guard said.

Fairchild had been through the routine many times, and he backed up to the slit in the steel door and put his hands behind his back. He felt the cold steel of the handcuffs wrap around his wrist as the guard clicked them on tightly.

"Step back into the cell," the guard said.

Fairchild complied, and a moment later the door opened. Two guards were standing there in black uniforms. They walked in carrying a waist chain and shackles and went through the process of hooking him up.

"Let's go," one of them said.

Fairchild felt a sense of relief. Was he going to be arraigned by a magistrate—maybe by video—and get a bond set? He hadn't expected to be arraigned since it was Christmas, but he figured stranger things had happened. If the magistrate set him a reasonable bond, his dad would have him out in a few hours.

The guards led him down three separate hallways of concrete floors and block walls, through two steel doors, to a small room. Inside the room was a steel table.

"Sit," one of the guards demanded.

Fairchild sat. There was no television, no computer. It didn't appear there would be a video arraignment. Maybe the magistrate would come in and arraign him face-to-face. After a few minutes, the door opened again, and Fairchild felt sick to his stomach. It was the state cop, Grimes.

"Merry Christmas, Rex," Grimes said cheerfully. "I hear you had a little problem last night."

Fairchild stared at the table, determined to keep his mouth shut.

"Remember the last time we spoke and you told me to fuck off?" Grimes said. "Well, sir, I did it. I fucked off right to the Charleston Police Department's narcotics squad and asked them if they'd keep an eye on you for me. I don't know whether you're aware or not, but it's real obvious you've got a drug problem. I figured it would be cocaine or meth. Turns out it's cocaine. That's a bad drug, Rex. Ruins your teeth. Makes you skinny. Just breaks you down physically over time. So I figured it wouldn't be long at all before you went to see your dealer, and I was right. Drug addicts are so easy to predict. They're just so damned stupid. My friends in the Charleston PD followed you, and now here you sit with a felony resale charge against you and a prior federal conviction. I have friends at the DEA, too, and I'm going to be talking to them about you. See if I can't get you back in the federal system. You have the right to remain silent, by the way. But I think it's time you talk to me before this gets away from you to the point where nobody will be able to help you."

"It was an ounce," Fairchild said. "The feds won't touch it."

"I think maybe they will after I tell them about your involvement in two murders. With your prior, you'll get at least five years in the federal system plus whatever I can manage to get you on the conspiracy charge."

"You don't have a conspiracy charge against me," Fairchild said. "If you did, you would have arrested me."

"You asked Rocky Skidmore to gather information for you about Donnie Frazier. You didn't know it, but Rocky Skidmore is too feeble to get out and do much of anything, so he put his stepson, Jimmy Baker, on it. Baker got what you wanted and passed it on to Skidmore, who passed it on to you. You passed it on to Big Pappy Donovan, and he passed it on to Darren Street. As a result, two men were murdered in a bar in Cowen. That's a conspiracy if ever there was one."

Fairchild's stomach knotted even tighter. He'd received a call from Rocky Skidmore and was told that there was a paid informant named Lester Routh in Cowen who had told Grimes everything because Skidmore's loose-lipped, drunken stepson had bragged about his involvement to Routh.

"Let's say you know what you're talking about, and I'm not admitting for one second that you do," Fairchild said. "You still can't prove I knew anything about the murders before they happened."

"You go ahead and try that on in front of a jury if you like," Grimes said. "You go ahead and admit you gathered information for Pappy, but you didn't have any idea what he was going to do with the information. Good luck with that."

"I'm not ratting anybody out," Fairchild said. "You can forget it. Go ahead and put me back inside. I know how it works. I'll do the time standing on my head."

"There's another way I can play this," Grimes said. "It'd be real easy for me to get the word out that you got popped on a felony drug case and started flapping your jaws to make a deal. How about I make sure you get released on bond and then put out the word that you've agreed to testify against Big Pappy and Skidmore and Jimmy Baker? How long do you think you'll last?"

"You can't do that!" Fairchild yelled. "That'd be the same as killing me yourself. It would make you a murderer."

"I don't see it that way at all," Grimes said. "You've done what you've done, and you're going to have to face the consequences one way or another. Either you talk to me, agree to testify, and I'll protect you and make sure you don't go back to prison, or you get put back out on the street with a big ole bull's-eye on your back. It's up to you."

"You can't do this, man," Fairchild said. "It ain't fair. It ain't *legal!*"

"I don't think you're really one to be talking about what's legal," Grimes said. "But you're right about one thing. Life isn't fair sometimes. You're about to experience it firsthand."

CHAPTER 47

I got through Christmas morning by not acknowledging to myself that it was Christmas morning. I was getting better and better at that kind of thing—not allowing certain emotions to be a part of my life. The gesture at Julius Antone's house on Christmas Eve may have been emotional to some extent, but I looked at it as simply fulfilling a promise I'd made to myself before my mom was murdered. I'd also felt some closeness to Katherine during our brief time together on Christmas Eve, but for the most part, my intention of protecting myself from emotional trauma by not allowing myself to become emotionally involved with anyone or anything seemed to be working.

I was driving through the deserted streets of Knoxville, looking for a suitable apartment, when my burner phone started ringing around 1:00 p.m. on Christmas day. It was Pappy, of course. Nobody else called me on that phone.

"We've got a mess to clean up in West Virginia," he said. "There's a cop up there that won't let this thing go. He's pushing people, and I'm afraid somebody will crack. If somebody cracks, the whole thing will come crashing down on you and me, and we'll wind up spending the rest of our lives in some shithole West Virginia state penitentiary."

I sighed and felt my stomach tighten just a bit. What had Pappy done? How many people had he involved in gathering information for me in West Virginia? Were they typical criminals, too damned dumb to live?

"I'm not going back to jail, Pap," I said. "I've always told you that. They'll have to kill me before they get me back inside."

"To each his own," Pappy said. "Me? I'm not interested in either. I'm not ready to die, and I'm not ready to go back to prison."

"What's going on?" I said.

"It's my fault," he said. "Well, that isn't true. It's your fault and it's my fault. I used a guy who I didn't know had become a drug addict, and you left a damned eyewitness alive. I told you you should have killed that dude who owned the bar. He's apparently telling the cops he can identify you now. The guy I used was too damned lazy or too messed up on drugs to do the job himself, so he enlisted an old buddy of his. But it turns out that guy wasn't healthy enough to do what we needed done so he sent his stepson to get the information we needed. The stepson did a pretty good job of getting what we needed, but he also likes to drink, and he ran his mouth to a guy up there who turns out to be a paid informant for the West Virginia State Police. It's a problem, Darren. We have to fix it."

I was right. He'd used a bunch of dumbasses, and now he wanted me to help him fix it.

"How?" I said.

"We're going to have to make some people keep their mouths shut."

"Are you talking intimidation or something more serious?"

"At this point, I think the cop has too much leverage for us to go the intimidation route. I think we're going to have to go all Michael Corleone on them."

Michael Corleone? I wasn't sure what he was talking about at first, and then I remembered *The Godfather*. At the end of the first movie in the trilogy, Michael Corleone, who had taken over his father's business interests, ordered the assassinations of all the rival New York dons, along with a Las Vegas casino owner named Moe Greene, a double-crossing

Corleone family member named Tessio, and his own brother-in-law. All of the killings occurred on the same day, while Michael was attending a christening for his niece.

"How many are we talking about?" I said.

"Five. The bartender, my guy in Charleston, some redneck biker named Skidmore and his stepson, Jimmy Baker, and the paid rat. His name is Lester Routh. And before you get your panties in a wad, I'm going to do four of them myself. All I want you to do is take care of the bar owner."

"Do you have a time frame in mind?" I said.

"We need to do it soon. I don't want this West Virginia cop gaining any more momentum. We just go up there, kill every damned one of his witnesses and informants, and he has no case."

"He'll come after us that much harder if we kill his witnesses," I said. "And besides, they aren't really witnesses. None of them saw a damned thing. I was wearing a disguise when the bar owner saw me and talked to me. Even if I wound up getting arrested, they couldn't convict me."

"I'll bet you thought the same thing when they arrested you for the murder you *didn't* commit," Pappy said.

"You're right about that," I said reluctantly. "I have to give you that one."

"Do you really want to take a chance on going to jail again? Do you want to sit in some county jail in West Virginia for a year while they get their act together and try you? You know you won't get a bond if they arrest you for two murders, and you know it'll take them close to a year to get you to trial. Do you really want to take a chance on that happening? I don't, not for a single second."

I pulled my car into the parking lot of an apartment complex and sat there in silence for a few seconds. If Pappy was right about the cop closing in—and I suspected he was—then I had a serious decision to make. Did I let the investigation play out and take a chance on getting arrested again? Or did I do as Pappy was suggesting and take out the bar owner while he took care of the rest of the witnesses? It certainly wasn't unheard of or unprecedented. The Mafia, drug cartels, gangs—they'd all done it successfully at one time or another.

"Get some kind of plan together and call me in a couple of days," I said. "I'll be thinking about some things myself in the meantime."

"So you're good with it? You'll take care of your end?"

"I'm not going back to jail. I'll do what I have to do."

CHAPTER 48

Katherine called me around four in the afternoon and I picked her up at six. We went to one of the older restaurants in town, the Copper Cellar on Kingston Pike. She was wearing red and green and was smiling when she climbed into the car. She was so young, so beautiful, and so positive that I found her intoxicating.

"Tell me about Darren Street," she said after we got settled in at the restaurant.

"Not much to tell," I said.

"Not true, and you know it. Where did you grow up?"

"Here. In Knoxville. I went to Farragut and then to UT and then to law school at UT. Same thing you're going to do."

"I know about your mother, and again, I'm so sorry. What about your father?"

"I don't think you want to know about my father," I said.

"I do," she said. "I want to get to know you. If you don't want to talk about it, that's fine, but if you do, I'd like to hear it. I'm genuinely interested."

"My father was a drunk," I said. "He beat me and my mother on a regular basis until I got old enough to put a stop to it."

"You put a stop to it?" Katherine said. "How?"

"It was the night before Thanksgiving when I was thirteen years old. He was drunker than hell. He always wanted spaghetti the night before

Thanksgiving, so that's what my mother made for him. He started cursing her and threw some of it in her face. Then he reached down and started unbuckling his belt, which meant he was going to start beating her with it. I knew it was coming because of the way he'd been acting that week, so I'd stashed an aluminum baseball bat near the refrigerator in the kitchen. When he started taking off the belt, I told him to stop, that he wasn't going to be hitting anyone in our house ever again. He turned his attention to me, which is what I wanted, and I grabbed that bat and I broke several of his ribs with it. Then I took his belt away from him and beat him senseless. I wound up dragging him through the house, out the front door, and down the porch steps into the yard. I told him to leave and to never come back. I told him if I ever saw his face around there again I'd kill him, and I meant it. So after a little while, he crawled out to the garage in back, got in his car, and left. He never even came back to get his clothes or anything else. I guess he moved in with his girlfriend; I didn't really care. A couple of years after that, he got drunk and ran his car into a tree. And that was the end of Billy Street. I didn't even go to his funeral."

"I'm sorry, Darren," she said. "It was incredibly selfish of me to ask you to talk about that, to bring up that kind of memory and that kind of pain. It must have been awful. And here we are, together on Christmas, about to enjoy a meal, and I ask you to talk about something so terrible. I truly am sorry."

"Don't be," I said as the waiter approached and took our drink orders. Katherine asked for red wine; I ordered a beer. "It was a long time ago, and I don't regret what I did."

"But you have to regret that your father was an abusive drunk," she said.

"I don't think about him, and I try not to regret anything. If I spent my time dwelling on things I've done or things that have happened to me during my life, I'd be institutionalized by now or I would have offed myself."

"Speaking of things that have happened to you, did Ben Clancy really frame you for murder?"

"He did, and he did it very effectively. I have to give him credit. He was very good at being a very bad man."

"So you did two years in prison for a crime you didn't commit. And then you escaped in a helicopter, of all things, made your way back here, and got yourself exonerated. That was quite a story. I was finishing up my undergrad work while all that was going on. It was fascinating, and every time I saw your picture in the paper or some kind of footage on the news, I always thought, 'Wow, that guy is cute. I'd like to get to know him.'"

"Well, here we are," I said. "Getting to know each other, although all we've talked about is me so far. How about a little quid pro quo?"

The waiter appeared again, and we ordered dinner. Katherine asked for some spinach artichoke dip as an appetizer and ordered a seafood salad as an entrée. I ordered grilled teriyaki chicken.

"You're far more interesting than I am," she said when the waiter left. "Do you mind telling me about some of your experiences in prison?"

"Talking about prison is far worse than talking about my father. I'd just as soon skip it if it's okay with you."

"It's fine," she said, her eyes sparkling in the candlelight.

"Listen, Katherine," I said, "before this goes any further, there are some things you should know. Did you hear about two men getting killed in West Virginia who were suspected of bombing my mother's house?"

She nodded. "Of course. I'm a criminal justice major. I pay attention to things like that. It was in the newspaper."

"I'm the prime suspect in those murders," I said. "The police think I did it. They also think I had something to do with Ben Clancy's disappearance."

She shoved her fork around in her salad and looked down. "Should I even ask you whether you had anything to do with those things?"

"Would it matter to you one way or the other?"

She looked up at me with those incredible sapphire eyes and said, "No, after everything you've been through, I don't think it would. After everything you've been through, I can't believe you're still able to function."

"I appreciate that," I said, "but just to put your mind at ease, I didn't have anything to do with any murders anywhere. I have no idea what happened to Clancy, and I didn't go to West Virginia and kill anyone."

"Have the police questioned you?" she said.

"I won't let them. I'm a lawyer. I know my rights. And besides, I was railroaded into prison by the FBI and a corrupt prosecutor once. I'm not going to give them a chance to do it again."

"Good for you," she said. "What are your plans after dinner?"

"I don't really have any. I figured I'd drop you off and go back to the motel. I need to find a place tomorrow. I don't like sleeping at the motel. I don't like anything about it, to tell you the truth."

"I don't have any plans, either," she said. "Would you consider coming to my apartment and keeping me company for a little while?"

"Sure," I said, "I'd like that." I wasn't sure what to expect, but I was feeling a little adventurous.

"If things go well," she said, "maybe you won't have to sleep at the motel. Maybe we can even exchange gifts."

CHAPTER 49

I can only describe Christmas night with Katherine as ethereal. My entire plan of protecting myself from trauma by refusing to feel was shot to hell. Katherine was perfect in a way I'd never, ever experienced. Everything with her was natural and easy, and when I left the next morning, all I could think about was that I didn't want to go. I wanted to stay with her; I wanted to drink her in, to look at her, to smile with her, to laugh, to touch her. I hadn't felt that way about anyone or anything in my entire life. I had no idea I was even capable of it.

Even with Grace, whom I thought I loved, it was different. I'd thought about Grace several times over the past few days, and I'd begun to wonder if perhaps she might have been one of the triggers Dr. Benton had spoken to me about during my one and only abbreviated therapy session at her house. Grace had been my lawyer through one of the worst periods of my life. Even though she had been an important part of getting me out of prison and getting the murder charge against me dismissed, looking at her each and every day had to remind me of those terrible times. I was beginning to believe that Grace was both a blessing and a curse, and even if my mother hadn't been killed, we would never have made it. Eventually, I would have pushed her away because she was—unintentionally, of course—a constant reminder of the two years when my life spiraled completely out of control, two years during which I'd endured being beaten, strip-searched, dieseled, stabbed, and constantly humiliated by people who had authority over me because I was a prisoner.

Katherine was an incredible, passionate lover, and she put me at ease. After we made love a couple of times, I actually slept for several hours without having a nightmare. That was something that usually happened only if I drank myself into a stupor.

I woke up at five thirty and slipped out of bed. Part of me wanted to awaken Katherine and drink her in again, but another part of me was telling me to leave, that I needed to slow down. I got dressed in the dark and walked quietly out the door as Katherine slept.

As I drove along toward the motel, I began to wonder whether maybe I should do as Laura Benton had suggested—start over. I could shut down my law practice, and get some menial job while I went to school to become something besides a lawyer. I still had the problem in West Virginia I had to address, but once I got past that, maybe, just maybe, I could start down the road to some kind of normal life with Katherine. I knew it was ridiculous to be thinking in those terms so early in the relationship, but I simply couldn't help it—I couldn't get her out of my mind. And the thoughts I was thinking were optimistic. They were about the future and what it might hold for Katherine and me. They were positive. It was a 180-degree turn from the thoughts I'd been having since I got out of prison, since I'd gone back to practicing law, since my mom had been killed, and since I'd done what I'd done in West Virginia.

Less than ten minutes after I left her place, I got a text from Katherine. It said, Please tell me you went to get us some breakfast and you're coming back.

I pulled into a parking lot and wrote back: Gotta find a place today. See you tonight?

She wrote: Can't wait that long. Can I help you look?

Don't see why not, I wrote. Let me take a quick shower and I'll call you.

Need someone to scrub your back? was the reply.

You're killing me, I wrote. I'll call you as soon as I'm ready to go.

I drove to the motel and took a shower. As soon as I got out, my burner phone, which was lying on the nightstand next to my regular cell, began to ring.

"What's up, Pappy?" I asked.

"We're going to have to step it up in West Virginia," he said. "I just got a call from my guy Fairchild. He got popped Christmas Eve with an ounce of coke on him. That state trooper, Grimes, set him up. Then Grimes came into his cell yesterday and tried to get him to roll on us again. He said he didn't tell the cop anything, so the cop said he was going to put the word out that Fairchild had ratted us out and made a deal. He figured Fairchild would be so scared of us that he'd roll, but Fairchild says he didn't. He says if I hear he's ratted us out, it's a lie. He's going to eat the charge and go back to prison if he has to."

"Was he out? He didn't call you from a phone at the jail, did he?"

"No, a magistrate set him a bond after Grimes left and his dad paid the bondsman. He said it took them until after midnight to process him out and he called me first thing this morning."

"Do you believe what he said about eating the charge and going back to prison?" I said.

"Doesn't matter. He's too much of a risk either way now. He might have been recording the call, but I didn't say anything they could use against me. The fact that the magistrate set a bond on Christmas makes me suspicious, though. We need to go up there now."

"Today?" I said. I wondered to myself what day it was. Wednesday. It was the day after Christmas, and murder was in the air.

"No sense in putting it off. You know your guy will be at his bar tonight. People get out and drink at Christmas. They get their fill of being around their families, and they head out to the bars. Catch him when he comes out to his car at closing and take him out. Do you have a clean gun?"

"Yeah," I said. "I have something."

"Good. I'll take care of my end."

"You don't need to kill anybody," I said. "If I take out their only eyewitness, it's over. All they'd have left to use in court is three rednecks: your boy Fairchild, who's a drug addict, the guy Skidmore, and his stepson. The informant won't be able to testify because he didn't see or hear anything from either of us. All of his information is hearsay, stuff he heard from Baker. The only thing the state could prove is that Baker asked around about Frazier, found out about Beane, and then passed the information along to Skidmore. Skidmore could say he passed it along to Fairchild, and Fairchild could say he passed it to you. You didn't tell him I was going to go up there and kill those guys, did you?"

"I didn't tell him shit. I just asked him to find out if Frazier was bragging about doing a bombing in Tennessee."

"So they can't prove anything. Just let me go up there and take care of my guy and that should be the end of it."

"I'm doing Fairchild and I'm doing the informant. I hate rats, Darren. Do you know how many guys I ran off the yard in prison because I found out they'd ratted people out to the feds or the cops? Dozens of them. They're the scum of the earth. And Fairchild is a loose cannon, man. I can't have him walking around anymore. The rat in Cowen? Lester Routh? I'm going to kill him just on principle. I might wait awhile, but he has to go. The other two rednecks, Skidmore and Baker, I'll let them be if it makes you feel better."

"I just think you're taking an unnecessary risk," I said.

"Then we're going to agree to disagree," he said. "How soon can you get up there?"

"Probably be best if I leave as soon as possible. Can you get me a car so I can leave mine here at the motel? They check every night and list the license plate numbers of the cars in the lot. I want mine to be here."

"I can have a car waiting for you at the Flying J in an hour," Big Pappy said. "Same ID as last time?"

"You can get that done, too? That fast?"

"If you have money and contacts, you can get anything done. I have both."

"When are you planning to go to Charleston?" I said.

"I'll be there by ten."

"Okay, make arrangements for the car. I'll get on it now."

I disconnected the call and immediately sent Katherine a text message: I need a couple of days to sort this out. It's going too fast. Besides that, I'm representing you in a criminal case and becoming romantically involved with a client is a conflict of interest and a stupid thing to do. Last night was probably the best night of my life, but I need a little time. I hope you'll understand.

I sent the text. A couple of minutes later, my phone started ringing. It was Katherine. I ignored it. As soon as it quit ringing, I got a text from her that said, I understand. I'll be waiting when you're ready. I looked at the text and smiled. She was too good to be true.

I dressed, retrieved my pistol and silencer from where I'd hidden them inside an air vent in the bathroom, put them in my backpack, and called a cab on my burner phone. I walked two blocks to where I told the driver to pick me up, and told him to take me to the Flying J.

CHAPTER 50

Mike "Big Pappy" Donovan tossed his prepaid cell onto the seat beside him and turned the eighteen-wheeler he was driving into the lot of a large warehouse he rented on the outskirts of Cincinnati, Ohio. He hit the button of a remote control he'd pulled out of the console and watched the door slowly raise. Once it was up, he pulled the truck and fifty-foot trailer inside, shut down the engine, hit the remote to close the door, and climbed out of the cab. He walked over and turned on the warehouse lights, then headed toward the small office. Once there, he turned on the coffee maker and sat down behind a metal desk. He needed to think for a minute.

Darren Street thought he knew some things about Big Pappy Donovan, but pretty much everything Big Pappy had told Street about himself was a lie. Big Pappy had wanted to gain Street's favor while they were in prison because he wanted Street to work on his appeal and get him out. It had worked, too. Street had done some brilliant work, and the result was that Big Pappy had walked out of federal prison after serving twelve years instead of the thirty-five the government had intended him to serve. But in the meantime, Pappy had told Street some things about himself that weren't true.

He'd told Street he grew up in Hawkinsville, Georgia, and that he'd played football there and went on to play at Mercer University. He'd told Street he'd gone back to his high school after earning a degree and had been teaching biology and helping coach football when he was accused by a crooked cop of dealing crack cocaine. He told Street he had snaked the cop's girlfriend in a bar one night, and that was the reason the cop hated him.

That was the only thing he'd told Street that was true. He had met the woman, Paisley Grant, in a bar in Hawkinsville, Georgia, one night when he was passing through. He'd wound up having sex with her in his truck in the parking lot. At the time—and Pappy didn't know this— she was dating a cop named Ronnie Ray. Pappy continued to stop by Hawkinsville now and then and continued to have sex with Miss Grant every time he came to town. Ray, who had been assigned to a federal task force working the drug trade in southern Georgia, set up an elaborate sting—most of which was fabricated—and got Pappy indicted and convicted of selling crack. That's how Pappy wound up meeting Street at the federal maximum security penitentiary in Rosewood, California.

What Pappy hadn't told Street was that he was actually born in Las Vegas, Nevada, to a jazz drummer named Art Donovan and a stripper and hooker named Felicity Bell. Pappy's father, upon learning of Felicity's pregnancy, had an attack of conscience and offered to marry the girl. She accepted. But Art Donovan's passion for jazz was equaled only by his passion for the ladies, and he was soon out the door and on the road. Little Michael was left with his mother. She turned back to the world of stripping, hooking, drinking, and taking drugs. One of Pappy's earliest and most vivid memories of his childhood was waking up in his mother's bed one night to find her having sex with a man he'd never seen. His mother was moaning, and he thought the man was hurting her. He climbed off the bed and went to the kitchen to get a knife. The amorous couple didn't even notice until little Michael plunged the butcher knife into one of the man's triceps. It was the first of many acts of violence that Michael Donovan would commit.

By the time Michael was four, Felicity's neighbors had made enough complaints to the Nevada child protection services that Michael was finally removed from his mother's home. His father obtained a divorce and stayed on the road, and the authorities couldn't even find him. They placed Michael in a temporary foster home in Las Vegas and started searching for a more permanent solution. They found it in Georgia. Art Donovan's brother, a trucker named Lucas Donovan, agreed, along with his wife, Desiree, to take in their nephew. Felicity willingly signed away her parental rights to the boy, and he was accompanied by a Nevada child services worker to his new home in Dalton, Georgia.

Thus began a litany of problems for Lucas and Desiree Donovan, because they had agreed to take in a child who had been ignored, neglected, unloved, and totally undisciplined. They did their best to try to change Michael and make him feel wanted and loved, but nothing worked. He was destructive. He set fires. He abused animals. He refused to take instruction. He had zero interest in school outside of the things he could do to terrorize other children and the teachers. He was far bigger than the other children his age, and he was a remorseless bully. He was given detentions, suspended from schools, expelled from schools.

His first serious run-in with the law came at the age of thirteen. Michael—who would not earn the nickname "Big Pappy" until he entered federal prison—and two of his delinquent buddies had laid out of school and had been smoking weed. They needed money for more weed around three in the afternoon, and Michael said, "I know what to do." He walked to his house—his aunt and uncle were both at work—and he retrieved a pellet gun his uncle used to shoot at rats that sometimes came around an outbuilding in back of their house. The pellet gun looked just like a semiautomatic pistol. After Michael retrieved the pellet gun, he went to a telephone booth and called a cab company. He asked the dispatcher to send a cab to pick up him and his two friends. When the driver got there, Michael got into the front seat next to the cabbie while his buddies got into the back. Michael asked the cabbie to take them to Brook Run Park. When the cabbie pulled into the lot to drop the boys off and asked for the fare, Michael pulled the pellet pistol from beneath his shirt and put it to the cabbie's temple.

"Gonna need all your cash, man," Michael said.

The cabbie was so terrified that he opened the driver's side door and tried to get out, but he tripped and got hung up on his seat belt. The cab was still in drive and began to roll forward, dragging the driver along. The driver was pulled from the vehicle onto the ground, and the rear tires ran over his legs, breaking both of them between the knees and the ankles. Michael and the boys ran, but within two days the Dunwoody police had found them, using security footage from cameras in the park and near the phone booth where they'd made the call. The cab driver identified Michael, and the other two boys agreed to testify against him in exchange for leniency.

The juvenile court judge sentenced him to two years in the Youth Detention Center in Atlanta. While he was there, Michael beat two older boys senseless, raped another, and had two more years added onto his sentence. He was scheduled to get out at the age of seventeen, but he continued to fight with other boys and terrorized the guards. Two more assault charges got him the maximum sentence he could get under the juvenile laws of Georgia—they held him until his eighteenth birthday.

When Michael was released, he went back to Dalton. His uncle Lucas, who felt guilty about not being able to help the boy, offered him a job with his trucking firm, LDD Trucking. He took Michael, who had grown to six feet six inches and 250 pounds by then, under his wing and taught him how to operate an eighteen-wheeler. He taught him how to maintain the vehicles; turned him into a mechanic and a welder and anything else he needed to be in order to keep a truck on the road.

Lucas also taught Michael the ins and outs of the freight business. He stressed to Michael how important it was to be friendly and honest with the customers, to put their needs first, and to make sure their freight arrived on time and undamaged. Michael enjoyed the freedom of being on the road, and he quickly saw that he needed to develop a personality—a persona, really—that would help Lucas's business grow and eventually allow Michael to open and operate his own firm. Michael was disingenuous about kissing people's asses, but he was good at it. He knew he'd grown into a handsome young man, he knew he had an infectious smile, and he knew his massive size made people want him to like them. He took advantage of all those things, and within two years, by the age of twenty, Michael Donovan had started—with the help of his uncle—Donovan Trucking, based out of the same town as his uncle's firm.

Michael had one truck, and that was the way he wanted to keep it, because he had no intention of doing things the traditional way. Michael had worked hard at learning the business, but he also still liked to get out on the weekends, and he knew there was a huge amount of money to be made in the cocaine business. His truck was a perfect form of distribution; he simply had to become a little creative. The feds had declared war on drugs, and the wide-open cowboy days of the early eighties were gone by the time Michael got into the coke business. But there was still a huge demand out there, and the profit margins made the risk more palatable. He found a supplier in Atlanta through a kid named Randy Hayes. He'd done a couple of years with Hayes in Atlanta juvy, and Hayes had talked about his family connections in the cocaine trade. Once Michael had a supplier, he needed distributors for his product, and he wasted no time procuring them all along the eastern US seaboard.

Michael's truck hauled legitimate loads of everything from clothing to lawn furniture to car parts to kitchen appliances. He procured freight customers in Florida, Georgia, the Carolinas, Tennessee, Kentucky, Virginia, West Virginia, Ohio, Pennsylvania, New York, Maryland, New Jersey, and Delaware. His drug business started when he was fronted one kilogram of coke by one of Randy Hayes's cousins. Michael broke the kilogram down into thirty-five ounces and stuck them into a sealed piece of PVC pipe, which he then placed inside a tubular axle on his trailer. He paid $16,000 for the kilo, and over the next two weeks, he sold the thirty-five ounces for $2,000 apiece, which meant he made $54,000 on one kilo in two weeks.

Over the next five years, he built the cocaine business to the point where he was hauling fifteen kilos a month—all of it in the axle of his trailer—and netting nearly $1 million each trip. He had become rich, cautious, and ruthless. He trusted no one. He had the brains to find lawyers and accountants who were willing, for a healthy sum of cash, to help him launder and hide his money offshore. Two attempts had been made on his life—one in Dayton, Ohio, and one in Charlottesville, Virginia. Both of them had ended with him killing the person who was trying to rob and kill him.

And then, at the age of twenty-eight, the crooked cop who had become infuriated because Michael had had sex with the cop's girlfriend set Michael up and packed him off to prison for what was supposed to be thirty-five years. Before they sent him off, Michael conned a woman named Linda Lacy into believing he loved her, and he used her to keep his trucking and cocaine business running—although on a smaller scale—while he was inside. He spent eleven years stomping guards, taking over hustles, and ruling yards as a shot caller when he wasn't locked down in a hole for what he'd done to the guards. He made millions off his prison hustles, all of which he smuggled out to Linda through corrupt guards. Darren Street came along in his eleventh year, and by year twelve, he was out, thanks in large part to the work Darren had done. Six months after he got out, he caught Linda cheating on him with an old inmate buddy of his whom he'd given a job. He shot them both, cut them up and bagged them, and took them to yet another buddy who ran a huge junkyard near Lexington, Kentucky. Linda and her lover wound up in a car compactor, and later in a smelter.

So when Darren called him for help in finding the men responsible for murdering Darren's mother, Michael—who had become Big Pappy by then—was glad to help. He didn't really think Darren would have the stones to clip those two crackers, but Darren had surprised him. The problem was, he'd left an eyewitness, and now things were getting out of hand. Cops in West Virginia and Knoxville were sniffing around, a paid informant had popped up out of nowhere, and his old buddy Rex Fairchild had turned out to be a pathetic, unreliable druggie.

Even Darren was suspect now. His mother had been killed, his son taken away, and his girlfriend had dumped him right before Christmas. He sounded unsure of himself over the phone. Pappy wondered, if it ever came down to it and the cops managed to arrest Darren and get him back into jail, whether he would roll on Pappy to get himself a lighter sentence. Maybe he would even tell them Pappy had taken it upon himself to seek revenge for his old friend. Darren might tell them that Pappy had committed the murders.

Pappy shook his head and pushed himself up from the chair in which he'd been sitting. Thinking time was over. He walked to a locked cabinet in a corner of the office, opened it, and gazed over his choices. The cabinet contained an arsenal of weapons: pistols, rifles, shotguns, assault weapons—all of them untraceable—along with boxes upon boxes of ammunition and a selection of knives, holsters, and body armor. There were even some flashbang and antipersonnel grenades. The cabinet also contained several changes of clothing and a selection of fake beards, mustaches and wigs, hats, and fake identification cards.

Pappy made his selections and walked back out into the warehouse. He lifted the door on the trailer, pulled a ramp down, and then climbed inside the trailer. He backed a 2013 silver Ford Focus sedan out onto the floor of the warehouse and placed his weapons, clothing, and disguise in the trunk.

He walked to the cab of the truck, climbed up, and grabbed the remote control for the warehouse door. He pushed the button on the remote and folded his huge frame into the Focus. He pulled out of the warehouse, onto the road, and headed east.

It was a little more than three hours from Cincinnati to Charleston, West Virginia. Depending on where and when Pappy found him, Rex Fairchild didn't have long to live.

CHAPTER 51

Katherine Davis walked into the house on Clinton Avenue, removed her coat, and sat down on the couch in the living room. Her aunt, Detective Dawn Rule of the Knoxville Police Department, came in shortly thereafter and handed her a cup of coffee.

"You sounded pretty upset on the phone," Dawn said.

"Where's Uncle Jim?" Katherine said. "He might be interested in this."

"He got called out to some shooting in Sevierville. A policeman was involved, so the TBI has to look into it. What's going on?"

"Something is happening," Katherine said. "I mean, one minute Darren is telling me he wants me to go apartment hunting with him today, and the next he sends me a text and says we're going too fast, he needs some time. Have you talked to the trooper in West Virginia? What's his name? Grimes?"

"Not in a week or so. It's the holidays, Katherine. I take some time off during the holidays."

"I didn't take any time off," Katherine said. "I thought I had him hooked. He spent last night at my place."

Dawn Rule set her coffee down and stared at her niece. "When I first proposed this . . . this . . . idea to you, I didn't expect you to have sex with him. We set up the DUI charge, you went into his office and sold him on your damsel-in-distress act, and everything was going fine.

All you were supposed to do was get to know him, see if you could get him talking about his mother, maybe make an admission to you that he was involved in the murders in West Virginia or the disappearance of Ben Clancy. I didn't expect you to jump in the sack with him."

"You're judging me. I'm a big girl, Aunt Dawn. I can jump in the sack with whomever I please. And besides, he's excellent between the sheets. A little tentative at first, but—"

"Spare me the details, please."

"I actually like Darren," Katherine said. "The things he's been through? Unbelievable. Most people would have put a bullet in their head or gone completely insane by now. Did you know he and his girlfriend have broken up? You might want to go at her again. Something obviously changed."

"No, I didn't know that, but it makes me feel a little better knowing you weren't sleeping with him while he was engaged to someone else. A jury would love you for that."

"Stop," Katherine said. "You told me on the front end this would be dirty. It's the kind of thing I want to do. I want to catch bad guys doing bad things and make them pay for it."

"I thought you just said you liked the guy."

"I do. I really do, and I feel sorry for him. But if he killed two men in West Virginia and maybe another here, then he has to pay for that. I mean, that's what a lot of people in this family have been all about. Dad was an FBI agent until he had the aneurysm. Mom's still a prosecutor, Uncle Jim is a TBI agent, you're a detective. I'm about to go to law school, and I'm going to be either an FBI agent or a prosecutor, maybe both before it's over. I can't let personal feelings get in the way of doing the job, right?"

"It isn't a good idea to have sex with people you're investigating, Katherine."

"First of all, I like having sex. Men practically throw themselves at me, and I've learned to take advantage of it. If that makes me a bad person, so be it, but I don't feel badly about myself. Secondly, I'm not really investigating him, am I? I'm not a cop. I'm not on your payroll. I'm not even a paid informant. I'm just a girl who got charged—falsely, I might add—with driving under the influence of an Ambien pill so I could get close to Darren Street and use the tools I have to get an admission out of him. Now you're criticizing me for doing exactly what you thought I might do. And when you get right down to it, you've probably broken more laws than Darren Street setting up the phony charge. You didn't kill anybody, but we're splitting hairs, aren't we? You're being hypocritical."

"Sometimes we have to bend the rules a little. The sooner you learn that, the better off you'll be."

"Oh, I'm learning, all right. So . . . are you going to do anything about what I told you earlier? I told you something must be going on. I know where he's staying."

Dawn shook her head. "I told you earlier. It's the holidays. I'm not working."

"Can't you get a warrant or a subpoena and search his room?"

"On what basis? That he told you he doesn't want to see you for a little while?"

"Make something up."

Dawn threw her hands in the air. "He's a lawyer, for goodness' sake! And a good one, from what everyone says. If I make up a reason to search his hotel room, he'll find out. He'll find out, and he'll sue the hell out of the city and the police department and me."

"You just said you have to bend the rules sometimes."

"Bend them, not snap them in half."

"I'll do it myself, then," Katherine said.

"Do what?"

"Search his room, provided he isn't there. If he is there, I'll charm my way in and take a look around."

"What will you be looking for?"

"I don't know. Anything unusual. Not many places to hide things in a motel room."

"If he isn't there," Dawn said, "how do you propose to get inside?"

"Don't you remember what one of my dad's favorite hobbies was? He could pick any lock out there, and he taught his daughter well."

"You're crazy," Dawn said. "If you get caught, I'll deny all of what we've done. I'll get everyone in line. You'll be out there on your own."

"I won't get caught," Katherine said. "I'm going to bag you a murderer."

CHAPTER 52

By the time I got to the Flying J in the cab, I was fighting myself. The night with Katherine had a great deal to do with it, I was sure, but I also just couldn't find it in myself to drive all the way to West Virginia and execute a man who hadn't done a thing to me. In fact, he'd allowed me to mete out a violent form of justice to Donnie Frazier and Tommy Beane in his bar, and he'd walked into the bathroom while I shot them. He'd taken his time about calling the cops, and for all I knew, he couldn't really identify me. I'd been wearing the beard, the glasses, and the hat. We'd spoken for a little while about my mother, so perhaps he could recall my voice, but I knew from my experience in courtrooms that eyewitness identifications were often unreliable, and that voice identifications were even less reliable. After I got out of the cab, I paced around for a while. The December wind was cold, and the sky was foreboding. I immediately saw the car Pappy had left for me—a Dodge—but I didn't want to get into the car and start driving. Instead, I took out my prepaid cell and dialed Pappy's number.

"People are going to say we're in love if you keep calling so often," Pappy said.

"I'm not going to do it," I said.

"You're not going to do what?" he said. There was a chill in his voice I'd never heard.

"I'm not going to West Virginia. I'm not going to kill the bar owner. It's stupid. They can't convict me on what they have. They can't even arrest me, or they would have done it by now. If I go up there and kill the guy, all I do is piss them off and take a chance on leaving some forensic evidence somewhere. He didn't do anything to me, and I'm not going to kill him."

"Where are you?" Pappy said.

"I'm at the Flying J, but I'm about to go back to the motel."

"No. No, you aren't. Get your ass in the car, drive up there, and do what needs doing."

"I'm a damned lawyer!" I yelled. "If they were going to arrest me, they would have done it. I know what I'm talking about. They don't have a case."

"Don't grow a fucking conscience on me, Darren," Pappy said.

"It doesn't have anything to do with growing a conscience. It has to do with whether they can make a case on me, and they can't. Just let it be. Go on about your business. This will blow over. It'll go away."

"I'm not willing to take that chance. Now, for the last time, take care of what you should have taken care of in the beginning."

"Or what? You going to come down here and kill me? Bring it on, big boy. I'm not any more afraid of you than I am of anyone else. You know damned good and well I'm not afraid to die."

"Listen to yourself," Pappy said. "We've been through a lot together, you and me. You helped me out a bunch, and I've helped you out a bunch. But this is serious shit, Darren. This could be the difference between staying out of prison and going back in for life. Fairchild will be dead in the next three to four hours. That rat in Cowen will be dead within a week. I expect the bartender to be dead, too. If you don't take care of it, I'll do it myself, but there will be consequences."

"I appreciate everything you've done," I said. "I owe you money, and I owe you my gratitude. But I'm not killing him. You're wrong about him needing to die. And if you kill Fairchild in the next three or four hours, don't you think the cops will be all over Sammy? They'll have his place staked out. I'll walk right into a buzz saw."

"Figure something out," Pappy said.

"No. I'm staying here. I'm not killing him."

"I hate to hear that," Pappy said. "I guess I'll be seeing you before long."

The call disconnected, and I called a different cab company to come and pick me up. While I was waiting, I tried to figure out what I should do. Somebody would be coming to pick up Pappy's car soon, I was certain of that. I could wait and find out who the person was, maybe take a photo, but I didn't think it would do me any good. I could call the cops anonymously and tell them the car was about to be used in a murder, but the prison code was still ingrained in me. I just couldn't turn myself into a rat. Then something dawned on me, and I started searching on my phone for a number for Sammy's in Cowen, West Virginia. I had a phone number in just a couple of minutes. I went back to the hotel, waited until ten o'clock, and dialed the number.

"Sammy's," said a voice on the other end. I knew it was him.

"Do you recognize my voice?" I said.

"What?"

"Do you recognize my voice?"

"No."

"Good. I was at your place a while back. I asked you if you loved your mother. Took care of some business."

He was silent for several seconds, and then he said, "What do you want?"

"There's a man that wants to kill you. He's headed that way. He'll probably try when you walk out to your car at closing time."

"What? Why? Why would anyone want to kill me? I ain't done nothing to nobody."

"A state trooper up there named Grimes has told some people you're going to testify against me if they arrest me, that you can identify me. Is that true?"

"I ain't told him nothing."

"You're lying, but it doesn't matter. There was another man involved in this with me, and he doesn't want to go to jail. He's willing to kill people to stay out, and you're one of the people he's after. I tried to talk him out of it, but he's on his way up there right now. You need to do whatever you need to do to stay out of his way."

"But . . . but . . . what do I do? Oh Lord, mister. I wish I'd never laid eyes on you."

"Either wait for him with that sawed-off shotgun you were telling me about or call your buddy Grimes. I could've just let him kill you, but you did me a favor. I wish you'd kept your mouth shut, but you didn't. So now we have to deal with the situation as it is. I'm giving you fair warning about what's coming. Up to you to figure out what to do. And I'd appreciate it if you'd tell Grimes you've changed your mind about being able to identify me."

I hung up the phone, and a pang of guilt hit my stomach. I hadn't exactly ratted Pappy out, but I'd warned his victim that he was coming. I had no doubt Sammy would call Grimes, and that something bad would happen at Sammy's bar later that night.

I had no idea how it would turn out. All I could do was wait.

CHAPTER 53

Pappy was still fuming as he rolled the Ford Focus off the interstate into Charleston, West Virginia. He had been a shot caller on federal maximum security prison yards for years, and he wasn't used to people refusing to do what he told them to do. So when Darren refused, Pappy took it as a slap in the face. Darren had disrespected him, and being disrespected was the ultimate insult in the eyes of an inmate. Pappy was no longer an inmate, but as far as he was concerned, the rules still applied: you disrespect him, you pay the price.

Right now, though, he needed to deal with Rex Fairchild. Pappy didn't know whether Fairchild had ratted him out to the cops or whether he'd done what he said and told the cops to go to hell, but Fairchild had simply become too much of a liability. One of the first rules of dealing drugs was to stay out of your own product. It was a rule to which Pappy had adhered strictly throughout his adult life. He'd never used any drug, not even marijuana. He drank a little beer once in a while, but never to excess. He didn't smoke cigarettes, but he'd made about three million selling them in prison over the twelve years he was inside. Pappy chuckled to himself. Were it not for the fact that he was a drug-dealing criminal, a sociopath, maybe a psychopath, and a killer, he'd be a stand-up citizen. But Fairchild? He'd crossed the line. Not only had he hidden his drug addiction from Pappy, but he'd kept using after Pappy told him to quit, and then he'd gotten busted with an ounce of powder coke on him. Pappy knew an ounce of powder wasn't that big of a deal as far as being a serious crime, but he was worried that Fairchild's addiction to the drug would eventually loosen his lips.

It was the day after Christmas, a Wednesday, and Pappy thought Fairchild's car lot might be open for business. He'd just been busted and would need money to pay his bondsman and a lawyer. Pappy knew Fairchild's old man helped him out a lot, but he didn't think Daddy would be in a very generous mood after the latest cocaine bust. Pappy drove by the car lot and saw that it was, indeed, open.

It was ten thirty in the morning, and a cold, steady drizzle was falling. Pappy didn't see any customers on the lot. He'd done his Google Maps reconnaissance back in Cincinnati and turned onto Thirty-Sixth Street SE and parked in a corner of the Kanawha Elementary School lot. School was out, and Pappy didn't believe there would be security cameras that covered that part of the lot. Even if a camera covered the area, he was wearing a disguise and had a long overcoat with a hood and a stocking cap in the back seat. The tag on his car couldn't be traced back to him. He reached into the back and grabbed the overcoat and the stocking cap.

He pulled the stocking cap down over his head, donned the coat, and got out of the car. He opened the trunk, retrieved his weapons, stuck them into the pocket of his coat, closed the trunk, and started walking toward the car lot with his shoulders hunched and his hands shoved into his pockets.

As he came up on MacCorkle Avenue SE where the lot was located, cars whooshed by him, tossing plumes of water from their tires. The car lot was in the middle of a block, and Pappy scanned the area around it. He didn't see a soul other than the people flying by in their cars. He cut off the sidewalk and headed straight up to the trailer that served as Fairchild's office. He opened the door and stepped into a paneled room with a desk to his right. There were nondescript prints of different models of cars on the walls. There was a chair behind the desk, two more in front of it, and a laptop computer sitting on top, but there didn't seem to be anyone around. Pappy stood inside the door and listened. Within a minute, he heard a toilet flush. He took two steps, removed a silenced Smith & Wesson nine-millimeter, semiautomatic pistol from his pocket, and aimed the pistol at the door. The door opened, and a man Pappy had never seen before started to emerge from the bathroom before freezing in horror.

The man, who was of medium height, maybe thirty, with a receding hairline, raised both of his hands.

"There's no money here," he said.

"Where's Fairchild?" Pappy said.

"He isn't working today."

"That isn't what I asked you. Where is he?"

"He's at home, I think. He told me he had a bad weekend and asked me to cover for him today."

"The Internet says he lives on Upper Falcon Road. Is that right?"

"Yeah, yeah, that's where he lives."

"Who are you?"

"I'm Dave, Dave Van Fleet. I'm his brother-in-law. Please don't hurt me. If you have a problem with Rex because of the drugs, if he owes you money, just go away. I won't say a word to anybody about you being here. Like I said, there's no money."

"Can't do that, Dave," Pappy said.

"What are you going to do? Kill me? Please, I have a wife and two kids. I haven't done anything to you."

"Are you a good person?" Pappy said.

"What?"

"*Are you a good person?* Did I stutter? Are you a decent fucking human being?"

"I don't know. I mean . . . yes, I think so. I try to be a good person."

"You know that saying that sometimes bad things happen to good people?"

"Yeah, but—"

Pappy squeezed the trigger twice. Both bullets struck Dave Van Fleet in the head, and he fell back into the bathroom.

"It's true," Pappy said as he stood over the body. "Sometimes bad things happen to good people."

CHAPTER 54

From the conversations Pappy had had with Fairchild over the phone, he knew Fairchild had a live-in girlfriend named Rita. He didn't know whether Rita would be at Fairchild's trailer when he went looking for him there, but he didn't really care. The murder of Dave Van Fleet at the car lot had kindled a bloodlust in Pappy. If someone got in the way, they were going to die. If someone saw his face and could ultimately testify against him, he'd hunt them down and kill them.

The drizzle had intensified into a downpour by the time Pappy made his way to the outskirts of Charleston onto Upper Falcon Road, which was narrow and lined with mobile homes. Fairchild's trailer sat in a curve with no neighbors in sight or across the street. As Pappy approached, he saw two cars in the gravel driveway. He passed by once, drove a half mile or so down the road, turned around at an intersection, and headed back. He pulled into the driveway, got out of his car, and hurried up to the trailer's small front porch. He ascended the stairs, pulled the nine-millimeter from his overcoat pocket, and turned the doorknob. It wasn't locked. He walked in to find Fairchild sitting on his couch. He was shirtless, the television was on, and there was a round mirror on a table in front of him. On the mirror was a razor blade, a short straw, and a small pile of white powder.

"Moron," Pappy said as he raised the silenced pistol. It burped twice. Both shots struck Fairchild in the chest and he slumped back on the couch. Pappy walked up close to him and shot him again in the forehead. He saw a flash of movement to his left, heard a low growl, and was immediately knocked off balance by a hundred-pound Rottweiler that had come out of one of the bedrooms. He felt teeth sink into his left forearm as he tried to push the dog down onto its back. The dog was strong, however, and began shaking its head. Pappy could feel flesh tearing from bone in his arm. Pain shot through the limb like a lightning bolt, and he cursed loudly. He wanted to shoot the dog in the head, but he was afraid he'd shoot himself in the arm at the same time. He finally slipped the pistol barrel against the dog's chest and pulled the trigger. The dog howled, rolled over, and began crawling away. At about the same time, Pappy looked up and saw a small blonde woman standing in the hallway ten feet away, pointing a shotgun at him. The shotgun belched fire and smoke, and Pappy felt a searing burn in his right ear. He aimed the pistol at the woman and fired twice. Both shots struck her in the chest. She fell back into the hallway, and the shotgun clattered against the wall and landed on the floor.

Pappy straightened up and walked over to her. He shot her once more in the forehead. The dog was still whining as he hurried out the front door. He reached up and felt his right ear, which was still burning as though it was on fire. Part of it was gone.

His blood was all over that trailer. He knew it wouldn't be long before the cops came, gathered the blood samples, extracted DNA, and ran the DNA samples against the DNA he'd given them when he was in the system.

The DNA would match. It was over for him, and he knew it. They'd be coming soon. He'd kill as many of them as he could before they ultimately took him down, but before that happened, he had one more place to visit.

Knoxville, Tennessee.

CHAPTER 55

I took a cab from the Flying J back to my hotel, got in my car, and started looking around for furnished apartments. I didn't want to have to go out and find and buy and haul and arrange furniture. I finally found one that I thought I could stomach around one o'clock, called the rental agency that was managing the building, and learned they wouldn't be back in the office until Monday. I thought seriously about texting or calling Katherine and telling her I'd had a change of heart, but instead, I went to a bar a couple of miles from the hotel, had three drinks, and watched part of a lousy bowl game that was on television. I still had some decent bourbon back at the room, so I decided to go back there and watch the rest of the game. During the day, I'd wondered several times whether Pappy had found Fairchild and what had happened. I wondered whether he was on his way to Cowen to kill Sammy. If he was, I knew I probably wouldn't have to deal with Pappy again.

About an hour after I got back to the room, there was a loud knock on the door. I went and looked through the peephole. Detectives Dawn Rule and Lawrence Kingman were standing outside.

"What do you want?" I said through the door.

"Need to talk to you," Rule's voice said.

"Not in the mood right now."

"Open the damned door, Street," Kingman said.

"Do you have a warrant?" I said.

"There was a bloodbath in Charleston, West Virginia, this morning. Thought you might like to hear about it."

"Don't know anybody in Charleston," I said.

"You know Michael Donovan," she said. "We think he's responsible."

I opened the door but didn't invite them in. "As you can see, I'm right here, so I couldn't have had anything to do with anything that happened in Charleston, West Virginia," I said. "And by the way, how in the hell did you find me?"

"We've been keeping an eye on you," Rule said. "We tend to do that with people who are suspected of committing multiple murders."

I'd been careful. There was no way they'd been following me. I supposed they could have triangulated my cell phone signal, but that would have required them to get a subpoena from the phone company, and that would have required approval from a judge. I didn't believe they had enough evidence against me to go to a judge.

"You're lying," I said. "I'll get to the bottom of how you found me eventually, and I'll sue your asses."

"Mind if we come in and take a look around?" Kingman said.

"There isn't a snowball's chance in hell you're coming in this room without a warrant," I said.

"Your buddy Big Pappy Donovan killed three people in Charleston a few hours ago," Rule said.

"First of all, he isn't my buddy. He was the shot caller on my yard in prison and I helped him with his appeal. Haven't seen or heard from him since I got out. Secondly, if he killed anybody, I don't know a thing about it."

"Heard the name Rex Fairchild?" Rule said.

"I don't even know why I'm talking to you. Why don't you guys just get the hell out of here and leave me alone?"

"Fairchild is dead, along with his girlfriend. Donovan killed them at Fairchild's house. Shot Fairchild's dog, too, but the dog lived through it. The dog bit him, though, and Donovan's blood is in the house.

Donovan didn't know Fairchild's girlfriend had a teenage daughter. She was in the laundry room during the shooting, but she came out when Donovan went out the front door, and she saw him walk across the porch, down the steps, and get into his car. She identified him from photos the Charleston police showed her. They'll match his DNA up soon, and he'll be toast. Fairchild's girlfriend got a shot off from a shotgun. We don't know if she hit him, but he might be wounded. Oh, and just for good measure, Donovan also killed Fairchild's brother-in-law, who just happened to be filling in for Fairchild at his car lot in Charleston. Shot them all with a nine-millimeter, same caliber gun that was used on Donnie Frazier and Tommy Beane in Cowen a while back."

"Why are you telling me this? Since you're standing here looking at me, it's obvious I didn't have a thing to do with it."

"Because this could be a chance for you to help yourself out. Help us find Donovan, and maybe we help the West Virginia State Police pin the killings in Cowen on him, too. Maybe we forget what you did up there and what you did to Ben Clancy. I mean, we could certainly understand why you'd want to kill the men who bombed your mother's house and why you'd want to get even with a prosecutor who framed you for murder."

I was half-drunk, which was why I'd opened the door in the first place, but I wasn't so drunk that I'd become stupid. This was a classic cop trick. A lie to try to get me to make admissions they would later use against me.

"I haven't done anything to anybody," I said. "I've told you that before, and I'll tell you again and again. All you're ever going to hear from me is that I didn't have anything to do with any of the things you're talking about. And just out of curiosity, what is your theory of the motive Pappy Donovan would have to kill Donnie Frazier and Tommy Beane?"

"Loyalty to the man who got him out of prison," Kingman said. "They killed your mother; he did you a favor and got some revenge for you."

"You have absolutely no proof of any of this, of course," I said.

"We will if you tell us he did it."

"Not gonna happen," I said. "Not now, not ever."

"Where is he?" Kingman said. "You stay in touch with him, don't you?"

I slammed the door in their faces, turned around, and walked over and sat on the bed. They pounded on the door and yelled for a little while longer, but eventually, they went away.

* * *

Once they were gone, I picked up one of my burner phones and dialed Pappy's number.

"What the fuck do you want?" he barked.

"The cops have already been here. They know it was you who did the killings in Charleston. Three? You had to kill three? What's the matter with you, man? Have you gone insane? They said you left blood there. Is that true?"

"Fucking dog, man, and Fairchild's bitch girlfriend blew part of my right ear off. How do they know it was me?"

"Fairchild's girlfriend had a teenage daughter who was there. I guess you didn't see her, but she saw you. She identified you from photos."

"Shit!" Pappy yelled.

"I told you not to go. If you're headed toward Cowen, I guarantee they'll be waiting for you."

"What did you tell them?" he said.

"I told them I haven't seen you since prison. And then I told them to get the hell out of here."

"It's almost over," Pappy said. "I decided not to go to Cowen. I've patched myself up at my place in Cincinnati. I'm going to get some rest, and then I'm heading to Knoxville."

His tone sounded ominous.

"You're coming after me?"

Some part of me knew this was inevitable after I'd refused to do the bartender in Cowen. You just didn't say no to Big Pappy Donovan. It was an insult, a sign of disrespect, and I knew the penalty for disrespect could be death.

"You're a smart guy."

"What the hell, Pappy? Why me?"

"You're the one that got me into this in the first place. I helped you out, did you a huge favor, and you repay me by dragging me into a pile of shit. If you'd killed the bartender like you should have, we would have been okay, but you didn't, so I wound up getting shot and bit by a dog at Fairchild's place. They're going to match up my blood through DNA, and then they're going to come after me. But before they do, I'm going to take care of the man that got me into this."

"You didn't have to do a thing. You didn't have to help me, and you damned sure didn't have to go to Charleston. I told you not to. You made your own choices."

"And you made yours. You're about to find out that when you deal with the devil, you pay the consequences."

I took a deep breath and let it out slowly. I could hear the resolve in his voice. He was coming. I was a little afraid, but I knew I wouldn't back down from him. I'd been in dangerous situations before, had been afraid, and had found the courage to do what I had to do. "Are we going to do this like men, or are you going to sneak up and bushwhack me like some bitch?"

"Did you just call me a bitch?" Calling a man a bitch was another unforgivable insult in prison.

"I asked you a question. What's it going to be? I think I've earned enough respect for you to tell me when you're coming. All I'm asking for is a fighting chance."

"Tomorrow," Pappy said. "You pick the time and the place. I'll even let you pick the weapons. Guns or knives?"

"Are you serious? You think I'm going to do some kind of O.K. Corral shootout with you?"

"You can rat me out and call the cops. You can try to set me up and have an army of police waiting. Or you can be a man and live up to the consequences of the choices you've made. And that means me and you, a fight to the death. Old school. A duel. Just the two of us. No seconds, no doctors. I've always thought I was born way too late, anyway."

He was like a runaway train headed straight for me, and there was nothing I could do to derail him. The tone in his voice told me he'd crossed over the edge into a psychopathic state. I had, unfortunately, visited that same state of mind myself. There was no reasoning with him at this point. I could have easily called the police, and they would have set up an ambush. They would have either arrested him or killed him. I suspected they would have killed him because he would have started shooting as soon as he smelled a cop. And even in my semi-drunken state—I'd sobered up considerably, given the content of the conversation—I knew part of what he was saying was right. I'd known that he was a killer when I called him, the day Dawn Rule and Lawrence Kingman first told me about Donnie Frazier. I'd known he'd killed his girlfriend and her lover, and probably more. I'd known he was a drug dealer on a large scale. I'd known I was throwing my lot in with a dangerous and perhaps even psychotic individual. Now that things had blown up, was I going to turn tail and head to the police? Or was I, as he said, going to be a man and live up to the consequences of the choices I'd made?

"There's a place outside of Petros," I said. "It's where I went to practice shooting before I killed Frazier and Beane. It's in the middle of nowhere. We can do it there. I'll text you directions. It isn't hard to find the gravel road that leads to the range. Once you get on the road, you drive exactly one and one-tenth of a mile. You'll top a rise, and the range will be on your left."

"Time?" Pappy said.

"If we're going all old school, we might as well do it tomorrow at dawn. I'm assuming you can get here by then."

"I'll be early. Weapon?"

He was a massive, tremendously strong man, and he probably had some experience with knives. I had none. I was strong, too, but nothing like him. I was probably quicker than he was, but the only way to cut him with a knife would be to get close to him, and if I got close to him, he might get his hands on me. If he did that, I knew it would be over.

"Pistols," I said. "No rifles, no assault weapons, just pistols."

"Sounds perfect," Pappy said. "We do it just like they did back in the day. We start with our backs to each other. We walk five paces, we turn, we aim the pistols in the air, we count to ten, and then we lower them and start shooting."

Five paces each would put us about thirty feet from each other. Ten yards. He wouldn't miss from that distance, and I hoped I wouldn't, either. I'd become very proficient with the 0.22, but I wasn't sure how I'd do when I was looking down the barrel of a gun. He'd already told me he was wounded, though, and maybe, just maybe, he would have lost enough blood to give me some small advantage. Maybe his hands would be shaky. Maybe his vision would be blurred just a bit.

"Fine," I said. "I'll meet you at dawn."

"There will be no quarter given," he said.

"None expected," I said, and I disconnected the call.

CHAPTER 56

Will Grimes looked around the mobile home. He was standing about five feet from where Rex Fairchild had been shot. The bodies had already been removed, and the Charleston Police Department's forensics examiners were still going over the place. There was an occasional pop and flash as the investigators took photographs. Sergeant Eric Young, the officer who had helped Grimes squeeze Rex Fairchild, was standing next to him.

"I assume the crusty coroner has already been here," Grimes said.

"Yeah," Young said. "He's a piece of work."

"What was his opinion?"

"He said they're dead. Trauma caused by gunshot wounds."

"He's always so insightful," Grimes said. "How'd you find them?" He'd received a call from Young at around eleven-thirty that morning and had driven back down from Elkins.

"Somebody went into the car lot and found the brother-in-law and called 9-1-1. Around the same time, Fairchild's girlfriend's daughter called dispatch. They found Fairchild on the couch right there. He'd taken two in the chest and one in the head. The girlfriend was over there in the hall. Same gunshot wounds, two in the chest and one in the head. He shot their Rottweiler, too, but not before the dog took a chunk out of him. We've got blood samples from the carpet that will confirm who the shooter was."

"Dog dead?"

Young shook his head. "The dog was the only one that made it, outside of the daughter and the shooter," he said. "The dog took one to the chest, but from what I've heard, he'll live. The girlfriend also got off a shot from a shotgun. Forensics picked some pieces of what they think is an ear out of the wall right there. We should have plenty of DNA."

"So Big Pappy Donovan is wounded and on the loose. He won't know about the daughter, so he won't know we're already onto him. I assume you've put out an APB on him?"

"We have, but the girl couldn't tell us much about the car. Just that she thought it was silver and small. We're checking around the car lot to see if we can find it on some security camera footage."

"Did you get anything out of Fairchild yesterday when you talked to him at the jail?" Young said.

"Nothing. He was terrified of Donovan. I guess he had a good reason to be."

"Does this shut down your case against the lawyer?"

"Didn't have much of one in the first place. I haven't been able to get the district attorney to take it to a grand jury. Fairchild was my only direct link to Big Pappy Donovan, and Donovan is the only link to the lawyer. So I guess this pretty much shuts me down."

"Do you think this Donovan is finished, or do you think he'll go after your other witnesses?"

"I hope he comes after them," Grimes said, "because I'll sure be waiting."

"He'd be stupid to come after anybody else," Young said. "If that's his blood on the floor, my guess is he'll take off. He'll try to get so deep in the weeds nobody will ever find him."

"Maybe," Grimes said, "or maybe the snakes are starting to eat each other. Wouldn't surprise me to see the lawyer turn up dead next."

"That'd be just fine with me," Young said. "You won't see me shedding any tears over a dead lawyer."

Grimes shrugged his shoulders.

"Maybe they'll kill each other," he said. "Make the world a better place."

CHAPTER 57

After I hung up the phone, I lay back on the bed and closed my eyes. So much had happened in such a short time, and now it was coming to what I knew would be a violent and terrible conclusion. One of us would not walk away from the clearing in the mountains near Petros. If I died there, I knew Pappy would dispose of my body, and no one would ever know what became of me. If I somehow managed to kill him and survive, I knew where I'd take him; I just didn't know how I'd get him there. It wouldn't be as though I could just throw him into the trunk of my car.

The worst thought that struck me, though, was that if I died, how few people would really mourn the loss. My mother was gone, my son was half a world away, my ex-wife hated me, Grace had kicked me out, and I'd distanced myself from nearly everyone I knew. I had no close friends in the legal community, no close friends at all, really. Bob Ridge and I hadn't spoken since my mother's death. I knew, as a cop, that he probably had to stay at arm's length because I was a suspect in the West Virginia murders and the disappearance of Ben Clancy. But even if he'd reached out to me, I would have found a reason to avoid him. The irony of all that had happened was that my best friend was a psychopathic killer, and now, at dawn the next morning, I would meet him in a remote patch of wilderness and try to kill him before he killed me.

At the thought of shooting Pappy to death, my eyes flew open and I got up from the bed. I walked outside, crossed the street, and bought a thirty-two-ounce bottle of water from a convenience store. If I was going to be in a fight for my life in the morning, I didn't want to have a hangover. On my way back to the room, I stopped by my car and retrieved a small gun-cleaning kit from the trunk. I went back inside and unscrewed the cover of the air vent in the bathroom and took out the pistol. I left the silencer, the box, and two clips of ammunition inside the air vent and replaced the cover. I walked to the desk near the bed, laid out some towels, and began obsessively cleaning and oiling the pistol. I always cleaned and oiled it after I shot it, but I wanted to make absolutely certain it was in pristine condition. I used a product called M Pro 7. It had no odor, so I wasn't worried about using it in the room. That turned out to be a good thing, because just as I'd finished up and reassembled the pistol, there was a soft knock at the door.

My first thought was that it was Pappy. He could have been lying about being in Cincinnati. He could have driven to Knoxville, but how could he have found me? There was simply no way he could have known where I was staying. I thought back on our conversations over the past few days. Had I told him where I was? No, I hadn't. Maybe the person who delivered the car to the Flying J for Pappy was following me and knew where I was staying. I ran into the bathroom, unscrewed the vent cover again, grabbed a clip of ammunition, and slid it into the pistol. I set the silencer and the box on the bathroom vanity, popped a round into the chamber, and went back into the room.

Instead of going to the door, I went to the window and pulled back the blinds. Standing outside the door in a long, brown leather coat was Katherine Davis. I *had* told her where I was staying, although I hadn't told her which room I was in. But my car was parked right in front of the room. I sighed and walked to the door.

"Surprise," she said when I opened the door.

"Yes," I said. "I'm surprised."

"Can I come in?"

The pistol was in my right hand, which I was hiding behind the door.

"Can you give me one second?" I said. "I was on the phone with a client. Private conversation. It'll just take me a second."

I closed the door and stuck the pistol under the mattress. I fixed the bedding back the way it was and went back to the door.

"Come on in," I said.

She walked in leisurely, smelling of lemon and musk. It was one of the sexiest smells I'd ever breathed. Her hair was flowing, her makeup perfect, her eyes gleaming.

"Did you find a place?" she asked.

I nodded. "Think so. Management company won't be back in the office until Monday, so I won't know for sure until then."

"Where is it?"

"Cherokee Bluff, not too far from the office. They're apartments. Nice but not outrageous."

She sat down on the bed and crossed her legs. She was wearing jeans and calf-high boots beneath the coat. "Did I do or say something last night that offended you?"

"No," I said as I sat down in a chair about ten feet from her. "Everything you did and said last night was almost too good to be true. I'm having a little trouble processing the feelings."

"You've been through a lot lately."

"Yeah, well, I'm about to go through some more."

"Really? What's going on?"

"The police were here earlier. A couple of detectives. You know Dawn Rule or Lawrence Kingman, by any chance?"

She shook her head. "Don't think so."

"I thought maybe you'd run across them through the grad program. Anyway, some psycho apparently killed three people in Charleston, West Virginia, this morning, and they think I either had something to do with it or know something about it."

"Why would they think that?" she asked.

"They're still holding on to this theory that I killed two guys in West Virginia who supposedly bombed my mom's house. The killings today were apparently somehow related to that, or at least that's what they think. They're grasping at straws; they have nothing but unfounded suspicions."

"So you talked to them today?"

"Not for long. I'd stopped by a bar earlier and had a couple of drinks and my judgment wasn't the best, so I opened the door and talked to them for a few minutes. But they were just being cops, trying to trick me into saying something incriminating, so I shut the door on them."

"Why don't you come back over to my place, Darren?" she said. "You told me you don't like it here."

"Look around. What's to like?"

"Then come back over. We'll drink some wine. We'll get some take-out, whatever you like. And maybe we can exchange gifts again."

"I'd like to," I said. "I really would. Thank you for the invitation, but I can't do it tonight. I just have too much on my mind."

I couldn't tell her I had a date with a psychotic killer and that I had to prepare myself mentally for what was coming.

"I can ease your mind," she said.

I got up, walked to the door, and opened it.

"You're kicking me out?" she said. "You're really going to make me leave?"

"Tomorrow," I said. "After tomorrow, things will be different."

She rose from the bed, walked to the door, and lingered a few inches from my face. "What happens tomorrow?"

"I can't tell you. Now, please, this is extremely difficult for me, but I have to ask you to leave now."

"But I'll see you again?" she said. "Do you promise?"

"I hope so, Katherine. I really do."

CHAPTER 58

The gunfight at the clearing near Petros was scheduled for dawn on a Thursday, two days after Christmas, but there was no way I was going to show up at dawn. I thought Pappy would probably get there and get familiar with the place as soon as he could, and I wanted to be there first. So as soon as Katherine left, I went into the bathroom and replaced the air vent, then picked up the silencer, the box the gun came in, and the extra clip of ammunition. I retrieved the pistol from beneath the mattress and went out and got in my car. I drove around several blocks, doubled back, ran red lights, and pulled into and out of strip malls and apartment complexes until I was certain I wasn't being followed.

I then drove to a small storage space I'd rented when Grace had kicked me out. Inside the storage space was my camping gear and some heavy clothing, along with most of the rest of the things I'd accumulated after my mom was killed. The weather forecast said it would be cold and there could be some light snow in the mountains west of Knoxville on Thursday, so I put on a set of warm clothes, a pair of leather gloves, a leather coat, a pair of boots, and a stocking cap, then picked up a flashlight and a box of ammunition for the pistol. I drove to a convenience store, bought a couple of large cups of coffee, and filled my car with gas before I got onto the interstate.

I planned to keep the car running with the heater on most of the night. I knew I wouldn't be sleeping, so I thought I'd drink the coffee a couple of hours before dawn. It would be cold, but the caffeine would have the same effect.

From there, I went to my mom's grave. I stood over the headstone as the wind howled around me. Surprisingly, I wasn't sad or afraid. I almost felt lighthearted. I said, "Mom, if you know what's going on, you know I might be joining you very soon. I've done some bad things and I know you might not be too happy with me right now, but when you were alive, you always had my back and I always had yours. If there's anything you can do to help me out tomorrow, a little nudge here, a push there, a big gust of wind that throws him off balance or sends a bullet off target, I'd appreciate it."

I got back into my car and pulled onto the interstate. As I drove west out of Knoxville toward Petros, I picked up one of my burner phones. I'd left my regular cell back at the hotel. I dialed my ex-wife, Katie's, number. I wanted to talk to my son, Sean, just in case. I didn't know what I'd say to him, but I wanted to hear his voice. The phone went to voice mail. I asked Katie to please have Sean call me on my burner number—that it was important—but I knew she wouldn't. The next number I dialed was Grace's. She didn't pick up, either.

"I just wanted to tell you I'm sorry for anything I've ever done that hurt you," I said on her voice mail. "I never intended to hurt you. I never wanted any of the things that have happened to happen. I want you to know I appreciate how kind you've always been to me, how good you were to my mom and my son, and that I'll always love you."

I was on the gravel road that led to the shooting range in just over an hour. Small flakes of snow were dancing across the headlights like tiny flying fish, and the darkness beyond the reach of the headlights was complete. I pulled my car into a small stand of trees about a hundred yards from the clearing where the targets were, turned off the engine and the lights, took the Walther P22 pistol out of my pocket, and got out. I walked around with the flashlight for a little while, then went over to the targets. I illuminated a target with the flashlight, backed up thirty feet, and emptied a clip into it. I popped another clip in and did the same. I walked up to the target and checked it. The pattern was tight—all of the rounds were close to the bull's-eye. If I could stay calm, I at least had a chance.

I went back to the car, opened the trunk, picked up the box of ammo and reloaded the clips with .22-caliber long-rifle hollow points. The wind was whistling through the leafless tree branches all around me, and I shivered. I thought about cleaning the gun again—the kit was in the trunk, too—but since it had been spotless when I got there and I'd only put twenty rounds through it, I decided against it. I got into the car, started it, and turned the heater up. I looked at the clock on the dashboard. It was only 10:35 p.m. I wondered how long it would take Pappy to get there. I'd positioned myself in a place where I knew I'd see him come in. He couldn't drive without headlights; it was just too dark. He would come over a rise that led to the firing range. It was in a natural bowl, almost like a box canyon. Three sides were flanked by steep banks that led to a ridge farther up the mountain.

Time crept by. I got out of the car and walked around several times. I kept impulsively checking the Walther to ensure it was ready to go. Finally, at 5:58 a.m., I was walking about thirty yards from my car, just finishing the second cup of cold coffee I'd bought earlier, when I saw the glimmer of lights coming up the other side of the rise and heard the crunch of tires on gravel. A vehicle topped the rise and stopped. It turned slowly to the left, and its headlights illuminated the target range. It had to be him. Big Pappy Donovan had arrived. The sun wouldn't rise until 7:45 or so. The first light of dawn would appear about a half an hour before. We had a little more than an hour to wait.

I walked over and huddled against the trunk of a giant white oak tree. It protected me from the wind and gave me a clear view of the spot where the headlights had gone out. I couldn't hear the engine running, and I couldn't see the vehicle, but I imagined I could hear Big Pappy breathing. The breaths were slow, deep, and measured, the breaths of a predator stalking prey.

I stayed near the tree for more than an hour, when suddenly I noticed faint slivers of light beginning to emerge above the mountain ridges in the distance. Five minutes later, I stood and began to walk toward the range. I could make out the shape of Pappy's vehicle; it was a small sedan of some sort. Another five minutes passed, and I saw the interior light come on. The door opened, and the huge man climbed out of the driver's side. He took several steps toward the range, and I stepped out of the tree line.

He saw me and stopped. I did the same. I was ready to pull the Walther out of my pocket and start shooting, just in case he tried to ambush me.

"I'm glad you came," Pappy said. "Wasn't sure you would."

"I told you I'd be here."

"I was afraid I was going to have to hunt you down in Knoxville. It would've been hard, but I would've gotten to you eventually."

"I'm saving you some trouble, then."

"Are you ready to die, Darren?"

"I am. Are you?"

"Not today."

The snow had stopped completely, but the wind continued to swirl. I took my gloves off and dropped them on the ground. As I looked at Pappy, I noticed something that seemed a little unusual. He was wearing a short coat, but he appeared even bulkier than usual. I cursed under my breath. The son of a bitch was wearing a bulletproof vest.

"You're wearing a vest?" I said.

"And you're not?"

"No, I'm not."

"Then how stupid are you? Who comes to a gunfight these days without a vest?"

I should have known he'd do something like this, and I cursed myself for being so naive.

"I thought this was supposed to be old school," I said.

"It is, but we're not using flint-lock pistols and musket balls, are we? I reserved the right to use the technology available to me, although I don't think I communicated that to you very effectively."

I'd planned on aiming for center mass and trying to pump as many hollow points into his chest as quickly as I could, but now I'd have to aim for his head. He had a large head, which helped, but at thirty feet and in poor light, it would make things more difficult.

"How's your ear?" I said.

"Fuck you, let's do this."

We walked toward each other slowly. He'd always made me feel small, but walking toward him in the dim light in the mountains, knowing what was about to happen, made him appear gigantic. The gun in his right hand looked to be a nine millimeter, and I was sure it was, like mine, loaded with hollow-point bullets that expanded on contact so they inflicted maximum damage. Neither of us said a word as we approached each other. I watched his gun hand intently because I didn't trust him. We came within inches of each other and he turned around. I did the same.

"Five paces," he said, and I walked off five paces. I turned back around to see that he was doing the same.

"Pistol toward the sky," he said, and he raised his right arm.

"Ten . . . nine . . . eight . . . ," he said. I wondered for a brief second whether he was counting down the last ten seconds of my life, but then I began to hone in on my target. I breathed deeply and slowly.

"Seven . . . six . . . five."

I was surprised to realize that I wasn't frightened. It was as though I'd accepted whatever outcome the universe had in mind for me. I wouldn't question, and I wouldn't try to force anything. My heart was beating normally, and my hands were steady.

"Four . . . three . . . two . . . one."

I saw his hand begin to drop as he took aim. I did the same, and I did it quickly. I fired two shots before I heard his weapon explode. I felt the concussion as a bullet whizzed by my left ear. I fired again, and again. Was I missing him?

He fired two more times. The second shot knocked me backward onto the ground as I felt my right collarbone shatter. The pain radiated through my arm and chest like fire at first. It was so excruciating I almost passed out, but then it eased and turned into a dull, aching throb. My pistol immediately fell to the ground beside me, and my right arm was rendered useless. I reached over with my left hand and picked up the gun, which caused pressure on my right arm and sent pain shooting through me again. I expected to see Pappy hovering over me with the nine millimeter pointed at my forehead. Instead, I looked over, and he was on his knees, clutching at his throat with both hands. I couldn't see his pistol.

I managed to get to my feet and staggered toward him, raising the Walther with my left hand. I held my right arm against my stomach, but pain still shot through my shoulder, arm, and neck. When I got to within six or eight feet of him, I could see he'd been shot through the throat, and blood was spurting from the wound. There was another bullet hole in his right cheek.

He looked up at me with an expression of pure hatred as his throat gurgled. I took a few more steps and was less than three feet away. His pistol was on the ground by his right knee. He started to reach for it, and I fired one last shot with my left hand. The bullet went into his forehead just above the bridge of his nose, and he went straight over on his back.

"No quarter," I said out loud, and I turned and began to walk slowly toward his car.

CHAPTER 59

I was relieved to see Big Pappy's keys were in the ignition. I sat down in the driver's seat with the door open and the interior light on and began to examine my wound. The entry was almost directly in the middle of my right clavicle. I was certain the bone was broken or fractured. It was bleeding, but not badly. I cursed myself for not thinking to buy and bring along a first-aid kit. I'd known the chances of my getting shot were pretty high but honestly hadn't expected to survive if I was wounded.

I removed my coat and shirt and started feeling around my upper torso with my left hand for an exit wound. I found it beneath my right armpit, about halfway down my rib cage. It, too, was bleeding. There wasn't a torrent of blood coming from the wound, but there was more than was coming from the entry wound. The entire right side of my upper body was throbbing in pain. It radiated in waves from the collarbone, down my arm and through my rib cage. I took some deep breaths—which hurt like hell—and tried to think. I reached down and pushed a button, and the trunk popped open. I forced myself to stand and walk to the back of the car. I started going through the trunk with my left hand. There were several weapons—pistols and knives and assault rifles—enough ammunition to fight a long battle, some bags of dehydrated food, several gallons of water, a tent, a wad of cash, and, to my great relief, a first-aid kit. I pulled it out and opened it.

Two things caught my eye immediately: antiseptic wipes and rolls of gauze. I opened the antiseptic wipes and wiped down both the entry and exit wounds. I had to do it gingerly because of the pain. When I started stuffing gauze into the entry wound and applying pressure, I thought I might pass out. Once I had both wounds cleaned and stuffed with gauze, it was time to empty the trunk. It took me about ten or fifteen minutes, but I eventually got everything out and laid it in a pile beside the car. I stuck the cash in my pocket, got into the car again, started it, and drove it over to where Pappy's body lay. I backed up to him, got out, and spent another ten agonizing minutes loading his 270 pounds of dead weight into the trunk. Once I had him loaded, I got into the car and headed for Gatlinburg.

I pulled up in front of Granny Tipton's house around eight thirty in the morning. When she opened the door after I knocked, the color drained from her face.

"My goodness, Darren, what's wrong?" she said.

"I'm hurt," I said. I'd made a makeshift sling out of one of the rolls of gauze in Pappy's first-aid kit, and my right arm was across my stomach.

"You look terrible," she said as she wrapped her hands around my left arm. "Let's get you inside."

We walked into her dining room, and she sat me down in a chair.

"What happened?" she said.

"I'm sorry to come here, but I didn't know where else to go. Big Pappy came after me. It's a long story and something you really don't need to hear, but he came after me and he shot me. I probably need a doctor, Granny, but I can't go to a hospital or to anyone who will talk about this. Do you know anyone?"

She nodded. "I know a man. He's helped us out several times over the years. I'll call him and get him to come. I thought you and this Pappy were friends."

"So did I," I said. "It didn't work out that way."

"Where is he?"

"That's his car out there. He's in the trunk, dead."

"You killed him?"

"It was him or me."

"Let me help you get the coat and shirt off. I need to take a look."

I gasped as she removed the sling, my coat, and my shirt. The pain was becoming more intense as time passed, and the area around the entry wound had become red and swollen.

"I'm going to go call the doctor right now," she said. "I suppose you want the body in the barn with the pigs."

"If that's possible," I said.

"I'll call Ronnie and Eugene, too. What about the car?"

"It needs to disappear."

"Is there any way you were followed? Does anyone at all know you're here?"

"I wasn't followed. Nobody knows I'm here."

"Where's your cell phone?"

"At a motel in Knoxville where I've been staying."

"I thought you were living with Grace."

"That's another story."

She stepped back and gave me a stern look. "These aren't small favors, Darren."

"I know that, and I'm truly sorry for dumping this on you. I had nowhere else to go."

She turned and walked out of the room. I could hear her talking quietly on the phone for a few minutes, and then she returned.

"The doctor will be here in an hour," she said. "Ronnie and Eugene will take care of the car and what's in it. How long do you need to stay here?"

"As soon as the doctor is done with me, I need to go," I said. "As long as he says I can travel—hell, even if he says I can't travel—I'm leaving."

"How? Do you plan to walk back to Knoxville?"

"I was hoping for one last favor," I said.

"What's that?"

"I need a ride to Petros."

"I'll get Eugene to take you."

After Granny walked out of the room to call Eugene, it finally dawned on me that I'd survived. I'd survived a gun battle with a vicious murderer. I wanted to tell someone other than Granny, to share the news with someone who cared about me. But there was no one. I thought about Grace. She would have been horrified. I shook my head at the thought of her, and I realized that I missed her terribly.

CHAPTER 60

The doctor cleaned and stitched the wounds, set my collarbone as best he could, and put my arm in a real sling. He gave me enough pain medication to last for a month. My collarbone was broken, he said, along with one rib. He didn't have an X-ray machine, so he made the diagnosis by pushing on my ribs. When I screamed, he deemed the rib broken. He said from the amount and color of the blood he was seeing, he didn't believe any internal organs had been damaged. Once the wound and the bones healed, I'd be good to go. I gave him $1,000 of the cash I'd taken from Pappy's trunk—there was $25,000 in that wad—and thanked him. Eugene gave me a ride to Petros to pick up my car. Eugene had never been much of a talker, and he said very little on the way, which was fine with me. The less he, or anyone else, knew about what happened there, the better. When we got to the range, I asked Eugene to dispose of the pile of Pappy's things that I'd left on the ground. He agreed and loaded everything into the back of his Jeep.

I drove my car back to Knoxville and pulled into the motel around two in the afternoon. I'd been gone for less than twenty-four hours, I hadn't had any sleep, and I'd been shot. The pain medication was helping some, but I could still feel twinges whenever I moved. I went into the room and immediately sensed that something was wrong. I couldn't quite identify it; it just seemed that the room was a little different from when I'd left. It felt like someone had been there, and there was a distant, faint smell of lemon and musk hanging in the air.

Katherine? Had her perfume lingered that long?

My cell phone was on the table where I'd left it, and I walked over and picked it up. I'd received two calls, both from Dan Reid. He'd left me voice mails both times and asked me to call him back. He said it was important. Before I did, though, I walked out the door and to the motel office. The motel was managed by a young Indian couple who also lived there. I'd gotten to know them on a shallow level. I was friendly; they were friendly. I knew their names—Chanda was the wife and Kishan was the husband—and they knew mine. Kishan was behind the desk when I walked in. He was slim with jet-black hair and dark eyes, and he sported a thin mustache above his upper lip.

"Hi, Kishan," I said as I walked in.

"Ah, Mr. Street, you don't look so good," he said. "What happened to your arm?"

"Went skiing with a friend in Gatlinburg this morning. Didn't work out."

"Ah," he said. I could tell he didn't believe me.

"Listen, Kishan, did you by any chance notice anyone around my room last night or this morning?"

"I saw a young lady. She didn't drive in; she walked from somewhere, but I saw her coming out of your room. Same lady I saw earlier yesterday. Very pretty."

"Black hair? Blue eyes?"

"Yes. Very pretty."

"When did you see her?"

"Last night near midnight. I thought you were there. I was taking out the trash and saw her come out of the room. Is there a problem? Should I have called the police?"

"No, Kishan, no problem at all. Thank you for keeping an eye out."

I went back to the room, wondering two things. How did Katherine get into my room without a key, and what the hell was she doing in there? When I got back to the room, I picked up my cell and called Dan Reid.

"Sorry I missed your calls," I said when he answered. "I've been a little under the weather."

"I have something for you on your girl, Katherine Davis."

"Something good or something bad?"

"I don't know. Actually, I probably do. I don't think it's good."

"What is it?"

"I finished my background check on her, looked into her family history. Guess who her aunt is? Her mother's sister?"

"No clue."

"I'll give you a hint. She's a redhead and a detective. Works for the Knoxville Police Department."

"Dawn Rule?"

"You got it."

"Shit. They're using her to try to set me up, and she's playing along. I wonder if the DUI charge is even real."

"It isn't," Reid said. "After I found out she was related to Dawn Rule, I tracked down the cop who supposedly arrested her, Earl Anderson. I showed him my old FBI identification and told him I was investigating some possible official misconduct. He couldn't talk fast enough. Said he warned them about it, that he didn't want to be a part of it, that he'd always liked you. He said he agreed to do it because Rule and Kingman promised him a promotion as soon as it was over."

"Son of a bitch," I said. "They'll stoop to anything, won't they?"

"Maybe, but in their defense, they think you committed three murders."

Four now, I thought to myself. *Four. Plus I had somebody's face melted.*

"What are you going to do about it?" Reid said.

"I'm not sure, but thank you. I mean it. You did a great job."

"Appreciate the business," Reid said. "Let me know if you ever need me again."

"I will," I said.

"I heard a rumor that you and Grace split up," he said.

"I'll get her back," I said. "I just need some time."

"She's out of your league."

"I know, but I'm going to get her back, anyway. I miss her."

"You never know, do you?" Dan said.

"Beg your pardon?"

"How things will happen, how they'll turn out. You just never know."

"You're right about that, my friend. Absolutely right."

CHAPTER 61

I signed the paperwork to move into the furnished apartment on Friday and hired a small moving company to take my things out of storage and haul them to the apartment. I simply couldn't do it with the sling, and I paid them with some of Pappy's cash. I received phone calls and texts from Katherine all that day, but I ignored them until Saturday afternoon, when I replied to a text with: I'm in my new place. Can you come New Year's Eve and help warm things up? I don't have any plans.

Casual? she wrote.

Very.
Should I plan on staying?
Sure. Let's get drunk together and celebrate. I'll pick up some champagne.

Wouldn't miss it, she wrote.

I gave her the address and asked her to show up around eight.

On Monday, New Year's Eve, not long before Katherine was scheduled to arrive, I bought some takeout from an excellent Chinese place that was only a few blocks from my apartment and put it in the oven to keep it warm. I'd also bought four bottles of expensive champagne the day before, all on Pappy's dime. I opened one of them after I put the food in the oven and put it in a bucket that was half-filled with ice and water.

Katherine showed up right on time and walked in wearing tight blue jeans that were rolled up a few inches above her ankles. She had on a light sweater, horizontally striped in navy blue and white. Over it she wore a short tan jacket with the sleeves rolled up. On her feet were navy-blue pumps with four-inch spiked heels. As always, sexual allure oozed from her like sap from a maple tree.

"You look great," I said when she walked in.

She kissed me on the cheek. "What happened to your arm?"

"I have a friend in Sevierville who likes to ride horses. He invited me, so I went. Got thrown off."

"Is anything broken?"

"My collarbone and a rib. You'll have to be gentle tonight if you stay."

"Oh, I'm planning to stay, and I can be gentle. I can be anything you want me to be."

She looked around the apartment. I'd lit candles and placed them on a couple of tables and on the gas fireplace mantel. "This is nice. A little impersonal, maybe, but nice."

"I don't have a lot of personal things left," I said. "Pretty much everything I owned was destroyed when Mom's house was bombed."

She reached up and touched my cheek. "I'm so sorry."

"Let's not talk about sad things," I said. "It's New Year's Eve. I have great Chinese food, and I have even better champagne."

"Sounds wonderful," she said. "What can I do to help?"

"I guess just help me get the food plated. I'm not very handy right now."

We set about getting the food out of the oven, and I poured champagne. As we sat down at the table, I offered a toast. "To learning from the past and moving toward the future."

"Cheers," she said, and we both drank some champagne.

"That's good," she said. "That might be the best champagne I've ever tasted."

"I like it, too. Drink up. Maybe we'll get drunk and dance naked around the apartment."

She took another drink from the glass, and I refilled it immediately. "Why don't you tell me more about yourself? I mean, I know the basics, I guess. I know you'll graduate with a master's in criminal justice in May and then you're going to law school in the fall. I know you're beautiful and charming and the best lover, by far, I've ever been with, but I want you to tell me about Katherine. Where is Katherine from? Where does she see herself going? What makes her happy? What makes her sad? What's her definition of beauty?"

"No politics," she said. "No religion."

"Later. Another time. Where are you from?"

"Chattanooga," she said. "My dad was an FBI agent. When I was young, we moved around a lot, but by the time I was in the fifth grade, they sent him to Chattanooga, and that's where I went to middle school and high school."

"He and your mother still married? I know a lot of FBI marriages don't work out."

"They're still married, in a manner of speaking. He died of an aortic aneurysm when I was a sophomore in college."

"I'm sorry," I said.

"It's okay. He had a great life. He loved being an FBI agent, fighting the bad guys. And he went quickly. The aneurysm popped and he died immediately. He didn't suffer."

"So your mom is where? Still in Chattanooga?"

"Right, she's a prosecutor there."

"Assistant district attorney?"

"She is. She handles mostly sex crimes, and she's good at it."

"Brothers and sisters?"

"One of each. My brother is a boring banker in Nashville, and my sister is married with two kids in Chattanooga. She and my mother are very close."

"Are you the youngest?"

She nodded. "I'm the baby. My sister is close to my mother, but I was the apple of my daddy's eye."

"I bet you were," I said as I kept refilling her glass and mine, but I was sipping and she was drinking hard. The bottle emptied quickly, and I opened another.

"Are you trying to get me drunk?" she said as I came back to the table.

"I just want to have a good time," I said. "I need to loosen up a little. You don't have to drink if you don't want to."

She picked up her glass, which I'd just filled, and drained it.

"Let's loosen up together," she said.

I started bragging a little, telling her about what an excellent wrestler and football player I was in high school. I'd had several offers to go to smaller colleges in both sports, but I'd wanted to stay in Knoxville, close to my mom, and I'd wanted to go to the University of Tennessee. I was nowhere near big or strong or fast enough to compete with the guys at that level, and I'd known it, so I'd satisfied my competitive itch by playing intramural football and joining a wrestling club. She seemed interested in everything I had to say, she asked questions, she laughed a lot. Then I started telling her war stories about being a lawyer, and I shared more of what happened to me when I was locked up for two years. As I talked, I kept filling her glass. Within an hour of her walking in the door, she was drunk. She got up to go to the bathroom, and stumbled into the wall along the way. When she came back, I decided it was time.

"So you told me about your family, your mother and father and brother and sister," I said. "Do you have any aunts or uncles?"

She looked at me quizzically in her drunken state. "No auntseruncles," she slurred.

"That isn't what I hear. My understanding is that you have an aunt named Dawn Rule. She's your mother's sister, and she's a detective with the Knoxville Police Department."

She looked at me for a minute, then she looked down at her shoes.

"You know what else I heard? And I got this from an FBI agent so I'm sure it's the truth. I heard that your DUI charge is nothing but a sham, a ploy to get you close to me so you could try to get admissions out of me about the murders I supposedly committed in West Virginia. You're doing undercover work for your aunt. Only I don't regard it as undercover work. That's far too glamorous a term, as far as I'm concerned. You're nothing but a rat. A snitch. A worthless, lying piece of shit who gains the trust of others with one purpose in mind. And that purpose is to turn on them later and take every bit of trust they showed you and shove it right up their asses."

She stood and her glass fell to the floor and shattered. "I think I should go."

"You're damned right you should go," I said. "Don't ever come near me again."

I ran into my bedroom and picked up one of my throwaway phones as she staggered toward the door. I followed her out and watched her stumble to her car. I jumped into mine and began to follow her down the street at a distance. She was weaving all over the road. I called 9-1-1.

"There's a woman on Cedar Bluff Drive, four hundred block, who's all over the road," I said. "She's driving a blue Hyundai Sonata. The tag number is 492-OST. Yes, I'm calling from a prepaid cell. I don't want to give you my name. You need to get somebody out here quick. She's going to hurt herself or somebody else. I don't know if she's drunk or high or sick, but something is definitely wrong. Oh! Man! She just ran up on the curb and now she's back in the street and has crossed over the center line. I have to go. Send somebody."

I backed off from her a ways as she continued down Cedar Bluff. In less than five minutes, a Knoxville city cruiser passed me and pulled in behind her. He followed her for about a quarter of a mile and hit his blue lights. She pulled to the side of the road, climbed a curb, nearly hit a tree, and came to a stop.

I figured her aunt Dawn would get her out of it, or at least try to do everything she could, but that was okay.

Karma can be a bitch.

Katherine was gone, and I was once again alone. I went back to my apartment and resisted the urge to dial Grace's number.

CHAPTER 62

I laid low for the next three weeks, trying to get healed up and going about my business in a low-key manner. I hadn't heard a word from the Knoxville police, which I took as a good sign. No one had tried to kill me, so I figured Big Pappy Donovan's reach did not extend beyond the grave. I was sitting in a restaurant eating lunch when I got a text from Grace.

We need to talk, it said.

Change of heart? I replied, hoping it might be true. I'd found myself thinking about Grace more and more. I'd started to text or call her dozens of times, but I was afraid she'd flat-out reject me, and I just didn't need the pain.

Can we meet? she wrote.

Sure, where?

My place. Six o'clock?

I'll be there.

I knocked on Grace's door at precisely 6:00 p.m. It was Sunday, January 20. My right arm was still in the sling, but it was getting better. I hadn't had any problems with infections, and the gunshot wounds were almost healed. I carried in my left hand a vase of purple orchids, which were Grace's favorite flowers.

She opened the door and smiled, to my surprise. She looked at the flowers and said, "Those are beautiful, Darren."

"I know they're your favorite."

"Thank you. Come in."

I walked in as she turned and set the flowers on the island in the kitchen.

"What happened to your arm?" she said casually.

"Big Pappy Donovan shot me," I said. I'd decided I wasn't going to lie to her anymore.

She turned and looked me in the eye. The smile was gone. "He shot you? With a real gun?"

"Do you want to hear the whole story, Grace? Because I'll lay it all out for you. It will put you in a difficult position, but if you want to know, I'll tell you. I've been doing a lot of thinking over these past few weeks. I know I went off the deep end for a little while. I know I was crazy. But there were reasons: the two years in prison, Mom getting murdered, Clancy getting acquitted, Sean moving away. I let those things overtake me and I became irrational. I did some things I'm not proud of, but I think I can forgive myself and move forward. I think I've learned a lot, Grace. I've learned a lot about life and I've learned a lot about myself. I also learned that you had become the very best thing in my life and I turned my back on you in so many different ways. I even convinced myself that you were one of the things that triggered my Post Traumatic Stress Disorder. All I can do at this point is say I'm sorry. I'd love to try again if you'll have me."

She shook her head slowly and looked at the floor. "I don't know, Darren. I mean, I think you may have killed some people."

"I *did* kill some people. And then I lied to you about it. I killed the two men who bombed my mother's house, I helped kill Ben Clancy, and I killed Big Pappy. I killed four people, but two of them killed my mother, and one of them sent my uncle to prison for two decades on a bogus charge, framed me for a murder, drove James Tipton to suicide, and walked away from all of it. I killed Big Pappy because he was trying to kill me. Straight-up self-defense. The police will never, ever prove anything I've done. They won't ever have enough to arrest me, let alone try me and convict me. I probably shouldn't be telling you all this, but if we're going to ever be together again, if we're going to try, I want you to know that I've been honest with you. You understand why I did what I did. I know you do. The question is: Can you forgive me?"

I was on a limb, and I knew it. Grace could go straight to the police and tell them I'd confessed to four murders, but I didn't think she was anything like Katherine. She had substance and character, and I thought she still might love me. She'd also been to hell and back with me, and not all that long ago, she'd agreed to marry me.

"We can take it slow," I said. "We can make it work."

She began to sniffle, and I started toward her. She put her hand up and said, "No, please. I need to think."

I stopped and took a step back. "Okay. I just put a lot on your shoulders. Let's go back to the beginning. Why did you want to see me?"

"I'm not sure what to do now," she said. "I don't know what to say." Her sniffling had become more intense, and tears were flowing down both of her cheeks. "What do you say to a man who has just told you he's committed four murders? Justified or not? What do you say? How am I supposed to feel about that? What would it be like knowing that the man I'm with every day is capable of that kind of violence?"

"I think we're all capable if we get pushed far enough," I said.

"Maybe," she said, "but right now, at this moment, I don't understand it. I've never been pushed that far, and I've always been taught that when the law is broken, we have a system in place to address injustices and injuries suffered by innocent people. It's called the criminal justice system, Darren. You believed in it once. You're still a part of it, aren't you? Aren't you still practicing criminal defense law?"

"I've been a little preoccupied, but yes."

"Then you're a hypocrite."

"I guess I am, but look what the system did to me. It took two years of my life, twenty of my uncle's. It didn't offer to compensate me in any way, didn't offer me any help or counseling when I was released. The system can be cruel. Not just cruel, it can be downright barbaric."

"I know it isn't perfect, but what if family members of murder victims reacted the same way you did in every case? We'd have blood everywhere. Chaos. You're asking me to realign my entire sense of what justice is. You're asking me to accept that vigilantism has a place in our system of criminal justice, and I can't agree with you. I just can't."

"I didn't ask you to agree with me. I asked you to forgive me."

"I need some time to think about it."

She'd calmed down, and she pulled some paper towels off a roll on the counter and dried her face and wiped her nose. "I have something to tell you."

Something about the tone in her voice put me on alert. I knew what she was going to say before the words actually passed her lips.

"Do you remember the night when you came back and told me you'd been fishing? That you'd caught two big ones and left them where you caught them? And then you came home and all you wanted to do was have sex and have sex and have sex?"

I nodded, waiting for the two words I knew I was going to hear.

"I'm pregnant."

CHAPTER 63

Will Grimes stepped into the temporary office used by prosecutors during trials at the courthouse in Webster Springs, West Virginia. He'd just finished testifying in a year-old murder case involving a woman who had hired two teenagers to shoot and kill her husband for insurance money, and the prosecutor, District Attorney James Hellerman, had rested his case. The judge had taken a brief recess before the defense began telling its side of the story. Hellerman was already behind his desk, stuffing a dip of Skoal into his lower lip. Grimes sat down across from him.

"You did a fine job," Hellerman said.

"Thank you," Grimes said.

"You never know what a jury will do, but this is as close to a slam dunk as I've had in a while."

"So you think it'll be over today?"

Hellerman nodded and spit into a cup. "Bet we'll have a verdict by six o'clock."

"Wish they were all this cut-and-dried," Grimes said.

"Speaking of, did you ever find that guy you were looking for that killed those three folks in Charleston?"

"He disappeared into thin air," Grimes said.

"Where in the world do you think he ran off to?" Hellerman said.

"Who knows? Maybe he's dead."

"Any idea who might have killed him?"

"I have my suspicions."

"You think it might be that lawyer you were after, don't you?"

"He'd be my prime suspect."

"Are you still working that double murder in Cowen? The one where you think that same lawyer killed those two boys in a bar?"

Grimes shook his head. "No point. It's over. The lawyer was smart enough to put enough layers between himself and his crime that I couldn't get to him. Then one important layer wound up dead, and the other has vanished."

"The one that vanished, he's the man that killed the three in Charleston, right?"

"Right."

"Maybe he'll turn up one day."

"And maybe pigs will fly."

"Well, like I always say to you, Will, just keep grinding. That's what you do best."

Grimes leaned back in his chair and laced his fingers behind his neck. He'd been doing this long enough to check his emotions at the door, but the feeling of frustration of not having solved a brutal double murder, plus the murders in Charleston, frustrated him nonetheless.

"There's always something to grind on, that's for sure," he said. "People just keep on killing each other."

There was a soft knock at the door, and a bailiff stuck his head in. "Judge is ready to go."

"That one may have gotten away," Hellerman said, "but this one isn't going to. Let's go chalk up another one for the good guys."

CHAPTER 64

Two months later, Dr. Benton smiled at me from across the room. It was mid-March, and the signs of spring—my favorite time of year—were beginning to show. Daffodils bloomed outside in her garden. Bradford pear trees were covered in white petals. What was going on outside the windows of the room made me feel good, but what was going on inside the room grated on my nerves more than a little.

Dr. Benton just seemed so self-assured, so all-knowing. She had every answer, whether it be in the form of a platitude, a coping technique, or a prescribed medication. I was talking to her on a weekly basis now, part of an agreement with Grace to help me get past my mental struggles. The problem was, I no longer seemed to be having serious mental struggles. I'd killed or maimed everyone who had tormented me. I'd accepted what I'd done, and I'd forgiven myself. It still bothered me that Sean was so far away, but I'd gotten into the habit of staying in touch with him on a regular basis, so that anxiety had eased. My mother's will had finally gone through probate, so I had about $400,000 stashed in stock index funds. I was sleeping pretty well with the help of the same drug Katherine Davis said got her arrested for DUI.

Grace and I still weren't living together, and I hadn't given her ring back and asked her to marry me, but we were talking every day and getting along better and better. We laughed a lot, and she'd even started doing some good-natured needling. She'd called me Al Capone a couple of times, which, at some level, was probably pretty damned healthy. She hadn't pressed me for details about the shootings, but if she had, I would have given her second-by-second accounts. I also would have told her about having Rupert Lattimore's face melted, but I don't think that would have gone over too well. I'd heard Rupert had undergone several terribly painful surgeries and that more were planned. I'd also heard he looked like he'd been tossed straight into hell. As far as I was concerned, getting oiled up couldn't have happened to a more deserving person.

The cops had quit bothering me. Word of the fake DUI charge had gotten around pretty quickly once Katherine Davis caught a legitimate DUI. I'd called my friend Bob Ridge and told him what they'd done, and he'd talked to Earl Anderson, the patrol officer they'd conned into filing the charge. Bob told me the department was doing an internal investigation, but that nothing would ever come of it. Katherine Davis's real DUI charge was dismissed when the arresting officer failed to show up to court three times. I was certain that was arranged by her aunt Dawn. I was actually in the courtroom the day they dismissed the charge against her. I smiled at her and waved as she turned to walk out of the courtroom. And as for the state trooper in West Virginia, I knew I'd never hear from him again. By killing Rex Fairchild, Pappy had pretty much destroyed his case. I'd killed Pappy, and I thought my call to Sammy Raft had cemented things.

"Are you dreaming?" Dr. Benton asked me. Our hour was almost up, and I was grateful for that.

"Right now?"

"When you sleep. You told me you've been sleeping better. Have you been having nightmares?"

The truth was that yes, I still had nightmares, but they were less frequent and less intense than they had been in the past.

"It's been quite a while," I lied.

"That's remarkable, Darren," Dr. Benton said. "You must be extremely strong mentally."

"I've had a lot of practice."

"Yes, yes, you have, unfortunately. But you're still dealing with the triggers every day, correct? You're still going to court, still going into jails, still dealing with judges and clients and policemen and prison guards and all that."

"I'm pretty choosy about what I take right now because I've come into some money, but yes, I still have to deal with all those things on occasion."

"Amazing. When I first saw you, I honestly didn't think you'd be able to continue to practice law, especially criminal defense. You have to have developed some coping mechanisms subconsciously, some things you probably don't even understand."

I didn't want to mention killing people to her. Doing so had lightened my psychological load considerably. "I guess I have. And you're right. I can't really identify or articulate anything I'm doing, but I just seem to be getting along better."

"How are things with Grace?"

"Coming along. I think she's trusting me more every day."

"You've never mentioned what caused her to have trust issues in the first place, and she hasn't said a word. Would you be comfortable sharing what caused her not to trust you?"

"It was a combination of things," I said. "After my mother was killed, I became unavailable emotionally to her. I shut her out. She tried to help me, but the more she tried, the more I resisted. It just deteriorated to the point where she returned the engagement ring I'd given her and asked me to leave."

"That had to be difficult."

"It was. For both of us."

"But you stayed true to her and she stayed true to you, and now it appears your relationship is back on the mend."

Grace was hiding her pregnancy by wearing loose clothing. It wouldn't be long, though, before anyone who really knew her would point and say, "Is that a baby bump?" I found myself largely ambivalent about her pregnancy, mostly because I didn't know how things would turn out between the two of us. If we got back together and got along, I'd embrace the child. If things went south, though, I honestly didn't think I'd have much room for a baby. I hadn't told Dr. Benton about the pregnancy yet, mostly because I didn't think it was any of her business, and I certainly hadn't told her about my brief affair with the rat, Katherine Davis.

"Love is a powerful force," I said, because it seemed like the right thing to say at the time. I'd learned to work Dr. Benton.

"Maybe *the* most powerful force," she said. "How are you feeling about the future, Darren? Are you optimistic? Pessimistic? Afraid?"

"I'm uncertain," I said. "Optimism is a choice, and I've made that choice, but I've learned that I can't know what's coming. I know bad things happen. They've already happened to me, and I feel sure more bad things will happen before it's over. But I'll be able to handle the bad times better in the future. I feel fairly certain of that."

"Because you've developed coping mechanisms," she said.

Because I've learned that I'm not afraid to blow somebody's brains out when they deserve it; because my rule of law and your rule of law are two entirely different sets of principles.

But I kept my thoughts to myself. "I guess you could say that," I responded. "I guess you could say I've developed my own way of coping."

"Good for you, Darren," she said. "I wish I had more patients like you."

I chuckled. I couldn't help it.

"What's funny?" she asked.

"I'm sorry," I said. "I don't think you really want more patients like me."

"Why is that?"

Because you're a lousy shrink, and you'd probably eventually wind up dead and stuffed in that closet over there.

"I'm not anything special," I said. "A little different, maybe, but nothing special."

She rose from her overstuffed chair, indicating our session was over. "So I'll see you next week? Same time?"

I handed her $200 in cash and nodded.

"I don't know where I'd be without you," I lied. "Thanks."

"You give me too much credit," she said. "Your mental health really comes down to the decisions you make."

Damn straight.

I smiled and walked out the door.

ACKNOWLEDGMENTS

Thank you to Jacque Ben-Zekry, who shepherded me through this novel and cut me some slack during a very difficult time in my life. I wish her nothing but the best. Thank you, David Hale Smith and the folks at Inkwell Management for looking out for my best interests. Thank you to my son, Dylan, for helping me build a strong and loyal base of readers. And thank you to those readers for allowing me to do something I love to do and to make a great living while I'm doing it. And thank you to the rest of the Thomas & Mercer team—and when I say team, I mean it. There are just too many of them to name, but they work tirelessly together to help ensure the success of each book they publish, and I appreciate both their commitment to excellence and how good they've been to me. And finally, thank you to my Kristy, the love of my life, to whom I dedicate all of my novels. She inspires me each and every day, and after thirty-one years together, I still think she's the prettiest girl I've ever seen.

ABOUT THE AUTHOR

Photo © 2015 Dwain Rowe

Scott Pratt was born in South Haven, Michigan, and grew up in Jonesborough, Tennessee. He is a veteran of the United States Air Force and earned a bachelor of arts degree in English from East Tennessee State University and a doctor of jurisprudence degree from the University of Tennessee. Pratt's first novel, *An Innocent Client*—the first book in his Joe Dillard series—was chosen as a finalist for the Mystery Readers International's Macavity Award. *Justice Burning* is the second book in his Darren Street series, following *Justice Redeemed*. Pratt resides in northeast Tennessee with his wife, two dogs, and a parrot.